Saint Joseph

A Story of

Adventure, Mystery, and Romance

J. Salvatore Domino

To my father-in-law, Robert C. Rauter, one of my biggest supporters. Bob read my early work with enthusiasm and grace, even though it lacked the polish necessary to be widely recognized.

He never got a chance to read Saint Joseph. If I could send him a copy in heaven, it would be on its way immediately.

Table of Contents

Prologue

The Hidden Story

"The best place to hide a tree is in the forest."

I honestly don't know where that adage originated, but from the time I was a young man, it has guided my thinking into adulthood. As a boy, I saw those words inscribed on the bottom of a poster on the wall of a trendy boutique my mom frequented when she wanted a special gift. The framed artwork included a picture of a dark and misty forest filled with trees so dense you couldn't pick one from another. The profoundness of the statement, along with the shadowy artwork, spoke to me. I begged my mom to buy it for me, but it was expensive, and it wasn't practical. She declined with a headshake. Then, after a few seconds, she tried to appease me by saying, "Perhaps later."

Later never came, but every time I walked past the shop, I remembered the poster. A few years later, my parents purchased for me my first computer. Using a graphics art program and a color printer, I recreated my own version of that poster. I found an old wooden picture frame in our garage, which I painted to look new. My dad helped me mount my poster in the frame, then we hung my handiwork on my bedroom wall. I carried this poster with me when I went away to college, and to every city where I lived afterward. The poster is a sentimental reminder of my journey from a young, impressionable boy.

With age, the saying became less profound, more cliché, but I still like it, because it always reminds me to look deeper, below the apparent, to find the truth. More than any other advice I have received since.

When the other young boys in my neighborhood were playing baseball or standing on the corner smoking cigarettes, I was at the library reading a book. Many people viewed me as a nerd. Even my father, who was the "he-man" type, would tease me frequently over my lack of machismo. My mom soothed my insecurity by reassuring me it was nothing more than middle-child syndrome. She said my father loved all of his children equally.

Not that I couldn't compete with the others; I didn't want to. I knew that there had to be more to life than cars and sports and scoring with girls.

From the start, I knew being a writer trumped being a fighter. Writers live in a world of their own making; that idea seemed to appeal to me. The idea that I could change the world with my words meant I could become someone important.

At first, I experimented with songs. Being a songwriter had a certain alluring quality. It seemed like a way to become famous and get rich. It wasn't as easy as I thought. Then I tried writing screenplays. None of the songs or scripts I wrote was worthy of publication. I quickly found I didn't have the creative talent necessary to inspire make-believe. My logical brain didn't mesh well with writing fiction.

Maybe it was a lack of imagination, but non-fiction made sense to me. After all, the truth can often be stranger than fiction.

I liked puzzles and the way they came together to present a picture. Throughout high school, I had a deep investment in true crime and all the elements of solving crimes. While I had no desire to pursue a career in law enforcement, it fascinated me how investigators found clues and could solve a case by putting together the pieces of a puzzle. I challenged myself to solve the mystery before they would give me the answer at the end of the story. I wanted to find the tree hidden in the forest.

By the time I graduated high school, I had decided that journalism school might be a good way to learn to write compelling human-interest stories. Cleveland State University, in my hometown, had a journalism program. The school was close to home and affordable, which made my parents, who couldn't afford a lot, happy, and it satisfied my criteria for undergraduate work. Despite the school's proximity, I insisted on residing on campus. My goal was to fully experience college life, living independently and navigating the world.

I thought I was ready because before I ever set foot on campus, I had already written several books, which I hoped to polish up and share with my fellow journalism students. I even adopted a pen name, "Saint Joseph", an expanded version of my last name, St. Joseph.

My college literature classes showed me all the qualities my writing lacked. I quickly learned it was going to take more than polishing to meet the standard required for publication. My books were the butt of many jokes among my peers. It was disappointing, but you have to start somewhere. I consoled myself that it was my alter ego, "Saint Joseph," who authored those first books.

Since none would ever make it to publication. I put the pen name "Saint Joseph" on the shelf until the day I became a famous author.

Chapter 1

Going Deeper

It was my second year at Cleveland State University when an incident occurred that didn't seem important at the time, but looking back, I realized it changed my life.

It was fall, and the looming winter solstice brought shorter days and colder nights. Lake-effect snowstorms from Lake Erie to the north blanketed the campus. Except for scurrying between buildings to get to class, I spent more time indoors than out. Like in high school, I spent a lot of time alone because I struggled to fit in with other students. When I wasn't huddling in my dorm room, I hung out at the student union, drinking a cherry soda and watching the jocks showing off for the coeds who were rebelling against their fathers. It seemed the other kids were in college for a good time.

It wasn't that way for me. I was there to learn. When I tired of watching the student mating ritual, I would make my way to the library. Sticking my nose in a book was always the panacea for my isolation. If I couldn't be one of the popular students, at least I could be one of the smartest.

I felt I had something to prove, and I wanted that proof to come as a perfect 4.0 grade point average at graduation.

Then, one Tuesday, a few days before the holiday break, my journalism professor returned an essay to me without a grade. I was hoping to see an "A+" and some other praise, such as "Great Work", written across the front. Instead, across the top of the paper, she had scribbled a note, "We should talk about this paper." It concerned me that there could be a serious problem. I needed a good grade on this project, and in my estimation, it was fine work.

A hundred thoughts raced through my mind. *Did I misquote a source? Was there a plagiarism problem? Did I do something that would wreck my chances of achieving a perfect GPA?*

I scheduled an appointment to meet the next day with Dr. Elaine Sadeski at her office for a one-on-one conference. I wanted an explanation, and tomorrow couldn't come soon enough.

Pacing outside her office door, I watched other students come and go until my appointed time arrived. While I waited, I read the paper repeatedly, trying to discern the problem. When we finally met face to face, and I had my chance to defend my paper, I came prepared for any argument.

I handed Dr. Sadeski the paper, emphasizing the notation, and said, "You sent me a note."

Taking a seat, I watched as she reviewed the note and the paper. She pondered my future, and after a minute, she said, "Oh yes, I remember this essay."

Leaning in across the desk at me, she said. "Occasionally, I find something worth spending extra time reading and reviewing. I like to recognize exceptional work. Your paper goes into much greater detail than the essays I typically receive from my undergraduate students. It is excellent work. Keep doing this quality of work, and your GPA will thank you."

She took the paper and wrote A+, "Good Work" across the top. It relieved me to know she liked my paper. *But why the mystery? Why did she call me to her office?*

Seconds later, she answered my unasked questions. "There is another reason I called you to my office today. There is something else I wish to discuss with you. I verified some of the sources you referenced in your paper. You found evidence contrary to the accepted opinions. No other students in your class have taken the time to research and verify their data as thoroughly as you. That tells me you enjoy digging deeper for answers, finding the hidden truth."

At last, being the nerdy kid with his nose in a book paid off. All my years of reading true crime as a boy taught me how to look beyond the obvious. I could find arguments that differed from the commonly accepted viewpoint. I didn't mind digging down deeper for answers.

She continued, "If you have an interest in this type of work, you will make an excellent Investigative Journalist."

"Investigative Journalist?" I replied. "I want to be a novelist. Isn't that everyone's goal, to write the great American novel?"

She smirked. "That's how every journalism student starts out. Novelists are like stars in the sky. The number of great unpublished or unread novels is countless. Because no one reads them, they changed no one's life. The investigative journalist specializes in unveiling misdeeds. They find the facts that are camouflaged or overlooked by mainstream reporters. You, my friend, have a talent and an eye for the hidden story. You can change the world."

She reached back into the drawer and withdrew a printed document. It wasn't thick. Not much larger than a pamphlet. They titled the booklet, *Hypothesis-Based Inquiry: A Guidebook for Investigative Journalists.*

She handed me the booklet, saying. "Take a minute to look this over. I have been taking part in a working group of international journalists to formulate guidelines on how to better research and publish investigative reports."

I glanced at the cover; it looked official. It was an early draft version of a document that the International Educational and Communications Organization, a group known as IECO, based in Paris, France, would soon publish. The booklet, written in both

French and English, appeared to be a handbook, a compendium of rules for investigative journalists.

"There are rules?" I commented. "I thought investigators were supposed to break the rules. That's how they dig up dirt."

She laughed. "Only the bad ones, the shock jocks. Anyone can cheat and win. A talented journalist knows when to be a detective and when to be a pickpocket. If you can find the truth without cheating, the world will admire you, not scorn you. Society views many journalists as underhanded, only out for a buck."

Then she got serious again. "Not too many schools in the U.S. are teaching this method of reporting. Writing a Hypothesis-Based Inquiry requires a lot of planning and research. Most news and media outlets do not have the time or luxury to let a story develop. They are busy trying to scoop each other and get the article out before the other guy. The result is they latch on to a headline that catches the reader's eye."

I understood what she was saying. She continued, "I've been trying to teach journalists to wait and produce a complete story that will prove to be the definitive answer. Everyone needs to make a living, so writers gravitate to stories that sell, regardless of the depth of the investigation."

Her vision of writing the complete story resonated with me. I wanted to know more.

"I am hoping one day my counterparts at IECO and I will convince enough people to adopt our brand of reporting. I want to see the journalism community held to a higher standard," she said.

I'm not sure why her advice intrigued me so. Perhaps at that point in my life, I was still malleable. Like a lot of college students, I was still finding my way. Her conceptualization of creating a more competent writing community seemed to fit my personality.

"Can I borrow this book?"

"Keep it. I will print another one. This is an advance copy. Once published, IECO will make it free to the world. Take your time, study it; it may sway your thinking. Next semester, I plan to teach a course using this method. I expect you to register."

Before I left her office, she encouraged me to continue finding the hidden story behind the story. That professor, Dr. Elaine Sadeski, planted a seed that has been growing in my head like a flourishing willow tree on the bank of a river. We concluded our meeting, and I promised to work diligently to meet her standards. I received an "A" final grade from that class, and I had Professor Sadeski to thank for her support.

The following September, I registered for her class on how to build a Hypothesis-Based Inquiry. She remembered our meeting and paid close attention to my assignments for the rest of my undergraduate period, encouraging me to find the buried facts shrouded behind the apparent ones. That training opened my eyes. With Dr. Sadeski's encouragement, I chose to pursue a master's degree with a specialization in investigative journalism. Little did I know Professor Sadeski's influence would go beyond Cleveland State. I had no idea she would reappear in my life years later.

I spent the next few years learning the how, what, and why of researching deep into the hidden stories that surround us every day. Along the way, I honed my writing skills using the booklet. When IECO published the final version of Hypothesis-Based Inquiry, I ordered an official copy. From then on, I would use it as my bible for how to present the information in a cohesive and unchallengeable report.

Near the end of my junior year of college, I informed my parents of my choice to attend graduate school at Northwestern University in Chicago. My father couldn't afford the tuition at Northwestern. He encouraged me to stay closer to home and seek part-time employment to help reduce my student loan debt. After graduate school, he envisioned me returning to Cleveland, and following in his footsteps, finding a job, rejoining my siblings, and living happily ever after as one big happy family.

I hurt his pride when I told him my life goals differed from his. "No, I want to become someone important. I simply do not want to be an average guy. I want to change the world." My words weren't intended to make his life seem trivial. I was just too immature to understand how important his family was to him and the sacrifices he made for us. He just shook his head, hoping someday I would see things differently.

After four years of hard work, I achieved Magna Cum Laude at Cleveland State, falling short of Summa Cum Laude by just two decimal points. The one class I received a low grade, differential calculus, a requirement for graduation, prevented top honors. Still, when graduation day came, my parents were proud of my accomplishment.

Despite their opposition, I had decided I was going away. The day I left for Chicago, and my new life, was the most awkward I had ever encountered. I never realized how distant my father and I had become. He viewed me as immature and impulsive. I thought he was narrow-minded and old-fashioned.

Hurt by my rejection of his life, my father shook my hand and quietly said, "Goodbye, good luck."

My mom was less fatalistic. She kissed me goodbye and wished for me, "I hope you find the happiness you are after. Call us anytime you need help."

That was it. Cleveland was in my past. I left for Chicago and never looked back. As time went on, my family and I grew more distant. Oh, I called my parents on holidays and special occasions. We exchanged birthday cards and well-wishes. We were all too busy with our daily routines to do more. I was busy making my way in the world, while my brothers and sister kept my parents occupied with home life and grandchildren. They ate dinner together on Sundays, celebrated holidays as a family, and went to the grandkids' school plays.

I became the odd man out. Accepting that role in exchange for the freedom to do my own thing without outside influences. Call it confidence, or ignorance, but I wanted to make my own mistakes, my way.

I needed money, so while still in graduate school, I freelanced for a small internet-based news outlet, the *Newsie*, in a suburb of Chicago. They were creating an electronic online version of their print newspaper, hoping to retain their share of the local market.

As a fringe media player, the *Newsie* looked for stories that they could sensationalize and post as clickbait on the internet or social media. Their hope, of course, is that it will go viral, increasing their advertising revenue. Then other media outlets will have to join the frenzy or miss the readership. My long-term goal wasn't sensationalism, but an in-depth exposé that leaves a lasting impact on the reader. Nevertheless, working for this company granted me the freedom to work on my personal stories at my own pace. Even though I was starting out writing overplayed articles that were trending on the internet, deep down inside, I knew there were greater things to come. I could see my future. A chance at my Watergate.

Chapter 2

You Never Forget Your First Time

I never imagined I'd be the one to blow the whistle on my government. Throughout my life, I have been a believer. My naiveté and belief in the establishment's good intentions were a curse. After all, why would the people we trust to run our country misuse their power? Don't they realize we rely on them to watch out for those who can't take care of themselves?

Then one day, my wide-eyed optimism turned into doubt. The doubt into cynicism. My training and years of schooling, reinforced by internships and work with several media outlets, taught me to question everything.

Because I question everything, I've learned to dig down below the surface level and find hidden motivations in people's actions and words. There are times I even question my own motives. Was my investigation driven by the desire to see justice done or for personal recognition and power?

Whatever the motivation, I promised myself that every story I published would resonate with the name D.K. St. Joseph.

David Kern St. Joseph is the name on my birth certificate. As a child, my parents and siblings called me "D.K.", yet today, the D.K. moniker has never become known in my professional life. Only my parents and siblings refer to me by my full name. It's strange because every story I write always ends with what has become my signature line, *The Complete Story by D.K. St. Joseph.*

People in the business world focused only on my last name, St. Joseph. Since name recognition is so important and St. Joseph, minus the D.K., was easy to remember, an abbreviated version of the pen name, Saint Joseph, which I tried to adopt as a young boy, somehow became my identity as a journalist.

In the literary world, I am St. Joseph. Outside of work, it became even more abbreviated. My close friends and co-workers simply call me by one name, Joseph.

Once I gained focus and chose my career direction, I embarked on building my reputation. That meant looking for a story that was worthy of a full-scale investigation.

Becoming a talented investigator is not as easy as it sounds. Even though I spent years learning to investigate corruption, lies, and other forms of misinterpretation. I learned you can't just go out in the backyard and start overturning stones, hoping to find a gem. It takes weeks, sometimes months, of research before you even start writing your story. Only after you scratch the surface will you reveal if there is something below the shell that even warrants your time and effort. The majority of journalists lack the motivation to undertake deep, challenging work without any guarantee of reward.

Most journalists become reporters who produce three-minute stories for the evening news. Some become columnists, writing a new piece every day about everyday happenings. Or they eventually become editors, deciding which stories are newsworthy and which to bypass. They act in the present, letting people know what is happening now.

I became an investigator because I wanted to go beyond reporting the news of the day. I never take a news story at face value. Even if I have to ask the same questions three times to get all the facts, my goal is a complete and accurate story. To get it right, I keep researching the past to bring history into the present.

To discover illegal or unethical behavior, I often cross legal minefields. Understanding what is allowable from a legal perspective is essential to avoiding a violation of ethics. Still, I sometimes enter the realm of corruption or work with unsavory characters who are breaking the law, while I try to keep myself from doing something illegal.

Over time, I became known for my accurate research and clear-cut reports that play no favorites or hedge on conclusions. Although my work primarily involves events in the United States, I am not confined to any discipline. I will go anywhere the story takes me, from Cleveland to the Amazon rainforest. Fortunately, or unfortunately, as it may be, there are enough stories that need to be told right here in the U.S.A. to keep me busy for the rest of my career.

Investigating politicians, regardless of their political leanings, right or left, is of no consequence to me. Corporations are not exempt from my hypothesis. It could be defective drugs, automobile safety defects, and insider trading. The story could be about political payoffs, misappropriation of funds, or even murder. They are all fair game.

Yet, investigative journalism isn't exclusive to the US, Europe, or the West. We have members of our guild everywhere, including the Middle East, India, and Southeast Asia. Occasionally, I have assisted foreign journalists who have had difficulty researching data in the less-than-open environment of their home country. One problem many foreign journalists face is the lack of accountability in their society. In some foreign countries, when the person or group discovers they are being investigated, the journalist will simply disappear. Never to be heard from again. They vanish completely as if they never existed.

At least in the Western world, if I disappeared, someone might ask, "What ever happened to D.K. St. Joseph?". A simple question might lead to a new investigation or uncover a scandal.

♦ ♦ ♦

By the time I received my Master of Science from the Medill School of Journalism at Northwestern University, I was primed and ready for my first big score, but I would still have to wait a little longer. I had student loans to pay off, so I took a job with a small independent press in Chicago called the *Southsider*. The *Southsider* hired me because they liked the way I wrote my articles, which differed from just the typical news reporting. They felt the Hypothesis-Based format would appeal to their readers.

I chose to stay in Chicago because, in some ways, it reminded me of my hometown of Cleveland. Its Midwestern ideas and attitudes, a former industrial city, and a history of racial segregation, all had a familiar ring to me. But Chicago was much larger than Cleveland. I liked their lakefront, which consisted almost exclusively of green parks and clean sandy beaches, much less industrial than the Cleveland lakefront. Chicago let people enjoy the city, which often took their minds off the crime and pollution that surrounded them. Chicago has plenty of restaurants and nightspots for a young man to sow his wild oats.

I was maturing and quickly learned to take advantage of my time off to visit the city's nightclubs and music venues.

I remember one crazy experience that occurred during my time in Chicago. I met a girl named Coleen O'Sheen at a party hosted by one of my co-workers. Coleen and I hit it off right away. She liked my down-to-earth style. I liked her angelic face and petite figure. We met for coffee a few times, nothing serious, just conversation. I recall our first proper date was dinner at a trendy Northside restaurant and a walk along the lakefront. On our second date, we went to an outdoor concert at a park near her home.

Coleen didn't believe in premarital sex, an opinion she made clear to me one evening when things started getting amorous. I probably should have broken it off with her right then, but I liked her, and since it was only casual dating, more like a friendship, we continued.

About three weeks in, she invited me to her parents' house, where she introduced me to her family. Strangely, I had the feeling they were interviewing me for a job. They kept asking me about my plans, my career goals, and my family back in Cleveland. They were very solemn and pious people, not the fun-loving, accepting type. It made me a little nervous.

After that evening, I distanced myself from Coleen. I thought Coleen was cute, but a little too serious for my liking.

One evening after work, I was home making dinner when a knock came on my apartment door. I didn't have a lot of friends, so I thought it might be the Jehovah's Witness group or one of my nosy neighbors. When I opened the door, there stood Coleen.

Surprised but not necessarily unhappy, I said. "Hi Coleen, what are you doing here?"

"You have been avoiding me. Did I do something wrong?"

She was correct. I had been avoiding her. I hoped she would get the message. "No, I've just been busy."

"My parents liked you very much. My father said he would approve of our marriage."

Marriage? How in the world did marriage get into the picture?

After regaining my composure, I said. "Coleen, I don't want to marry you. We have only dated a few times. I don't want to marry anyone."

Her face turned white as a ghost. Somehow, she had imagined us as more than we were. The tears welled up in her eyes as if I had shattered her dreams.

"Is it the sex? You have to have sex?" She stepped closer. Dropping her arms to her sides in a surrendering stance. "If that is what you want, then take me. Take me right here and now. I won't be a virgin, but we won't tell anyone. We can still marry."

I wasn't about to marry anyone, and I certainly would not have sex with Coleen under these circumstances.

"No, Coleen, I don't want to do that. I do not want to marry you. We shouldn't see each other anymore. We are too different."

Without another word, she turned and stormed out of my apartment. I closed the door, wondering what had just happened. I only saw Coleen once after that, at a summer festival in my neighborhood. She gave me a look that would scare the crap out of a Hell's Angel. To this day, I thank God I escaped the clutches of that young woman and her family.

Except for the Coleen O'Sheen incident, I found Chicago to be a good place to live. At least in the summer. It could've easily become my new hometown.

Like so many small presses, the *Southsider* faced challenges in maintaining readership. The internet explosion was just beginning, and many of the small markets were still in print media, like newspapers or magazines. They used syndication with other small presses to help cut costs. My articles syndicated well, which helped pad their bottom line, and their syndication scheme made my articles viewable nationwide. A win-win situation.

At first, most of my articles were along the lines of consumer complaints. Someone contracted to have a garage built, and the unscrupulous contractor absconded with thousands of dollars in deposit money. Another time, a neighbor complained that a local body shop was running a chop shop, and the police wouldn't do anything about it. These small potato stories gave me a chance to hone my skills, but it wasn't the type of work I had envisioned when I went to graduate school.

After a few months at the *Southsider*, they gave me a weekly column. I titled it, *EXTRA, EXTRA Read All About It*, a play-off of the old-time newsboy who stood on the corner hawking a hot news special edition item to passersby. My progress to become a world-renowned investigative journalist was slow but steady.

There was another reason I enjoyed working in Chicago. Politics. Chicago and the State of Illinois have a long history of political patronage and corruption. It was a situation that lent itself to real investigative work. It seemed every day the media reported a complaint that, on the surface, seemed like business as usual, but could have a hidden story if someone took the time to do a little research. The environment piqued my interest. I didn't just want to report on news happenings; I wanted to investigate deeper into what made politics in Illinois work.

My first investigation wasn't a blockbuster deal. It focused on a local politician granting favors to a small group of supporters at the expense of the larger constituency. But then, that's always how it starts, isn't it? No big deal, until it becomes a big deal. That's when someone like me, a relative unknown, scratches the surface to find a gem of a story. It may not turn out to be Pulitzer Prize material, but it puts food on the table, all the while making me one of the most hated reporters in town.

The story was about an Illinois State Senator named Charles Djorn who was promoting bills benefiting certain contractors and investors in public works projects. Let's be honest, this type of thing happens daily in almost every country. The proverbial "It's not who you know, but who you blow" scenario.

Other people had investigated Djorn many times for impropriety. Yet he always found a way to justify his decisions and skillfully worm his way out of a tight squeeze. Whether he provided statistical data that showed his assessments benefited the constituency, or simply denied there was any inducement for his support of a publicly funded project. He was well shielded. Immune to mediocre investigations.

I took on the investigation partly because I believed I could find something more than the others had missed, and as much as I hate to admit it, I disliked this politician greatly.

Djorn was an ugly man, about forty-five or fifty years old. He was overweight, with a round, pockmarked face, likely a result of childhood acne or chickenpox. He was mostly bald, which he tried to hide with a bad comb-over. His ill-fitting clothes and arrogant facial expressions made him look even more unpleasant.

Still, somehow, Djorn found a way to attract beautiful women. This revolting man had convinced several women to marry him, but all his marriages ended in divorce. Yet whenever he made a public appearance, an attractive woman many years his junior hung on his arm. He would grope them or pat them on their behind, as people watched and laughed at his inappropriate behavior. I couldn't understand why these women let him belittle them. Was it money or power they craved? Maybe it was jealousy, but his always being surrounded by beautiful women stuck in my craw.

It wasn't just his treatment of women that bugged me; it was his dishonesty. Every time the guy opened his mouth, it seemed like he told a lie. He rarely believed his own bullshit. He did it for the shock value. He did it solely to test his limits. It angered me that other people would campaign for a pathological liar because it benefited them financially.

As an investigator, you should never allow your personal feelings to influence your work, but as much as we try to avoid it, it is human nature. When something gets under your skin, the only way to remove it is to cut it out. Cut deep and don't stop until it is out in the open. If you don't, it gets in so deep it becomes part of you. It changes who you are.

When it came to exposing Djorn, I knew what I had to do. I started by reviewing several of the investigations that other journalists and prosecutors had tried before me. I hoped to find something in their dossiers that they had missed. *Surely, there must be some hard evidence they overlooked?* I researched pages of interviews, hundreds of internet sources full of distorted facts, and reams of legal documents outlining procurement procedures, disclosure rules, and cost estimates for similar public works projects. Nothing stood out as improper, except that somehow, as you learned more and more, you smelled a rat. Whatever rules this man was breaking were subtle. In his mind, he was only bending the rules. The question became, at what point does bending become breaking?

As an investigator, I'm particularly good at analyzing empirical data. While most investigators look for the smoking gun, I like to understand how the gun works, what type of ammunition it requires, and the reason why someone would choose a particular type of gun. Sometimes a killer uses a high-powered rifle, other times, a derringer works best. Why did they choose the method they used?

One of the favorite defenses Djorn used was to claim he was acting on behalf of his constituency. He never said who he thought his constituency included. Was it the voters in his senatorial district or the people who funded his campaign? I started analyzing some projects that he sponsored or had a hand in approving, and the monetary awards the companies received from the projects.

After studying the data, I began to notice a narrow trend. Certain enterprises, engineering firms, construction companies, and delivery services were more often awarded contracts than their competitors. That could be an easily explained trend. One could simply surmise that the company was better at bidding on the projects and more efficient at completing them in an orderly fashion. It is possible to assume that they were the best choice during the bidding process.

As I analyzed more and more data, I noticed that these companies, the ones being awarded the contracts, were being paid at a rate nearly nine percent higher than other companies doing similar work. Nine percent is a significant figure, and it was coming at a cost to the taxpayers. I had just scratched the surface. Would I find something of value that was hidden?

I dug deeper into why they had consistently awarded contracts to a company that was being paid more money than their competitors. What was it that made them a preferred vendor?

It was easy to find that all the vendors in question were regular contributors to Charles Djorn's campaign fund. But so were the other contractors. Campaign contributions are nothing new in politics, and it wasn't the smoking gun I was hoping to find. The campaign contributions only represented a fraction of the millions these companies were earning, with Djorn as their benefactor. What I wanted to know was where the money was going.

While from outward appearances, Djorn appeared to be squeaky clean. My sixth sense told me there had to be more. I asked myself. *If not Djorn, who else might benefit from his abuse of power?*

All the previous investigations into Djorn were direct attacks on his campaign funding or voting record. They were attacking his fortifications. His office manager and his staff kept their behind-the-scenes operations well hidden. I needed to find a way to undermine his credibility.

I decided to investigate Djorn's business partners and family. I took a risk and dipped into my savings account to start a full-scale investigation into the Senator's business associates and family members. To shield my investigation, I hired private investigators to shadow Djorn's family members and discover who they were and how they lived.

It was no surprise to learn that the Senator's sister, who had no visible means of support, was a prominent socialite. She lived in a luxury home, owned an expensive Jaguar convertible, dined at the finest restaurants, and dressed in designer clothes. Djorn's brother owned multiple commercial properties, which conveniently enough were being leased to the same companies that were being awarded the state public works projects.

With research, I discovered that Djorn's first ex-wife, like her sister-in-law, lived a high-class lifestyle. And despite a court decree that Djorn pay his ex-wife several thousand dollars a month in alimony, I could find no evidence that he ever paid her one dollar in alimony. It made me wonder how she could afford such opulence. I concluded someone else must be paying his ex-wife's bills.

After countless internet searches, emails, and phone calls, I finally located Djorn's third ex-wife. Emily, her new last name Matthews, had relocated to a small town in rural Missouri. She had taken a divorce settlement from Djorn, a buyout for her freedom. The settlement was far less than what she deserved, prompting her desire for more. She hated Djorn and was willing to spill her guts to get revenge for his false-hearted ways.

She had detailed information on Djorn's business partners, their bribes, and cash payments to Djorn and his family members. With her help, I started piecing together a chart of payoffs and money laundering that would surely put this man, whom I disliked, out of business.

It took me three months of research and a few bribes of my own. During that time, I found receipts, obtained copies of contracts, and recorded testimony from people who worked at the companies

Djorn was favoring. I kept my profile low by hiding behind associates, using false names, and staying out of the public eye.

I employed an old college friend from Australia as an editor, thinking no one in his circle would care about an Illinois politician.

Using all the tools at my disposal and testing the story with a few trusted associates, my story finally broke to a considerable amount of uproar. News media outlets that had previously tried to expose Djorn scrambled to verify the data in my report. Djorn and his partners all tried to disavow my findings as inaccurate and politically biased. He was partly correct. Politically biased? Yes. But inaccurate? No.

My report went well beyond the old "sources say" reporting that most media outlets used to rush their reports to the press. I had evidentiary proof: copies of receipts, bank statements, and legal documents that were irrefutable.

The U.S. District Attorney's office had no choice but to announce officially that they would initiate a full-fledged investigation into Djorn and his supporters.

Within days of the publication of my story, Djorn held a press conference. As expected, he denied any wrongdoing, citing the data in my report as anomalies of which he was unaware, mere coincidences. But at the same press conference, he announced he would resign and not seek re-election to his third term for health reasons. Behind the scenes, Djorn had cut a deal with the U.S. District Attorney. In exchange for his resignation, he would walk away with no admission of guilt. The result was that Djorn, his family, and business partners got away with stealing millions from taxpayers.

His resignation was a hollow victory. Eventually, Djorn revitalized his career, oddly enough, picking up the mantra as a conservative law and order supporter. He would later resurface as a candidate for the U.S. House of Representatives. It took him nine years to rebuild his following, eventually getting elected to the House for a two-year term.

After Djorn's resignation, I started receiving death threats in the mail. I don't think they came directly from Djorn but from some contractors and service providers that were the beneficiaries of his underhanded dealings. When I put Djorn out of business, I also put many of his supporters out of business.

Then the phone calls started. When I moved to Chicago, I made the rookie mistake of publishing my phone number. I will never do that again. Prank calls started coming in at all hours of the night. Most often, they were hang-ups. Sometimes I could hear noise in the background before they hung up. The calls were so frequent that I had to disconnect my phone at night to sleep. That was the last landline phone I ever owned.

One winter day, a few weeks after my story broke, I stopped on my way home at a local diner for a hamburger. I had eaten at this place several times before without incident.

I was just finishing up my meal. As I stepped up to the cash register to pay the check, a large woman with a blonde bouffant hairstyle, quite a few years older than me, approached. She wore the most garish outfit of tight zebra-print Capri slacks, a red jacket, an overabundance of costume jewelry, and high heels. Her bright red lipstick and dark eyeliner were a poor attempt to conceal her age. At first, she seemed friendly, like she was flirting. She wasn't my style.

She started asking me questions that were more like statements than questions. "You're that reporter fella? The one who wrote about Charlie Djorn?"

I knew something was up. Our meeting wasn't an accident. I refused to argue with her. "Excuse me, ma'am, I have an appointment."

She kept talking. "St. Joseph, isn't it?"

I repeated. "Sorry, ma'am, I don't have time," as I brushed past her toward the exit.

She followed me out the door and onto the sidewalk in front of the building when a heavyset guy, the bruiser type, stepped in front of me.

"It's him, Bill," she shouted.

Before I could even understand what was happening, an enormous fist smashed into my midsection, doubling me over and causing me to fall to my knees. In the blink of an eye, he hammered a second blow to the side of my head. The second punch felt like it came from a sledgehammer. It nearly knocked me unconscious. I fell to the frozen concrete, completely defenseless.

"Kick his ass, Bill," she shouted.

A second later, a kick from a size twelve construction boot landed squarely in my chest. What little wind I had left in me disappeared. I curled into a fetal position, helpless.

"You cost me my business, asshole," Bill said.

It took a few seconds for me to regain my presence of mind. When I did, I saw Bill and the blonde woman getting into a blue pickup truck and watched them drive away. For the first time in my life, I had gotten my ass kicked. This wasn't the kind of pushing and shoving you get into as a child that hurt your feelings more than your body. This time, they hurt me badly.

I probably should have called the police. A smart person would have gone to the hospital. I did neither. I rolled onto the sidewalk and sat, waiting for the pain and shock to subside. I waited just long enough to feel safe stumbling to my car and returning home.

By the time I arrived back home, my face had swollen to a freakish lump. A size twelve bruise graced the left side of my chest. My head ached. Likely the result of at least a mild concussion. It took a couple of days for the beating's effects to wear off.

I had just learned my first lesson in investigating bad guys. Bad guys don't like to be investigated, and they will make you pay. Since then, I've been more cautious around unfamiliar people and mindful of my surroundings. It was a tough way to enter the world of investigative journalism.

From a career perspective, that story put me on the map. My writing style, which began with an assumption that drew the reader in and ended with an assurance that the facts I had given were proof that my theory was correct, made my reporting unique. It was a different way of presenting an argument. For that, I can thank my IECO bible. My peer community of Investigative Journalists found it to be a high-quality exposure to political wrongdoing.

Regardless of the effectiveness of the outcome, they heralded my report for its content and format. I was now an accepted member of an exclusive club. The best part was that I would no longer have to work for obscure internet media outlets. I could now bring my stories to the major news outlets that would welcome me with open arms. Or so I thought...

Chapter 3

A Team Of One

While Chicago, the City of Big Shoulders, treated me well, being a columnist at the *Southsider* was too limiting and paid less than what I deserved. I also found the winters in Chicago to be noticeably colder than the ones I remembered from Cleveland. After suffering through two brutally cold winters in Chicago, I looked for my next adventure. It wasn't long before I found a job opening in sunny Los Angeles. The pay was nearly twice what I earned at the *Southsider*. Important because I still had student loans to pay off.

The cost of living in California was higher than in Chicago, but I found an inexpensive apartment in the Koreatown neighborhood of L.A. An outsider might describe Koreatown as somewhat sketchy. That was before it became the trendy locality it is today. The apartment wasn't fancy. It was an old building that the owner converted from a single-family home into three one-bedroom efficiency units. My unit had a small kitchenette, a walk-in shower, and a large room divided into a living area and a bedroom. I had a parking space behind the building for my car. The two other neighbors, who were Hispanic immigrants, kept to themselves, possibly to avoid drawing attention as undocumented individuals. Although I didn't fit in with the ethnic culture, Koreatown had a lot of historic buildings and excitement. Crime in the area was high, but I wasn't wealthy, so I wasn't a target for petty crime. As long as I kept a low profile, no one bothered me.

In Los Angeles, my life changed in other ways. Tired of being a skinny weakling, I took up an exercise routine that included bicycling and jogging along Santa Monica Bay. Later, I started weightlifting at a nearby gym. The Los Angeles lifestyle agreed with me. It wasn't long before the nerdy reporter became the muscular journalist.

As my confidence grew, so did my love life. Attractive women were everywhere in L.A., and they were easy to meet. The women in California were unlike the women in Cleveland or Chicago. The girls in the Midwest were into serious relationships. They wanted a life partner. Their goal was marriage, a house, and a family, all in that order. I had no intention of accommodating any of them, at least not at that point in my life.

In Los Angeles, the women were either trying to become movie stars or trying to marry a movie producer. My job title, Investigative Journalist, made a big impression. Most probably thought associating with me would make them famous, or at least help them meet a lot of famous people. It worked. My title made me a hot commodity. My paltry sex life improved, at least until they figured out that being a journalist meant spending most of my time reading or writing. Despite my new confident look and better physique, on the inside, I was still the same nerd. When they learned that I barely made enough money to pay my bills each month, they ghosted me. With their hopes of my bringing them fame or fortune dashed, they moved on to someone more exciting or wealthier.

The press that I worked with focused primarily on the entertainment industry. My articles were about movie stars and sports icons. The job paid well, but the pieces I wrote were mostly fluff. I wrote big headlines and brief articles. It wasn't the type of hard-hitting journalism I sought for my career. It wasn't headlines I was after. I wanted to be an investigator.

For me, investigating means exactly that, don't assume anything; reality is not always as it appears. People are all too often influenced by the facts that are handed to them. They look for and accept logical explanations. Experience has shown there is nothing less logical than the truth. Even an eyewitness can have their facts wrong.

In Los Angeles, I struggled to find my comfort zone in a city so different from my Midwest upbringing. Still, I made every effort to fit in and become part of the community. I had neighbors that I would see almost every day, yet I never spoke with any of them. That wasn't unusual in Los Angeles. Years can pass in L.A. without neighbors becoming friends.

But I was a Midwesterner. Growing up in Cleveland, I knew everyone in my neighborhood, and everyone knew the St. Joseph family. If I misbehaved as a child, like throwing a rock through a window or knocking over a garbage can, a friendly neighbor would politely inform my father. By the time I got home, my father would be ready with my punishment.

It wasn't that way in Koreatown. Two or three times a week, I watched the neighbor who lived in the building next door load a set of golf clubs into the back seat of his car and drive off. He would be gone for hours, only to return home later in the day, unpack his clubs, and put them back in the garage. Any reasonable person would assume him to be an avid golfer.

Finally, one spring day, I decided to break the ice and approach him, intent on making a new friend. Extending my hand, I introduced myself as his neighbor. Then, with a pointing motion, I showed which apartment was mine so he would know where I lived. We started up a conversation about the neighborhood and the other neighbors. He seemed friendly enough.

When I innocently asked him. "Where do you golf?"

He shook his head as he said, "I don't golf any longer. I have a bad back and haven't golfed in years."

Confused, I replied, "But I see you load your clubs into the back seat of your car all the time."

He explained, "Oh, those are the days I visit my father in a nearby nursing home. He suffers from advancing Alzheimer's and has anger issues. The staff at the home has their hands full, keeping him from starting trouble. They asked me to help if I could. When he was younger, he was a dedicated golfer. I bring him his clubs on the days when I visit him. It seems to calm him down. He sits in his wheelchair and polishes his clubs, counts his tees, and talks about the time he birdied a hole on this course or made a twenty-foot putt on that course. Perhaps it reminds him of his younger days? Funny how little things affect someone's mind. It's the least I can do for the man who raised me."

I learned two things that day. One, my neighbor loved his father very much. Second, even when we witness events with our own eyes, it's easy to arrive at the wrong conclusion. I saw him with golf clubs and assumed he was golfing. I was wrong. Only after learning the whole story, with all the facts, did I fully understand the truth behind his actions.

The beating I took after the Djorn incident taught me that investigating people is risky. It's a common response for investigated individuals to react negatively towards you. Most likely, they will only challenge your reputation. They simply call you a name like dirtbag or asshole. However, people can become irrational when you threaten their way of life. At the extreme, they threaten you with physical harm.

Individuals may act irrationally, but corporations under investigation are particularly surly. Corporations, unlike people, have money, they have power, and they have attorneys. Attorneys whose only job is to protect their clients by any means necessary. They will use their clout to discredit you. Corporate attorneys, who are usually very smart, may also be just as corrupt as the client they are protecting, making it a double whammy against anyone starting an investigation.

One thing you learn quickly in this business is to tread lightly in the early goings. If you ruffle too many feathers too early, the party you're investigating hunkers down. The word gets around to all the witnesses that live on the periphery, and getting them to talk becomes exceedingly difficult. In the early stages of an investigation, you want them to see you as a harmless annoyance who's only after easy money.

It's important to distinguish my role as an investigative journalist from that of the private detectives you see on television. We have little in common. A private detective is great at uncovering a crime or wrongdoing, allowing the police or media to dig deeper into its origin.

My job is to go further, uncovering wrongdoing and then assembling a compelling story from a chaotic mass of facts and circumstances. I treat it much like a doctoral thesis, one I must defend beyond a shadow of a doubt. Only then can I publish the final analysis and relevant facts to the public for review. Because of the complexity of our investigations, investigative journalists are held to a higher standard than reporters, or "shock jocks" who deal with opinion and sensationalism to attract an audience of followers. In my community, accountability, ethics, and professionalism are standards we demand. Remember the IECO guidebook my college professor gave me? They wrote it to prevent the maverick style of journalism that has become commonplace.

Due to the sensitive nature of this work, journalists often work alone or hire assistants and contractors who are not aware of the full investigation details to handle routine tasks, such as phone calls, stenography, and office work. I have sub-contracted Private Investigators who were unaware of the larger investigation to follow suspects or interview informants.

While I may use hired help to gather information, the burden of assembling all the data into a complete picture falls exclusively on me. It becomes a matter of trust. If one of my contractors or assistants were to inadvertently "spill the beans" about my investigation, suspects would run for the hills. Just a simple comment like, "I heard he has been having an affair.", in the wrong social circle, could torpedo weeks of work.

That means that at least in the early stages of an investigation, I become, for lack of a better description, a one-person team.

Chapter 4

Want Success? Copy Me

My years in Los Angeles went by in the blink of an eye. The Southern California lifestyle made a different man out of me. Physically, I wasn't a puny little boy any longer. Mentally, I was more confident interacting with people. While I gained more experience and made more business contacts, reporting on people who were famous for being famous wasn't my career goal. I had bigger fish to fry.

With some of my student loan debts paid off and my financial picture looking better all the time, I decided it was time for me to do what I do best: finding the hidden story behind the perceived version.

I spent weeks trying to find a job in New York City. Most successful journalists operate out of New York. That didn't work out. None of the major news magazines wanted me. I didn't have the experience they wanted to lead an investigative team, and I didn't want to start as an entry-level beat reporter and work my way up. I kept looking for job opportunities that would fit my career goals. Soon, I realized that there is no place on the globe better than in Washington, D.C. to find a cover-up. Conversely, no place is better suited for an investigative journalist to ply his trade.

I learned in L.A. and Chicago that working for a newspaper or magazine offers security and a steady paycheck, but not a lot of freedom. Being a freelance journalist carries greater risk and greater reward. I didn't have any job offers, but I felt it was time to take a risk. So, after weeks of deliberating, I packed up my belongings. Bidding the sunny skies of L.A. goodbye, I moved across the country to where the cherry trees bloom in the spring, my nation's capital. I found an affordable townhouse in Bethesda, Maryland, that I would use as my home base.

I didn't have a steady paycheck, but I knew it was there; I would make my mark.

Today, people ask me how I choose the stories I write. How do I decide who will be the next giant that I intend to bring down? It's easy. I like to think of myself as the little David who must face the mighty Goliath. Most times, it is an accurate description of the situation. It's especially true when you are investigating a large corporation. Corporations make worthy adversaries. They have lawyers with powerful legal minds who know how to straddle the line between good and evil. Corporations have money, money that is used to market themselves as the solution to whatever problem you might be having. And last, corporations use their money and influence to elect or manipulate lawmakers. Then use them to help make their dubious activities legal.

When you take on a big-money corporation, you also take an enormous risk. If you fail, your reputation goes down the toilet. If you succeed, it brings with it a level of satisfaction that you can enjoy for years to come.

I hit the ground running in D.C. with a portfolio filled with a list of big companies that were worthy adversaries. There were many to choose from, yet the decision came easily. There was one modern business that grated on my skin. Those for-profit business schools that promote themselves as institutes of higher education. Most often, they are little more than paper mills that rip off unsuspecting students and defraud federal student loan programs, all in the name of healthy profits. I knew they were ripping people off, so I began at the beginning.

For starters, I made a list of reasons to investigate this business. It wasn't long before the preliminary data alarmed me. The numbers I calculated showed that students who enroll in these for-profit schools are less likely to complete a program than in any college program offered by state schools. Their rate, as low as thirty-five percent, is well below the rate of public four-year colleges and private four-year universities.

For-profit students take on debt at a rate almost double those who have gained acceptance into four-year public colleges.

Graduates of for-profit schools earn nearly ten percent less in the first ten years after completing their program than students graduating from a public college.

I assessed the target audience of these schools. Finding a pattern was quick. Students at for-profit business schools are disproportionately older and more likely to be minorities or female. And they are more likely to be single parents than students at community colleges or four-year public universities. They were people searching for success without a clear direction.

The business model was like a blueprint for making money.

One of the most alarming statistics I found showed that students who enroll in for-profit programs are four times more likely to default on student loans than those who attend four-year public colleges. The cost to the nation and society is tremendous, despite being unseen on any corporate balance sheet. We pay for it through taxes and strained social programs. Sometimes, it manifests itself in another way, as these clients turn to crime to resolve their financial troubles.

While some might argue it is business. I will argue it is a dirty business. A business that requires oversight. In the absence of oversight, those companies that act with impunity must face financial consequences for their missteps. Either through monetary settlements or revocation of the licenses.

Numerous exposés have been written about this subject. Most efforts only exposed the issue, failing to generate consequences for the owners. Retribution was my goal. To put the fear of God, or at least the fear of D.K. St. Joseph, in them.

I sorted through the list of for-profit schools I had assembled. I could have chosen any of a dozen for-profit schools for my story. Of all the companies on my list, the one I disliked most was Middle America University. Middle America purported to be a twenty-first-century business school. They advertised a curriculum that would prepare their students for real-world challenges. Claiming to have direct access to high-paying careers at forward-looking corporations across the globe.

My initial investigation found an alarming array of statistics that told me this company had a lot to hide.

The University, and I use that term lightly, began operations from brick-and-mortar sites in eight cities across the United States. They carefully chose the cities, including Atlanta, Detroit, St. Louis, and the one closest to my current home, Baltimore. Other cities with classroom-based schools were Memphis, Birmingham, Little Rock, and Las Vegas. All cities they operated within had high populations of minorities and high poverty rates. Their campuses were always in the inner city in lower-income, high-crime areas.

I had the displeasure of visiting one of their schools in Baltimore during my investigation. I posed as a prospective student, eager to see what my college experience would be like before I signed on the dotted line. What I saw appalled me.

Middle America had rented space in an old, formerly vacant, shopping center in the Orangeville area. One of Baltimore's poorest neighborhoods. A former department store, the exterior of the now dilapidated building, showed signs of years of neglect. Maintenance people had patched the brickwork in a dozen places, none of the patches matching the other. Painted plywood siding covered sections of the front that were once plate-glass windows. Students took their lunch breaks on picnic benches outside near the parking lot.

Inside, the school hadn't invested a penny in improvements. The walls showed peeling paint, and dangerous-looking asbestos covered the plumbing and heating ducts. The bare concrete floors and open ceilings made the noise level unbearable. They created classrooms in the open retail space using temporary dividers. Conversations bled over from room to room during lectures. It was a horrendous learning environment.

The school used television infomercials to promote its curriculum. The ads featured high-profile billionaires, who presented "How I made millions...", success stories. They enticed the prospect by offering a free introductory seminar. Like the infomercials, the seminar featured a big-name politician telling his story.

The classes themselves were nothing more than presenters relating their success stories. They encouraged students to apply the same techniques that they claim led to their overwhelming success.

They taught the students very little about how to achieve similar results. None of the classes provided detailed information on financing, money management, or profit-and-loss situations. They didn't teach students negotiation skills, management competencies, or any form of technical skill.

The dropout rate was exceedingly high, at over fifty percent. Students who completed the curriculum were unlikely to achieve success beyond what they could have without the program. Only a handful of graduates reported success when applying for and securing a position at an established business. Still, Middle America used those few graduates as examples of the value of their program.

When the World Wide Web blossomed, Middle America was one of the first to recognize distance learning as a business model. They expanded to a global audience, tripling their student population. Their profits zoomed almost overnight. Through the widespread publication of video endorsements on television or sites like YouTube and Vimeo, they drove traffic to their website. Their advertising and marketing schemes appealed to a disadvantaged population. They suckered in candidates who couldn't gain acceptance into traditional colleges.

The school's recruiters then used high-pressure sales tactics to enroll students who had little or no prospects for success. Using hard-sell pitches, the recruiter or salesperson always tried to exploit a weakness in the prospect's situation. They might manipulate a single mother of two by convincing her, "Think about how much you can help your children."

Or they would review their credit score and debt-to-income ratio and promise them a solution to break their cycle of poverty. Ultimately forcing the prospect to feel guilty or afraid if they do not enroll. They weren't selling education. Instead, they sold dreams of a more secure future.

Besides their high-pressure recruiting tactics, their instructors engaged in a methodical and systematic series of sales pitches to convince students to buy books, extra seminars, or even clothing. The instructor would receive an incentive based on a sliding scale of transactions. The more they sold, the higher their commission.

Before you turn away and say, "Why should I care if these people fail to get an education or get taken advantage of?" You may wish to consider the impact these businesses have on the economy and your pocketbook. They collectively make billions annually while returning little back to society.

There was a second reason I investigated Middle America University. I not only believed they were failing to live up to their obligations towards their customers, but they were also being bankrolled by hedge fund investors. Big-money people who knew of their inferior operation but took the profits, anyway. Call it what you want. To me, it was a criminal enterprise.

Previous articles written about the school focused on the lack of education the school provided. I made my investigation different by concentrating on finding evidence that the investors were committing fraud, involved in predatory lending, or even money laundering.

For me, Middle America would become a massive undertaking. I wanted it to become that once-in-a-lifetime investigation that every journalist seeks to attach to their name. With a little luck, I could produce a document that becomes an example for business schools and colleges to use in their curricula.

To investigate, I wished to start by interviewing those who had unpleasant experiences. To be fair, an unhappy customer isn't always the fault of the provider. Lack of communication between parties is common in these situations. So, you must first categorize the problems they experienced. Was it determined by performance or financial factors?

Many consumer websites specialize in reviews and ratings. Social media can also be an excellent source of data. It took me weeks to sort through all the social media complaints. I tried to separate the ones that are sour grapes from the ones that have a legitimate claim of misrepresentation or fraud. Reviewing a large percentage of the positive reviews about the school allowed me to maintain a level of fairness. If some students felt they were getting what they needed, I wanted my report to include that data as well.

Through extensive interviews, I found that about half of the students who gave the school positive grades did so because they believed that a positive review would help them in the long run. They worried negative reviews would affect both their ability to get their Certificates of Completion and ultimately a job after completing the coursework. I spoke with one reviewer, who stated, "The evaluations I posted did not reflect my actual opinions on the courses. I wanted the school to look good to enhance the value of my certificate."

With no ability to subpoena their financial records, I had to find other evidence of wrongdoing. Corporate financial statements provided to investors only provide a small measure of evidence.

Fortunately, there is a way to query court records for lawsuits filed against the school. I used PACER, an electronic government service for court records, where I could get copies of court filings. The site provided sufficient information to identify the plaintiffs who were suing Middle America. It was no surprise, as I dug deeper into the lawsuits and complaints against the school. The same names kept popping up.

Once I had a list of names, my actual work began. I started contacting people, hoping to find someone willing to talk, anyone with knowledge that would be useful in my investigation. Many of the complainants settled with Middle America and signed non-disclosure agreements. They refused to talk.

The process of gathering information took weeks, which turned into months. For those months, I had little income, and my bills started piling up.

Finally, I made some headway. It starts small. The person you are interviewing utters something like, "I always thought they were hiding something." You work to make them expound on that comment. Then, after a while, the comment changes to, "Everyone knew they were hiding something." Eventually, the conversation changes to a definitive, "They were hiding it. I have the emails to prove what they were doing." Then suddenly it becomes as if someone had set up a course of dominoes and you pushed over the first, causing them to fall in order while you watch in delight.

As the evidence mounts, you could challenge the interviewee, who, caught off guard, allows another revelation to spill from their lips. As my investigation grew, the interviewees became like rats from a sinking ship. To save themselves, or at least justify their actions, they turn on each other. "It wasn't me; it was his idea."

Such was the case with Middle America University. I had no legal authority to charge the business or the principals involved, so my best course of action is to garner enough evidence to embarrass the authorities at the state and federal levels to bring charges against the operators. I intended to put these guys out of business. For that, I needed to find evidence of criminal wrongdoing.

After extensive interviews, I was able to record two industry insiders, both of them long-time lobbyists for the industry group known as the Association of Private Sector Colleges and Universities (APSCU). One participant, a hard-hitting attorney, J. C. Westfall, admitted that the school's recruiters were under pressure to register as many students as possible, as quickly as possible, without qualifying the student for the program or curriculum. The goal was sales. Westfall said. "The recruiters had a saying, 'Get one more ass in every class'."

The other admission came from an APSCU member who would only speak under anonymity. She admitted to a conscious effort to qualify the students for Federal Student Loans and Grants, even though the program would not provide the student a degree useful to get the career the person wanted.

By the time I completed my research, which documented the abuses and fraudulent actions of the school, several other investigations were already in progress by law enforcement and the Department of Education. My timing wasn't great.

I tried peddling my exposé to several major outlets, like the New York Times and the Washington Post. They rejected my manuscript for several reasons. It was too long for print media, meaning it would have to be run as a series. It was too in-depth for them to trust my work without having one of their teams verify my data. One rejection claimed my article hit on too many controversial subjects, which they wanted to avoid. Besides, to the major media companies, I was a nobody. They had people on their payroll whom they trusted to write their articles.

I knew it was good, so I kept working to find a publisher. I finally found an internet-based news outlet called the *Lumorist*. They were looking for articles with national appeal, and their digital format would allow the story to run as a series.

They worked the article over several weeks through social media, and of all places, through television ads, until it caught on and their readership skyrocketed. It became the subject of water-cooler conversations all across the country.

My story added fuel to an already smoldering fire that was burning Middle America University's house down. Under pressure from the lawsuits and the media, with my report being a keystone effort, the school shuttered its doors. In a separate action, the members of the school's board and investment council negotiated a settlement to repay a portion of tuition to former students.

The story about Middle America University brought me the recognition I had been seeking from my peers in the journalism community. Even today, they still consider the piece a model for Investigative Journalists worldwide to follow.

Later that year, they nominated me for a Phillip Meyer Journalism Award and a National Journalism Award. I won neither of those prestigious awards, but my nominations were important. Those accolades meant I had finally grabbed the brass ring. It was unusual that someone so young, at only thirty years old, could achieve recognition so quickly. The unique format and writing style I used captured the attention of readers of all ages.

I had hit the fast track up the career ladder, and for that brief period, that story had brought me to the top of the mountain. The companies that rejected my work earlier suddenly started contacting me to request submissions for their publications.

I couldn't envision other aspects of my life, such as family, love, or travel, having such an important impact on my future.

Yet, there was more to come, much more.

Chapter 5

One And Donne

Because you're only as good as your last exposé, I was always in search of that next big story. Sometimes weeks or months would go by with no high-impact articles. During those quiet periods, I made a living writing shorter commentaries. I published them online, and sometimes they would get syndicated in print media.

When my work requires me to be in the public eye, as mine often does, I attend a lot of media conferences. Over the years, I have attended charity events, seminars, and symposiums. If you attend, look for me standing alone against a wall in a crowded ballroom or in the back row of an auditorium.

Meanwhile, my friends and co-workers mill around smiling, hugging, and shaking hands. Did I say friends? No, correct that, I meant acquaintances. One thing you learn early in this business is that it is hard to make friendships, the meaningful kind, because very few people trust you. They may respect your intensity; they may try to understand your drive for the truth. But trust? Trust is more difficult to come by. You see, everyone has a skeleton in their closet. Everyone has done something wrong or made a mistake that they would rather forget ever happened. When they see you coming, they immediately worry that it might be them you're investigating.

It is always this way at any social event, fundraiser, funeral, or wedding. I stand away from the crowd, alone. Out of courtesy, some will stop by and shake my hand. Smile and ask, "How have you been?"

Or "What are you working on these days?" I cannot answer the latter question. That would be too revealing. It might jeopardize a work in progress or endanger a confidential source.

I usually reply with the same old dredged-up response. "Oh, I've been terribly busy. No rest for the wicked, you know." Or I pretend to whisper, "I can't talk now, they're watching. Maybe later?" For fun, I occasionally pretend to have a British accent and joke, "I'm writing a story about the Queen. It's jolly good, you know."

However, attending events and fundraisers is an important part of the job. I must make connections and, more importantly, practice my interviewing skills. Social events are a great place to test your skills at making someone feel at ease while drawing as much private information from them as possible. It might even inspire me for my next inquiry.

When you lack a large circle of friends, your love life suffers, too. My love life will never be the inspiration for a romance novel. Aside from my short time in L.A., there have been few women in my life. Of the few women I have dated, none of the relationships were genuine. My career or hers usually got in the way of anything lasting. Despite some romantic moments, my achievements as a journalist outweighed my success as a Casanova.

Not being popular doesn't mean I don't have stories. One relationship story that impacted my life is how I first got involved with Melinda Donne. It's an intriguing tale from my early career, and it says a lot about my personal growth.

Melinda, an international war correspondent from Northern Ireland, was already a rising star in the U.K. and Europe. Her home base was a town near Belfast. She had an insatiable thirst for adventure. Melinda traveled the world reporting on political conflict and the violence of radicalism. She did it so we, the less informed readers, could get a better grasp on historic events.

Growing up in Northern Ireland meant facing an intense and sometimes violent environment daily. Having lived through a lot of political conflict, it was no surprise that international disagreements, both cultural and religious, fascinated her. She wanted to not only understand the reason behind the conflict but also to show the rest of the world they weren't alone or even that different.

A mutual acquaintance introduced us at a Mass Media and Political Communication conference in Virginia. Melinda saw the United States as fertile soil to bring her articles. She produced stories that often took on a different viewpoint than those reporters in the U.S. would publish.

We had a brief affair shortly after I moved to D.C. She wasn't a particularly attractive woman from a physical viewpoint. I remember her having a round face, fair skin, and dark horn-rimmed glasses. With her short, dark hair parted on the side, she reminded me of a young boy about to make his first communion. She had rather a muscular build for a woman. While you wouldn't call her obese or overweight, no one would describe her as petite. When she stood upright, her posture leaned more toward the masculine side. Her walk reminded me of a bull charging toward a matador's red cape.

She looked out of place in designer clothing, which she wore for business meetings, always trying her best to look professional. But even in casual street clothes, she had a rugged appearance. Her body style enhanced her authenticity as an adventurer who traveled to undeveloped parts of the world. She went places where the Barbie Doll type of news reporter that you see on the six o'clock news would never consider going. Melinda wasn't afraid to stand toe to toe with a tribal leader or a rebel army officer. Her boldness sometimes took these tough guys by surprise.

Despite her brawny physique, Melinda had a pleasurable excitement about her. There was a certain undeniable energy that was impossible to ignore.

She was in the States to hobnob with politically connected supporters to raise money for her latest endeavor. The story she proposed was about international terrorists who moved between the remote villages and towns in the Middle East, down through Pakistan and into India, and ultimately to other lands. For this mission, her travel plans would lead her through the jungles of India. Venturing into some of the scariest places on Earth.

Melinda and I spent a month as best pals, dashing around the Washington D.C. metro area. Together, we met with her sponsors, trying to convince them how her work will help eradicate terrorism once and for all. With their financial help, she would buy equipment, hire jungle guides, pay for needed travel expenses, and, of course, have money to bribe local officials in the small towns and villages along the way.

Her fund-raising schedule included weeks of clandestine meetings with maverick Congressmen and international lobbyists. After dozens of speeches before anti-terror groups, late-night parties with dignitaries, and countless bottles of Irish Whiskey, Melinda raised enough pledge money to fund her endeavor.

I thought once she raised enough money for her mission, that would be the end of our brief liaison. It surprised me when she invited me to join her on her journey. She promised me an adventure I would never forget. Despite my initial apprehension, I seized the opportunity to understand her work and that of other journalists like her. Besides, I liked Melinda. She was fun to be with. There's no better way to learn about the world outside of America.

Melinda had the entire mission planned out, down to the last detail. Her description of an adventure, unlike any I had experienced, intrigued me. She instructed me on what to bring and what to leave behind. I should leave anything but the bare essentials at home. My computer, mobile phone, and wallet would remain behind in a hotel safe. "You only need to bring cash and one credit card, nothing else," she said.

Melinda went on ahead to obtain the plethora of travel documents necessary for the journey. I was to follow her ten days later. We met at the Viraj Sarovar Portico Hotel in the city of Jammu, in Northern India. It was my last taste of luxury before we set out on our trek into no-man's-land. The next morning, we hired a car to take us to a remote village only a few kilometers from the City of Tral, India. Tral, despite all efforts, remains a hotspot for terrorist activity. It was there in this little war-torn hamlet where we would start our adventure. Melinda hoped to make a connection with Islamic groups moving back and forth across the border between India and Pakistan. Melinda brought with her sizeable sums of Rupee, Chinese Yuan, and American Dollar, which she would use to bribe local officials and hire guides to protect us in the forest lands.

Dressed for action in khaki slacks, an off-white t-shirt, and a safari vest, she had her short hair neatly tucked under a "Boonie" hat. She clad her feet in military-style warm-weather army boots. Melinda looked more comfortable and attractive in her jungle clothes than in her business attire. She carried with her a Glock G19 pistol and offered me one as well. Not being skilled with firearms, and not wishing to shoot off my toe or other appendages, I declined in favor of a Jungle Master Survival knife.

The area around Tral was teeming with military security. Even our international journalist credentials did little to impress the Indian soldiers, whose job it was to keep the peace. With some coaxing and a few well-spent rupees, the security officers allowed us to pass into the contested zone outside the city center. We met our private paramilitary guides at a ramshackle three-room hotel on the town's edge. Our chaperones, all former Indian military officers, not only knew the territory, but they also enjoyed the thrill of danger and the lucrative pay more than they enjoyed protecting us.

We loaded our belongings into the back of what looked like a broken-down, dark green Land Rover. Someone had partially cut the metal roof off, leaving protection only for the driver and front passenger. From outward appearance, the vehicle wouldn't make it a few kilometers, but it had fresh tires, and the engine sounded healthy. They had equipped the vehicle with the latest short-wave radio and a modern GPS unit. Between the front seats, the guides had mounted a partially sawed-off shotgun, its barrel facing upward so that it just fit inside the cabin.

Pantere, a young, slender, dark-skinned guide, drove while Nambu, the larger, more muscular, bearded leader, claimed the passenger seat. Melinda and I piled into the fixed second-row seats. Two other guides, Keshaw, who had long flowing hair, and Abhay, who told us his name meant fearless, strapped themselves to makeshift jump seats that looked like they had been made from old lawn furniture.

Our path took us to the southwest toward the Afghanistan and Pakistan border. The route provided us with magnificent views of the Himalaya mountains to the north and open land to the south. The road, which started as gravel, quickly changed to smooth dirt for about one kilometer, then changed again into a pothole-filled, unmaintained pathway. As we drove toward the forest land, we could see huge construction trucks to the south harvesting the massive teak and pinewood trees to be used to supplement India's burgeoning economy. The government will eventually clear the land to make way for farmland to help feed India's exploding population.

Pantere kept a blistering pace over bumps and dips and the occasional flowing stream. Clinging tightly to our seats was the only thing that prevented us from getting ejected from the vehicle. The Land Rover never protested as it barreled over everything that got in its way, until we arrived in a section that finally became unpassable by any type of motor vehicle, except for maybe a bulldozer.

The truck slid to a halt between some trees just off the wet pathway, with Nambu declaring, "We are here."

Here? I thought. *Here seems to be in the middle of nowhere.*

I was correct. In the middle of a jungle, several kilometers from civilization, we were about to embark on an even deeper journey into the unknown. We grabbed our gear and stood by while Pantere marked the spot with the GPS and disabled the electronics so they would be useless to anyone but him. The guides, working quickly, used a camouflage tarpaulin to conceal the truck, adding tree branches for extra camouflage. When they finished, the vehicle was barely visible from five feet away. The likelihood of anyone finding it without the GPS coordinates was slim. With little fanfare, Nambu glanced at his compass and said, "This way."

We stepped deeper into the jungle, with Nambu in the lead.

Before leaving the United States, I did some research on the area we were hiking. The experts classified this particular area of the globe as a subtropical pine forest. I knew very little about the region's flora. To me, it was just a jungle, an area frozen in time. Its canopy of tall Himalayan pine and teak trees and its thick undergrowth of berberis and rhododendron could characterize it as scary. The tall grasses grew quickly to fill in between the trees and create a wildness that was home to a thousand rare and sometimes dangerous wildlife species.

We always let one of the hired guides take the lead. They knew the terrain and how to avoid dangerous animals, sinkholes, and traps placed by native hunters.

Even though our trek took us only a few kilometers from areas that were being bulldozed for agricultural uses, we were invading the natural habitat of rare and endangered species. As we marched our way deeper into the forest, we observed golden langur monkeys, barking deer, and in one clearing, a small herd of gaur, a type of wild oxen. Flying squirrels flitted from tree to tree as Beech and Pine Marten hung from the tree branches and scurried away when we approached. One of our guides, Nambu, pointed out an already trampled pathway, a herd of Asian elephants had created for us. We followed the path for several kilometers until it inexplicably disappeared into the trees.

We also worked to avoid tribes of indigenous people who still called the jungle home. They lived in harmony with and depended on the forest for their livelihood. They had watched for years as civilization had stolen the resources they used to survive and was eradicating their homeland. Even the less warlike tribes would chase you from their hunting grounds, endangering not only our mission but our lives as well.

It was a scary place even during the daytime. The heat was stifling, the smells of the indigenous plants overpowering. The thick canopy in certain areas made it easy to forget it was daytime. Sometimes, we would find a small clearing where the sun peeking through the trees reminded us of its oppressive heat. We walked for hours at a time, mostly in silence or speaking in a whisper, the guides using hand signals to warn us of a dangerous drop-off or pack of wild animals.

The advice Melinda had given me regarding the equipment to bring along was spot on. I will forever be grateful for her guidance in choosing a well-fitting pair of army-style boots. The boots saved my feet on more than one occasion when I took a misstep into a thorny bush or a pit of quicksand.

The guides, experienced in military-style operations into the jungle, moved quickly through the dense forest, using machetes to cut a narrow path through the bush and employing ropes to climb up and rappel down ravines. Melinda, with her muscular build, had no trouble keeping pace. I thought I was in good physical condition. I could run miles on a paved street or treadmill. Yet, not being a true outdoorsman, I found it difficult to keep up. We stopped to rest far more often than the others wanted. I was slowing them down, which made me question my choice to join her on her quest. Melinda made excuses for me. She pushed me along, encouraging me. Why? I didn't know.

Chapter 6

It's A Jungle Out There

Nightfall came early in the jungle, making it impossible to travel more than a few hundred yards after dusk. Any attempt to hike deeper into the tangle might meet with disaster. The first night, we camped in a deeply forested area outside of any town or village. Melinda wanted to keep our presence secret until she could arrange a relatively safe encounter with one of the terrorist groups that used this area to travel undetected between countries.

We camped early on day one. Setting three two-man camouflage pup tents in a small clearing near a stream. We kept our fires small, only large enough to boil water for tea. For nourishment, we consumed military-style food called Meals Ready to Eat, commonly referred to as MREs. To supplement our dinner, one of our guides, Keshaw, collected edible berries from the scrub bushes. The sour-tasting berries were no treat when eaten by themselves, but added flavor to our bland MREs.

We sat upon stools made from piled-up rocks and tree branches we had earlier cut down to clear spaces for our tents. Melinda kept her firearm in an accessible location, ready for any intruder, man, or beast that would threaten our encampment. In minutes, our eyes adjusted, faintly seeing into the brush around camp. We kept our focus, watching for anything that might threaten our well-being.

We broke into two-man teams and took turns standing guard and sleeping, each team taking a three-hour stint. Even though I wanted desperately to climb into my tent and pass out, Melinda insisted that she and I take the first guard shift. Her rationalization that it would ensure the two of us got a longer period, six contiguous hours of uninterrupted sleep, was spot on.

The day-long trek through the jungle exhausted me. My back, hips, and legs ached from lugging heavy backpacks. Mentally, the stress of only stopping for brief water breaks or to relieve ourselves was wearing me down. It was only day one, and I was already questioning my decision to take this adventure. I realized I was in over my head with no exit strategy. Because our campsite was nothing more than a clearing in the trees, less than one hundred square feet, relieving yourself in the camp was out of the question. No one wanted to deal with another person's mess. So, we had to slip discreetly into the bush to take care of it. How quickly I learned to appreciate modern plumbing.

For safety's sake, Melinda, the sole woman, had to be accompanied by a male guard and still try to maintain her decency. As Indian men aren't used to a woman boss, Melinda chose me as her partner.

By the time our three-hour guard shift was ending, the brutal daytime temperature was abating. Melinda and I would have the luxury of sleeping in the cooler night air.

Just before retiring for the night, I relieved myself one more time, hoping to avoid a nighttime excursion into the bush. I waited as Melinda slipped behind a tree and attended to her personal hygiene before we roused the two guides who were chosen to take over the next watch.

We crawled into our tent, and even though we had sleeping bags, it was too hot to climb inside. We lay on top of our bags, using them as a mattress. Despite spending the last few weeks together as chums, having fun, and becoming close friends, we had yet to be

intimate. Melinda simply didn't attract me in that way. She made a
wonderful companion, strictly in a platonic sense. This remote jungle
camp seemed like an unlikely place for that situation to change.

I stripped down to my underwear and lay on top of my
unfurled bag. Melinda undressed down to her panties, and though it
was dark in the tent, I could see the shadowy outline of her breasts as
she pulled her T-shirt over her head. Although she lay next to me on
her side, almost naked, it was too hot to do anything but sleep. In
seconds, we were both sound asleep.

By the time I awoke the next morning, I found Melinda already
dressed and helping the others break camp. She wanted to continue
toward our rendezvous point before it got too hot. Trying not to be a
hindrance, I jumped in to help. In minutes, we were following our
guides toward our next stopping point.

Melinda planned our route to intentionally skirt civilization
and avoid the small villages and hamlets that were, in reality, only a
few kilometers away. She wanted to keep our presence hidden from
the local herders and tribal hunters. Despite lacking modern
communication, the word would swiftly spread, alerting authorities
and terrorists to our location. Secrecy was crucial.

Day two brought even more treacherous terrain. The jungle grew
denser, the gorges deeper. One false step and we might tumble down a
ravine into oblivion, or we may encounter a pack of wild boar or a
pride of jungle cat. When I made jokes about the route we had
chosen, Melinda defended her plan. She kept reminding me to keep
my wits about me. We were strangers in a strange land. Risking an
accident or injury could end the mission, or worse, cost our lives. We
were still days away from reaching the rendezvous point she had
targeted.

Nightfall awakened the forest with sounds that weren't audible during the daytime. Squeals from the monkeys and grunts from the big cats permeated the air. Screams from the smaller prey would suddenly go silent as the predators announced their latest kill.

On the second night, our guides found a small clearing with dry soil. We pitched our tents just in time for all daylight to disappear. As we replicated our plan of three-hour guard shifts from the night before, Melinda and I took the first watch, talking softly and keeping our ears open. By the time our turn ended, our tent seemed like a luxury hotel. Even though it was hot, I welcomed the chance to lie down on my unrolled sleeping bag to rest.

It was several hours into an uneasy sleep when I awoke to the sound of what sounded like an enormous beast; a lion or tiger pacing around outside our tent. I could hear heavy breathing and a low rattling growl. Something more terrifying than a human was right beside our makeshift shelter.

Melinda heard it too. She cautioned me in a whisper. "Don't move, don't make a sound." The breathing drew closer, snorting and sniffing the smell of human flesh. I could swear the beast had its nostrils pressed against the nylon wall of our tent. Any second, that monster could tear us apart. Fear kept me motionless, too frightened to act.

The danger didn't scare Melinda; instead, it seemed to excite her. Moving slowly to avoid creating a stir, she reached for her pistol, grabbing it with both hands. I cringed, almost expecting what was to happen next.

Before Melinda could fire, a shot from outside our tent rang out. The giant animal let out a groan. I heard a second shot, a pant, then nothing. One of the on-duty guards had dispatched the giant cat. In seconds, the other guides scrambled from their tent as the camp erupted into chaos. The group of Indian guides shouted and laughed, congratulating the lookout for eliminating the threat.

I poked my head through the slit that made up the tent's doorway. In the dim moonlight, I could see the guides dragging the carcass of an Indian Leopard away from our campsite, into the jungle. My heart was still pounding. I turned back to Melinda. "Has anything like this ever happened before?"

"Aye, it happens, part of the adventure. We are in the jungle, after all."

As the commotion outside our tent subsided, I tried to lie back down and return to sleep. But Melinda wouldn't let me. The excitement had her turned on. She slithered up next to me and slid her hand into my underwear. "Let me calm you down," she said.

Shocked by her advance, I said. "What? Now? I don't think I can."

She took my hand and pushed it between her legs. I could feel her excitement. She whispered. "Believe me, you don't want to miss this chance. I promise you won't forget this night."

She was right. Melinda was a demon, a wildcat. It was one of the most erotic nights of my life. I could still hear the jungle guides milling around outside our tent as she held me with an iron grip. We could hear the sounds of jackals and wild dogs attacking the remains of the vanquished predator only a dozen meters away. Yet, the yelping and screaming from the scavengers outside the campsite were no match for the panting and moaning inside our tent. After she finished, we lay back and listened to the sounds of survival. A few minutes later, Melinda was sound asleep next to me as I stared into the darkness of our nylon shelter.

Melinda was too much woman for me to handle. Traveling to unknown places was exciting. I could even handle a little danger. A flush toilet and a fluffy pillow were also enjoyable. Unlike Melinda, I wasn't suited to be a war correspondent. Despite what was one of the most memorable nights of my life, I realized her form of journalism and mine were worlds apart.

The next morning, I informed Melinda that I would not be joining them the rest of the way on her adventure. At first, she said straight out, "No, you can't leave now." I insisted I was leaving. She was livid. I think she thought of me as a coward, angrily calling me names like "baby" and "little boy", all seasoned with a few expletives to express her anger.

Perhaps she was right. My goal was to write life-changing stories, but not at the risk of endangering myself. I'm a journalist, not an adventurer. I was clueless about how to abort this mission and return to civilization. When she finally calmed down and accepted my decision, she instructed one guide, the young Keshaw, to accompany me to the nearest village, where I could find transportation back to civilization.

My guide and I hiked back to a small hamlet where he bargained with a family of goat herders on my behalf. They kindly offered me water and shade while I waited for a farmer with a truck to take me to town. From there, I could catch a bus to Jammu and eventually fly back home.

Returning home became its own travel adventure. The Indian people are a warm and friendly lot. On my day-long trip to Jammu, I met several friendly people who helped me find my way back to what I call the civilized world. A backpack and a few hundred rupees can result in a fascinating tale of travel within India.

In Jammu, I found an inexpensive western-style hotel with a concierge who helped me arrange my travel back to Europe and on to the United States.

Very few people know of my failed jungle experience. It wasn't my finest hour. My immaturity was apparent. My weakness haunted me until I found the courage to be myself and learned to use my talent to change the world.

Years later, I shared the story with a friend, a bartender. He helped me see things in a different light. "There is a reason certain places are remote and unoccupied. Certain places on earth must not be intruded upon. That's why few people go there. Don't feel bad about yourself. It just wasn't a place that you belonged," he said.

Even though Melinda and I lost communication with each other, I kept tabs on Melinda's career. She continued her quest to bring the inside story of extremism to the masses. A few weeks after we split, her report came out on how a group of Islamic terrorists moved freely across the border between India and Pakistan and how they recruited new villagers to help support their cause.

Incredibly, she returned to civilization with audio recordings and photographs as proof of her meetings with known terrorists. The U.S. State Department, the U.K. Foreign & Commonwealth Office, and the Indian Ministry of External Affairs all vowed to root out these groups and put an end to their operation. The last I heard, over ten years later, they were still operating with impunity.

Several years after our undertaking, I learned that on another of her missions into that same war-torn area, one of the extremist Muslim groups she was interviewing held Melinda in captivity. She suffered injuries in a daring rescue raid by Indian government troops. Although not fatal, her injuries and the trauma surrounding her capture and rescue were serious enough to force her to withdraw from active correspondence.

After her release, I heard she returned to her hometown in Northern Ireland to write her memoir. I waited and watched for her book to be published. From the limited time I spent with her, I knew her biography would be full of thrilling adventures. Adventures the world can only experience by reading her accounts. Regrettably, it took many years for her story to reach America's shores. Still, I wondered how different it would have made my life had I continued my friendship with Melinda.

I would never be a war correspondent, so I put the Melinda Donne experience behind me, at least for a few years. Instead, I made a name for myself within the international community by exposing wrongdoing. Using the Hypothesis-Based Inquiry model, my articles continue to attract the attention of journalists across the globe.

One day earlier this year, I received an email from the standards committee inviting me to take part in a discussion on updating the standards for journalists worldwide. It had been years since they published the original document, and it needed updating. Their first request came as a multiple-choice survey. As always, I took the survey seriously. I did a complete job, filling out all the required data and offering additional comments I thought might be helpful for journalists worldwide.

Developers and committee members at IECO, who guarded the standards, acknowledged my suggestions. We started an interactive discussion on how to best implement my ideas. Over time, I made strong connections with several committee members. Not only did they become familiar with my work, but they also welcomed additional suggestions and my thoughts on improving their process.

The core group of committee members was from Europe, the Middle East, and parts of India. All of them were brilliant writers in their own countries. They also recognized that the United States is still a major influence in world events. Having journalists from the U.S. and Canada as members of their workgroup added an element of credibility to their work.

A few months after that initial survey, it thrilled me when Jacques Allard, the IECO Chairperson of Communication and Education, contacted me. Jacques invited me to join their working committee to help produce an update of the guidebook to be published the next year. My career as an international journalist was growing in stature.

Chapter 7

Cupid Has A Plan

Working as a freelance journalist has its benefits. It allows me to choose which stories I feel need to be told. Freelancing also comes with a price. That price is that I have to sell every story I write to a magazine or news outlet, or I won't get paid. When it comes to marketing my articles, networking matters more than knowledge in business, so I had to connect with powerful insiders. That meant taking part in media conferences, attending workshops, often speaking at fundraisers, and other private events as a way of keeping myself in the spotlight for the sake of my career.

One holiday weekend, I received an invitation to a mixer sponsored by a high-profile media group. The attendance list included many influential figures in the world of mass media. It featured renowned advertising executives, journalists, and corporate lobbyists. I attended not only to hobnob with the movers and shakers but also to listen for potential situations that would lead to my next juicy storyline.

Although the sponsors framed it as a business meeting, the mixer resembled a lavish social gathering. Men, dressed in trendy custom suits, seemed to have come straight from Savile Row. The women adorned themselves in elegant party dresses, vying to be the belle of the ball. Like the other attendees, I donned my latest Armani tailored blue suit, a crisp white shirt, and my most colorful Jerry Garcia tie. While not an actor, I was playing the part of a business executive and media mogul. Despite my discomfort with the elite cliques, my career depended on making the right connections. I wanted to make my presence known. On the outside, I looked the part of a professional. Deep down, I desired to return home, slip into a worn t-shirt, grab a bag of chips, and browse the internet.

The evening's festivities began with a brief introduction by the chairperson of a local area advertising association, welcoming the attendees. Presentations by service providers and vendors who spent a lot of money supporting the group followed him. Their goal was to encourage everyone to use their products and services. After the invocation, we all adjourned to a ballroom with a catered buffet of hors d'oeuvres and free-flowing alcohol.

In minutes, most of the attendees were busy glad-handing each other or negotiating a future business deal. I took my usual spot, standing in the back of the well-lit room, my hand growing numb from the cold of the melting ice inside my cocktail glass that was my companion, hoping that at some point I would discover some of the enjoyment the surrounding others are exhibiting.

I smiled and nodded to a few acquaintances, occasionally exchanging greetings and well-wishes. Around twenty minutes into the chaos, a man named Derek Watting approaches me. Watting, a lobbyist and political fundraiser who contracted with several large corporations, attended these meetings to stay one step ahead of the rumor mill. He wasn't shy about approaching me. While you wouldn't call us friends, Watting and I had a history. He frequented the same conferences and fundraising events I attended. We share the purpose of connecting with influential individuals. We travel in the same political circles, and I had even interviewed him for several exposés I was working on because he seemed to have his finger on the pulse of everything trending in the D.C. area. You might say, Watting and I shared a mutual mistrust with each other.

"Joseph," he addressed me. "You look bored and a bit anxious standing here alone. Mind if I keep you company?"

Watting's presence wasn't to engage me in friendly chat but to discover, proactively, my participation in any upcoming investigations that could impact his clients.

Feigning happiness, we greeted each other and shook hands. "Derek, it's a pleasure. No, I'm just hanging around trying to keep my ear to the tracks." Scanning the room, I said, "Perhaps I'll make a new friend or two. You're welcome to join me against this wall."

"So, what is happening in the world of investigative journalism this week? Anything spicy I should know about?" he asked.

"Well, Derek, I could tell you. But then I would have to kill you. So, for your safety, I will just keep my work a secret, unless, of course, you have some information that might help me unearth a scandal or crime."

Derek laughed. "Joseph, I can't endorse what you do for a living, but I respect the way you do it. I guess we will never see eye to eye, and as long as you stay clear of my clients, I will stay out of your way."

"I suppose that is all I can ask, Derek."

With a brief pause, he leaned closer, as if about to share a secret.

"Hey, if you're interested in making a new friend, Marjorie Sykes is someone you should meet," he said.

Derek pointed across the room toward a stunning dark-skinned woman in a dazzling blue sequin party dress. "I have it on good authority that she is a fan of your work. Marjorie is with the United Poverty League. I will be happy to introduce you if you would like."

I found it odd that Derek Watting would impersonate Cupid. Then again, I always question everyone's motives. At first, I resisted. "Thanks anyway, Derek, but I still know how to announce myself to a woman. I don't need a wingman."

Growing up in Cleveland, I never saw myself as a handsome man. My persona through my college years was that of a scrawny little geek. Though I no longer appear geeky, I still perceive myself as a nerd. Today, I can bench press two hundred pounds and run a half-marathon with ease. Plus, my ability to grow facial hair has allowed me to model the two-day-old beard that is so popular with celebrities and athletes. I even bought one of those electric beard trimmers that helped me keep it groomed at the right length.

Now in my mid-thirties, most people I meet might consider me ruggedly handsome, like an athlete or outdoorsman, although I'm far more comfortable turning the pages of a novel than hiking up the side of a mountain or kayaking a whitewater stream. A few years ago, I cut my hair to a fashionable shorter cut on the sides and a longer wavy top. My hairstylist told me it made my medium blonde hair look lighter and more youthful. She liked to flatter me. I think she fancied me as a potential boyfriend. Something that would not happen. She was quite a few years older than me, overweight, and she smoked. She's not the type of woman I sought. Besides, I had more important things to accomplish.

Despite my new appearance, it hadn't led to many romantic connections. Dating seemed like too much work. The younger girls I met were too wild. The women my age all had baggage from previous relationships or were looking for commitment. I wasn't ready to be committed. I simply became accustomed to being single.

Still, I had to admit, Derek had good taste. Marjorie Sykes was taller than most of the women who surrounded her. She looked to be every bit of five feet eight inches, only a few inches shorter than me. Her athletic build gave you the impression she might be a former professional golfer or a tennis player. I didn't recognize her name from the sports pages, so perhaps she was just a physical fitness devotee. She was exceptionally beautiful, something of a rare sight at these events. *Why hadn't I noticed her before?*

Staring at your phone at one of these meet-and-greet events is not only in poor taste, but it also makes you look immature and unsophisticated. Yet, I craved more information about her. At the risk of being rude, I grabbed my phone and tried to remain inconspicuous while I did an internet search for the name Marjorie Sykes. It's incredible how quickly you can gather information about someone online. Her profile interested me. To my astonishment, the internet listed Marjorie as a thirty-nine-year-old professional. I verified it on several sites. I would have guessed by her looks that she was younger, late twenties at most. Surprise! She was three years older than me.

A post-graduate of Georgetown University's McCourt School of Public Policy, she held a master's degree in public policy. What's more, as Watting had stated, she was a board member of the United Poverty League, a large international charitable foundation, and a champion for equal rights. I always preferred a woman with intelligence over beauty. Marjorie appeared to have both. On an educational level, I could consider myself her peer. While many people might consider her cause, fighting poverty, to be of higher social standing than journalism. I will be happy to debate the value of our respective causes to anyone who will listen.

I stared again across the room, captivated by the tall, shapely woman. Her style was one of sophistication. She looked relaxed with her dark hair, dark eyes, and confident smile. Matching diamond earrings and a diamond choker necklace adorned her ebony skin. I looked at her manicured hands, her fingernails polished in a deep blue color to match her dress. The absence of any engagement or wedding ring on her left hand caught my attention. It made her status even more intriguing. Could Ms. Sykes be a single woman? Nothing on her internet profile mentioned she was in any relationship. If true, she is most definitely someone I would like to know.

I was growing tired of standing alone against the wall at social events, and I certainly didn't wish to spend the rest of the evening with Derek Watting or the other vultures who were slowly getting drunk around me. It was time for a bold move on my part. I took a deep breath, put down my drink, and walked across the room to introduce myself to Marjorie Sykes.

Walking forty feet across that room scared me more than trekking with Melinda Donne through the jungle. My stomach filled with butterflies as I drew closer to her. I almost turned away, choosing to join another group, but then I calmed myself. Look cool, dammit!

Up close, she was even prettier than from afar. Her skin was as clear and silky smooth as a woman many years younger than her profile suggested. She had long, sensual eyelashes which seemed to amplify her dark eyes. Her lips were as red and plump as ripe cherries. She wore her hair pulled back away from her face in a classy but conservative style.

As I approached, I straightened back to look taller and held my head up high to appear more confident. To my surprise, she broke away from the conversation she was having with another woman and greeted me with a warm smile and a firm handshake. It was as if she were expecting me to approach.

"It is such a pleasure to meet you, Mr. St. Joseph," she said. "I was just discussing one of your articles with a co-worker at the United Poverty League. Your story on the Middle America University scandal is one of my favorites."

I could understand why Marjorie cited the Middle America University story. My original impetus for the investigation was to paint a clear picture of corporate greed. They were robbing the poor to make the rich even richer. However, someone could interpret the same data that I used to make my case as a pattern of racial bias. Marjorie's organization fought against racial bias in all forms. The United Poverty League pledged to help less fortunate people, the school also targeted many of the league's members. While not my original aim, many readers viewed the story as an exposé on racial inequality. Marjorie may very well feel the latter cause took precedence over the original intent.

"I have followed your career ever since you wrote that article. I've read all your articles. You are an incredibly talented journalist," she said.

She was flattering me, as I had written the Middle America story many years earlier. If true, that meant she had been following my work for years. Possible, but unlikely. More likely, she had stumbled across the article by accident. Trying to keep the conversation light, I joked. "You must have a lot of time on your hands."

With all the confidence of a used car salesperson, she winked and said, "Don't sell yourself short, Mr. St. Joseph. You provide an important service. The world needs checks and balances to keep our society civil."

Her familiarity with my work pleased me. I always find it a tremendous ego boost when someone remarks positively about my work. The journalists' mindset is an emotional rollercoaster. We are proud of our work but always yearn for greater acceptance. Writers are a strange lot, experiencing both happiness and sadness at the same time.

It seemed she knew a lot about me and my career. It was my turn to learn more about her. I changed the subject to her work. "I understand you do charity work. Tell me, what's it like trying to change the world?"

"Mr. St. Joseph, if you ever want a challenge, try convincing people we could make the world a better place if we just cared a little more about each other," she said.

That was the third time she called me Mr. St. Joseph. That had to stop. I edged closer into her personal space. Close enough to smell the sweet scent of her perfume. "Please," I said. "Why don't we dispense with the formalities? My friends call me Joseph."

Fully aware that I was now hitting on her, she blunted my charge. She smiled, stared directly into my eyes, and said, "Should we become friends someday, I will be happy to call you Joseph."

Marjorie was no easy target. Knowing her better and earning her friendship would require greater effort. I did my best to maintain a pleasant conversation, dropping the names of our friends and colleagues, and comparing knowledge of current events. The entire time, I fixated on her intense dark eyes and the confident way she carried herself.

I would have been happy to spend the rest of the evening discussing our viewpoints, but Marjorie needed to make the rounds. Everyone at the mixer was a potential contributor or political supporter. She wasn't there for a social call. She was working. So, before we separated, I decided I wanted more time to know her better. We exchanged contact information with the promise to meet sometime soon for coffee or a drink.

Meeting Marjorie changed my entire attitude about attending this event. I was suddenly happy that I had attended this mixer. My status as the journalism community's number one pariah was ending.

For the remainder of that evening, I watched as she mingled with friends and made new connections. Each handshake was a chance to further her cause to balance the scales of equality. She had a certain charisma that you couldn't ignore. At least, I could not.

Chapter 8

Birds Of A Feather

For the next few days, my introduction to Marjorie Sykes consumed my every thought. Imprinted in my brain was the image of her long, lush eyelashes accenting her dark eyes and her irrepressible smile. Replaying in my mind, I remembered her warm, welcoming handshake. Our conversation at the mixer was too brief. I wanted to reach out to her again, without appearing too eager. I needed a reason, some excuse, to request a business meeting with her.

Luckily, the trending headlines were full of rumors about another charitable organization that got caught stealing contributions. Marjorie would surely know the inside scoop on the reported scandal. I used it as an excuse to contact her for a discussion about the subject.

Monday afternoon, I texted her with an invitation to meet on Tuesday for coffee at a trendy bakery in the Dupont Circle neighborhood. The restaurant called Joe and Dough served organic bakery items and creatively brewed coffee and tea drinks. I frequented this place often, so I knew I would be in my comfort zone. Marjorie knew the café and agreed to meet later Tuesday morning.

As I walked into the café, the smell of freshly brewed coffee and hot baked pastries set my mind at ease. My favorite barista, Caitlin, acknowledged me.

"Hello, Mr. St. Joseph, your usual?"

"No, Caitlin, I will wait. I'm meeting someone. I'll wait for them to arrive."

She nodded in approval as I took a seat at a bistro table along the wall. Without a cup of coffee, I fidgeted with the table's flower arrangement while my eyes remained planted firmly on the front door.

Marjorie arrived on time. She had exchanged her blue dress and sparkling jewelry for a more traditional gray business suit, white blouse, and black pumps. She changed her hairstyle to a long ponytail. The sexy starlet from our first encounter was now the consummate business professional. Yet despite her conservative attire, there was no disguising her charming qualities.

Spotting me at my table, she came directly over, greeting me again with a handshake and a warm smile.

"Hello, Mr. St. Joseph, thank you for inviting me to meet you today."

Motioning toward the seat opposite me, I said. "Please join me."

I tried to act poised by pretending our meeting had business implications, but Marjorie knew better. Her experiences with men made her aware of the distinction between business and pleasure. Besides, I had nothing to offer her on a professional level. Despite my planned charade, she knew this wasn't a business meeting.

We hit it off right away. I often say that great minds think alike. Instead of boasting about myself as a brilliant mind, I will focus on Marjorie. She displayed a high level of intelligence, yet had a way of making you feel comfortable. Our conversation lasted over two hours. We bonded over several cups of dark roast coffee and two of Joe and Dough's signature organic muffins.

We discussed everything from our careers to our political beliefs to our exercise routines. Race, religion, it seemed, no subject was off-limits. Even our jokes brought laughter to one another.

Marjorie's mission as a board member of the United Poverty League was to lobby corporations and philanthropic organizations. Her work funded anti-poverty programs that helped grassroots groups in cities and towns across the country. She was good at what she did, raising millions and helping countless impoverished families and individuals. She knew every corporate mogul and wealthy humanitarian in the country on a first-name basis. It impressed me that this woman, whose salary compared to a middle manager at most corporations, could strong-arm men and women who earned one hundred times her income. People whose net worth topped the Forbes 500 list year in and year out.

She had a rewarding career, but her job kept her on the road, traveling from city to city, sometimes five days a week. She sacrificed a home life, exchanging domesticity for the vocation of helping others.

When we compared political beliefs, it was no surprise that she was more on the liberal side. When you consider her work with the charitable foundation and the disenfranchised people she worked with daily, she had to be more open-minded. She believed it was everyone's responsibility to help the less fortunate.

In that regard, we differed. I describe myself as a centrist. My work, which often positions me in line with dishonest authority figures, has made me more skeptical and guarded. Unlike Marjorie, I wasn't ready to accept that all people are basically good. While we agreed on the cause of many social issues, we didn't agree on the solution.

I found Marjorie and me to be very much alike, at least in our thinking. We are so alike that within minutes, we started finishing each other's sentences.

But despite our simpatico mindset, our formative years happened in two very contrasting environments. Our upbringings differed greatly, and we reached this point in life from separate paths.

Growing up in Cleveland, Ohio, I lived in a typical Midwestern household. My parents, William and Nadine St. Joseph, were everyday working-class folks. My father worked for the postal service. He started as a mail carrier and later moved up the chain to a supervisory role. He earned a decent wage that included fringe benefits like healthcare and a retirement pension. My mother worked at the neighborhood grocery store to help supplement my dad's income.

Together, they earned enough to buy a new minivan every few years while trying to raise four kids and keep a roof over our heads. Every summer, we would pack up the minivan and take a car trip to the Adirondacks, Niagara Falls, or the Jersey Shore.

We weren't wealthy, but we lived the American dream. My parents knew that if they worked hard and raised their children with good values and a decent education, we would move up society's ladder. Their plan, like a lot of white middle-class Americans, was for each generation to succeed beyond the last. If they were lucky, they would live long enough to enjoy a quiet retirement in Florida. For them, the plan was working to perfection.

When I was born, my parents baptized me as a Catholic. Catholicism would forever saddle me with the compunction of being a less-than-perfect individual. It is a deficiency they hammered into me in catechism classes designed to make me a better person. Even though I do not practice my faith daily, I will always be Catholic. So, like a lot of non-practicing members, I attend mass on Christmas and Easter. I reserve my prayers for a wedding or a funeral to ease my guilty conscience.

When I reached twelve, my father transferred to a different post office. The promotion allowed us to move to a newer home in one of the up-and-coming suburbs. My parents wanted their children to have the advantage of excellent schools, low crime, clean streets, and manicured lawns. As planned, we were moving up the ladder of society. Optimism for the future became our way of life.

In terms of romantic relationships, my family strongly believed in the institution of marriage. Find someone compatible, get married, and live happily ever after.

My brother, William, and sister, Katherine, are traditionalists. They met their spouses in college and fell in love. After college, they married, found good jobs, and purchased their homes in a pleasant suburb of Cleveland. Today, they are raising families of their own and, like my parents, executing the American dream, each in their own way. Both William and Katherine are helping their children. They help with saving for college, learning foreign languages, and studying the arts. It is their way of ensuring the next generation will succeed even further than they themselves could accomplish.

Then, there is my younger brother James. The one gifted with a rock star personality. After college, he became an investment banker. He travels the world helping corporations finance their growth. Out of the four children, James led the most exciting life. He has made his home in places like New York City and Hong Kong and is currently in Singapore, where he met his wife, Elena. They are awaiting the birth of their first child.

I was the only holdout, choosing to pursue my career instead of marrying and starting a family. I had girlfriends, but I wasn't interested in settling down with only one person in one place. I moved around from city to city. With each move, I intended to bolster my career. My move to Washington, D.C., is where I found my greatest success. I earned decent money, more than enough to support a family. Yet, the idea of spending my life with one partner in a simple home never captivated me. It seemed too restrictive. Perhaps I hadn't met the right person to pair with?

While I considered my upbringing to be quite conventional. Marjorie's story was very different. Despite being a product of the poorer inner-city neighborhoods of Philadelphia, she spoke with pride about her childhood. Her father, Raymond Sr., a black man, was a public high school principal. He worked diligently to help inner-city youth overcome apathy, crime-ridden streets, and abject poverty. Although himself a college graduate, the American dream for him and others in his sphere was more like a nightmare. He spent his life fighting a system that kept poor people poor.

Besides his regular job, Raymond Sr. was a board member at his Baptist church. Her mother, Sofia, was Catholic. Marjorie and her siblings attended the Catholic school a few blocks away from their home. Growing up, the Sykes children had guidance from two churches. Marjorie felt their Catholic studies taught them discipline and humility. Through Raymond's Baptist influence, they learned tolerance and to be open-minded towards people of different faiths.

Sofia, a dark-skinned woman of Hispanic descent, emigrated with her parents from the Dominican Republic as a teenager. She worked hard to maintain her Spanish heritage by teaching her children to speak in her native tongue. Marjorie and her family members spoke Spanish often in their household. Being bilingual helped Marjorie identify with other ethnic groups, a talent that served her well at the United Poverty League.

Marjorie's mother worked part-time jobs as a librarian and a substitute teacher at the Catholic school. She had no chance for a full-time career. With four children at home, she needed the flexibility to be home in the early morning and evening hours to care for her family.

Marjorie's siblings included two sisters and one brother. Her older sister, Alicia, became a stay-at-home mom. Alicia is raising two children with her husband, Jay. Her older brother, Raymond Sykes II, runs a successful accounting firm. His firm handles the bookkeeping for a select group of small businesses in the Philadelphia metro area. Every spring, his company prepares income taxes. He helps neighborhood residents, often for free, for those who are barely scraping by or need help with the complexity of their tax returns.

It was when she told me about her younger sister, Franchesca, that the joy faded from her face. Her story about the young girl made me understand more about the battle she was fighting against poverty. Marjorie's old neighborhood was a high-crime area with lots of gang activity. Franchesca struggled to stay on the straight and narrow path her older siblings found so easy. In high school, she became involved with alcohol and drugs. One day, while Marjorie was away at college, Franchesca was killed in a gang-related shooting. Her death had a deep and lasting impact on Marjorie.

Reducing crime and eliminating guns from an increasingly violent community became Marjorie's life cause. Being from a suburban community in the Midwest, I never harbored a strong feeling about gun control. Some people had guns, others did not. My father and brother, William, were responsible gun owners. Together they hunted deer, turkey, or quail, depending on the season. That was the way we lived. Gun control is a complex problem with no clear-cut answers.

Despite both of Marjorie's parents being well educated and with good jobs, they struggled to move up in society. In an era when a white person could get a mortgage in an upscale neighborhood or receive a low-interest line of credit to buy a new car, blacks and immigrant families couldn't. Financial assistance and equal opportunity weren't always available to them.

The American dream, for all its promises, hasn't always been distributed equally to all people.

The more we spoke, the more it became apparent. While Marjorie and I sometimes think alike, we are not birds of a feather.

Dealing with secretive individuals in my profession can make one jaded. You suspect something hidden beneath the surface. Whenever I interview someone new, it takes a while for them to gain my trust. During the conversation, I listen for signs that I'm not getting the entire story.

I asked Marjorie about her work at the United Poverty League.

She replied. "You have heard of lobbyists? Those individuals who peddle influence using money and threats. Well, I am a sort of reverse lobbyist. I use charm and guilt to offer rich benefactors a chance to appease their conscience."

I challenged her. "You don't feel bad using guilt to induce them to contribute?"

"Actually, most supporters recognize how blessed they are. They are aware they have an advantage over others. They want to help. I give them a cause they can support."

"When guilt fails, does charm take its place?"

Her face became deadpan as she replied, "It brought you here today."

I think it stunned me. How could I be so obvious? She was right. Her charm compelled me to ask for this meeting. I hadn't noticed, but she had subtly gotten under my skin.

Conventional wisdom says you cannot fall in love with someone in just a few hours. It is more likely infatuation. Nevertheless, I knew how I felt. Looking at Marjorie across the table, I noticed something I hadn't seen in a while. Hope for a better world. Deep down inside, Marjorie believed she could make the world a better place.

The work that she does, the life that she leads, helping others with very little personal gain, speaks volumes about the type of person the Sykes family raised. She had integrity, intelligence, and compassion. Why has she remained single for so long? I sensed that if Marjorie and I were to become closer friends, I needed to become a better man, less self-centered.

I wanted to know Marjorie intimately. I wished for more time with her. Yet we couldn't stay any longer in that coffee shop. She had another meeting later that day.

Finding words to ask her out was a struggle. But I finally blurted it out. "Marjorie, I would love to see you again. Perhaps we could have dinner together? How does Friday work for you?"

She smiled the same bright smile that caught my eye the day we met. "Yes, Joseph, I would like that, but Friday won't work for me. I'm going out of town on Friday morning. After visiting my family in Philadelphia for a few days, I will go to a business conference in New York. I won't be in town next week."

It was then that I noticed she called me Joseph. Up to that point, she called me Mr. St. Joseph. Marjorie's education and training taught her to maintain a level of formality and respect when meeting with clients. I felt a rush go through my body, hearing her say my name in the informal context. I guess that meant at some point in our discussion, we had moved up to the "we are friends" status. Lord knows I needed more friends.

But her schedule threw a kink into my plans. I looked at my calendar. "Gee, that is too bad. I'll be gone for two weeks when you return. I'll be in Brussels for an IECO project. We are developing new guidelines for investigative journalists."

As we both searched our calendars for free time. It made me realize how much of our time revolves around our work. Both of us sacrificed our social lives to the demands of our careers. A couple of weeks between meetings might cool our infatuation with each other.

Then, as if she had just discovered a hidden treasure, she said. "Wait, I will be home a week from Saturday. Will you still be in town?"

"Yes, I leave for Brussels the following Monday."

She said, "Perhaps we could do dinner Saturday night?"

I couldn't pass up the opportunity to get to know her better. My mind flashed toward visions of a candlelit dinner at a romantic restaurant.

"I'm putting it on my calendar right now."

We were both entering our appointments into our phones when she made me an offer I couldn't refuse. "Unless you want to join me on Thursday? I'm meeting some friends at the baseball game. The Nationals are playing the Philadelphia Phillies on Thursday evening, and I have an extra ticket. Are you a baseball fan?"

I loved the idea of a public venue to take the pressure off what I considered would be our first date. I lied and said, "Of course, I like baseball. It sounds like fun. Since you are paying for the tickets, I will buy the peanuts."

She giggled, hinting that a bag of peanuts sealed the deal. "Sounds like a plan. The game starts at 7:00 p.m. Why don't you come to my house at 6:00 p.m.? We can ride together. I will text you my address," she said.

I agreed, and we parted company, both of us expecting a fun evening at the baseball game.

On my way home, I stopped at a newsstand and purchased a copy of the Baseball Digest magazine. I hoped to brush up on my baseball knowledge so I would have something intelligent to add to the conversation. Sadly, I was ignorant about baseball and didn't want to appear foolish. If there was ever a time I needed to be clever, this was one of them.

Having spent an afternoon with the most amazing woman, I was beyond excited. Something mysterious and beautiful was happening.

It began as one of the most rewarding and heartbreaking periods I have experienced. Little did I realize that Marjorie and I were hurtling towards the cliff's edge. A place that could be our demise if we weren't careful.

Chapter 9

Time For A Quickie

I was seated at my breakfast table, poring over my Baseball Digest, when a call came in from Lou Barnes. Lou was the editor of the *Lumorist*, a weekly news magazine that published a lot of my work. I didn't answer. My thoughts were focused only on baseball and Marjorie; it was too early for anything else. He left me a voicemail asking me to stop by his office; he had something he wanted to discuss with me.

I took my time finishing breakfast, showering, and thinking about Marjorie Sykes. I strolled into the offices of the *Lumorist* at about ten o'clock and went directly past the bullpen to Lou's office. Most visitors must schedule an appointment to meet with Lou. For D.K. St. Joseph, Lou had an open-door policy.

Lou was one of those guys who's been around forever. I would estimate his age to be in his late fifties. Age wasn't apparent, as he appeared old when we initially met a decade ago. He was a short man, maybe only five feet six inches. Yet, despite his diminutive size, still an imposing figure. Balding with gray temples, Lou always had an angry scowl on his face. The only difference between the way he looked now and ten years ago was a little less hair, and now he used reading glasses, which meant his eyesight was failing. I think wearing glasses angered him. He was always putting them on and taking them off. If you have ever seen a movie or television show depicting the gruff newspaper editor seated behind a messy desk, then you have seen Lou Barnes.

Lou made it clear he was the boss. When the *Lumorist* hired Lou, they tasked him to transition it from a lifestyle magazine that printed trending entertainment articles into a legitimate news outlet. While Lou knew the news business, he was old school; he struggled to adapt to the fast pace of the internet-based media required.

Every time I walked into Lou's office, it impressed me. The office was enormous, fitting for an executive of a large corporation. Behind his desk were large windows that brought natural light into the room, and when he gazed out, they gave him a splendid view of the city. Across from his large wooden desk, he had arranged a conference area where he could interview guests. On the opposite wall was a small butler pantry where Lou stashed alcoholic beverages, strictly against company policy. I remember thinking. Someday, I will have an office this eloquent.

He had a computer terminal and keyboard on his desk, although I can never remember seeing him use the keyboard. Stacks of paper were strewn about on his desk. There were a dozen articles Lou was trying to prioritize for the next edition. Some had pictures or graphics, along with a brief amount of text. He made notes on some that appeared in the "not ready" pile he created. Lou liked my articles because, unlike the modish articles his younger reporters pumped out, mine made sense to him.

He looked up from his stacks of papers and welcomed me warmly. "Come in, sit down. I have an important story that needs to be told, and I can't trust it with anyone else. Joseph, I really need you on this one."

I smelled a rat. Lou rarely called me. I was usually the one who came to him with my ideas.

"My apologies, Lou. There is a conference in Europe I must attend. In less than two weeks, I'll be leaving for Brussels, and I'll be away for almost fourteen days. There's no chance I will get a compelling article done in time."

"Actually, I think you can. You have done it before. For a talented investigator like you, this one will be a quickie."

He paused for a second, then his face turned serious. "Joseph. I need a front page. Just give me a story I can publish. I haven't had an impact story in weeks. Your style attracts lots of readers. You need to do this for me. I promise you it will pay dividends for both of us in the long run. If I don't get the readership up, the next time you are in this office, there may be a new editor in this seat. That's how badly I need your help."

I didn't want to do it. He wasn't my boss; I freelanced, which is why he was willing to plead with me to write this story. But Lou was an old friend. He had helped me in the past when I was a struggling newcomer. Rejecting his request would be like slapping him in the face. Especially if his job was truly in jeopardy, as he claimed.

I conceded. "Ok, you got me here. Tell me what you want."

"Come here, let me show you what we have," Lou said.

He handed me a manila folder. Inside, I found sheets of paper with names, addresses, a picture of the man I would investigate, and a newspaper clipping from a local newspaper in Philadelphia.

To my surprise, the article was one that I was familiar with. They had plastered the story across the internet news for days. It involved a case concerning an owner of a car dealership in Camden, New Jersey. They accused a man named Andrew Johnson of murdering his partner, James Parker. From the news and reports circulating on the internet, the case against Johnson was ironclad. The story Lou was proposing was, on the surface, a fluff piece. Any decent writer should be able to piece together an interesting argument.

"We have it on good authority that Parker had been misdirecting funds from their dealership, and Johnson killed him in a dispute over money. Johnson claims he is innocent, of course. Everyone is reporting it as a slam dunk."

Making his hands into a fist, Lou said. I want an article with a powerful punch. I sense there is more to this story. With your skills, you should have no trouble confirming these accusations and identifying all the parties involved. Uncover something surprising, something others haven't discovered.

"Lou, they have reported this story ad nauseam. Anyone can write this. I don't know what you expect from me. Are you after a bigger fish and not telling me the entire story?"

"No, you don't have to research it. Just give me one of your fancy stories. Something I can publish that will make the *Lumorist* stand out above the others. A better alternative for readers compared to what's currently being reported."

I hated being on deadline. Rushing an investigation leads to mistakes. You overlook even the most obvious clues. I couldn't imagine having time for a thorough investigation. If I got tied up in a new investigation, it could delay my European trip. I would be writing it every minute of my free time until I boarded my plane. Even worse, I might end up writing it from Europe, an enormous hassle. Against my better judgment, I agreed to help Lou out.

"Ok, Lou, I'll look into it, but no promises. It may be a bust."

Smiling as if he had just won a poker hand, "Fair enough. Go get 'em, tiger," he said.

Chapter 10

Take Me Out To The Ballgame

Thursday afternoon, I took a ride-booking service to Marjorie's townhouse in the upcoming H Street NE neighborhood of D.C., an area that was undergoing gentrification as rich government workers and corporate influencers tried to reclaim the area around the Capitol building. While the neighborhood residents were mostly black, rising property values and rents forced the working-class population to move to different areas within the city. Construction dumpsters were everywhere as the new owners, mostly white professionals, gutted and rehabbed the old buildings.

Marjorie's townhouse, a recently remodeled unit in a row of two-story brick houses, complemented her personality perfectly. Tall trees lined both sides of the roadway, arching over the street like a tunnel of green. Each building had a front yard with grass and flower beds that led to a porch. They, like Marjorie, had a distinctly urban feel, along with an upscale personality. I could see why she enjoyed living in this part of the city.

It was a beautiful, warm late spring evening. By game time, the sun will be low, so no hat, sunglasses, or sunscreen will be necessary. A perfect evening for a baseball game.

I dressed in my best pair of designer blue jeans and a crisp new maroon-colored tee shirt. I aimed for a casual appearance, without looking sloppy.

I texted Marjorie when I arrived and waited for her outside. I couldn't believe my eyes when she stepped out of her front door. She looked magnificent in a cream-colored, red pinstripe Philadelphia Phillies jersey that fit tightly around her athletic body. A short denim mini-skirt covered the tops of her long, smooth legs. Atop her head sat a bright red Phillies baseball cap, which accented her baseball ensemble, and she finished it with cream and red-colored sneakers. A thin white-gold chain that gleamed like diamonds against her dark skin hung around her neck, and a small white-gold loop hung on each ear. It was unbelievable how a thirty-nine-year-old woman managed to appear both seductively youthful and wonderfully adult. Walking beside her would make any man proud.

But it was always Marjorie's smile that caught your attention. It was like a magnet drawing you into her.

"The Washington National fans may not appreciate your jersey," I said.

She laughed. "They never do, especially when the Phillies win. Are you worried about what people will think?"

"No, you look perfect," I replied.

We climbed back into the ride-booking car for the ten-minute ride to the ballpark. I tried making small talk, doing my best to impress her with my knowledge of baseball, reciting a series of facts and figures that I borrowed directly from this week's Baseball Digest. Unfortunately, it only proved I was sorely out of touch with the sport. Clearly more of a baseball fan, she saw through my ruse.

I know it sounds creepy, but the entire time, I couldn't take my eyes off her shapely legs protruding from her little mini-skirt. I think she knew what I was thinking and slid over next to me, shoulder to shoulder. She put her hand under my chin and turned my head directly toward her face. Pointing her finger towards her intense dark eyes, she said. "Hey, I'm up here, not down there."

My face must have turned three shades of red, as I blushed with embarrassment. All I could do was apologize. "Sorry, I didn't mean to ogle you. Please forgive me."

She caught me acting like an adolescent boy. It is hard to explain that while I meant no harm, I am just a man. A man who loses control of his manners when a beautiful woman presents herself as Marjorie has today.

By the time we arrived at the game, Marjorie had captivated me. At the stadium, every passing eye fell to her. Even wearing a Philadelphia jersey at a Washington baseball game didn't seem to faze anyone. The word regal doesn't come to mind when you are describing a woman in a baseball jersey and mini-skirt, yet she walked with her head high, the snug jersey accentuating her curvaceous body, totally confident in her own skin. I admit feeling intimidated by the scene, as people wondered what I, an ordinary fellow, was doing in the accompaniment of this goddess.

We met her friends, Cheryl and Timothy Carter, at the ticket office. Cheryl and Timothy are Washington Nationals fans and season ticket holders of the box seats we would be enjoying. Cheryl, a staff member at Global Communities, an international development and humanitarian aid organization, often worked closely with Marjorie. Timothy held a position at the Food and Drug Administration. They lived in Georgetown, an upscale neighborhood of historic homes and shops in the District of Columbia's heart.

We exchanged greetings and handshakes. I explained to them I was a Cleveland Indians fan, so for today, I would join Marjorie and be rooting for the Phillies. They joked about my poor choices in baseball teams, but understood my allegiance to my companion.

We stopped at the concession stand, where I bought drinks for our hosts and the largest bag of peanuts available. Then we proceeded to our box seats right behind home plate, a perfect location that afforded us an excellent view of the action.

It had been years since I had gone to a baseball game. I had forgotten the look of the green grass; the loudspeaker blaring off-timed organ music, and the excitement that accompanied the anticipation of a victory by adoring fans.

The Washington Nationals fans packed the stadium, fully expecting a home team victory. Timothy and Cheryl were surprisingly good sports, holding no animosity, as Marjorie and I cheered for the opposition Phillies team. Since the Nationals were leading most of the game, Timothy and Cheryl were having fun at our expense.

From our close-to-the-field seats, we could hear the home plate umpire calling the balls and strikes, just as I am sure he heard Marjorie when she disagreed with his calls. Marjorie knew the names of Philadelphia's players, like her family. She called out encouragement to each of her team's players and hoots to the opposition Washington Nationals team.

The baseball game provided a perfect venue for two new friends to get acquainted without the normal pressure of a first date. Despite my inappropriate behavior in the car, Marjorie hadn't taken it as an insult. It may have been my imagination or perhaps wishful thinking, but I was picking up signals that said she liked me as well. She was flirting with me, only her behavior was more subtle. Little actions, like the bump of her shoulder against mine, started a playful exchange as our elbows fought for the dominant position on the armrest. When her hand patted my back as she pointed out scenes from the ballpark's video scoreboard, my back stiffened. The brush of her hand across the inside of my leg set my pulse racing. Once I could swear, she blew in my ear. An act that she laughingly denied.

Sometime around the eighth inning, she scootched in, pulling me close. Putting her head on my shoulder, she chirped, "Smile".

Then, with her phone, she snapped a selfie of the two of us. It was one of those pictures you often see someone post on social media, although I don't remember ever seeing it posted on any website anywhere.

For nine innings, I held my breath. Each time she nudged me, my heart thumped with anticipation. I could barely remember the statistics I had memorized from my Baseball Digest.

With Marjorie's help, the Philadelphia team took the lead in the final inning and secured victory with a quick three-up and three-down finish. Smiling, I thanked our hosts for a wonderful time, promising to return the favor another day. A debt we have yet to settle.

As we exited the stadium, I took her hand. Fortunately, she didn't resist. The stadium management arranged a ride-booking station on the far side of the parking lot. We followed the crowd as people with pre-arranged rides funneled toward the queue.

I was holding Marjorie's hand to avoid getting separated when a small boy broke away from his parents and cut in front of us, causing Marjorie to stumble. Her ankle twisted as she attempted to regain her balance. She tumbled onto the hard asphalt, skinning her knee and letting out a loud yelp from the pain. When the commotion died down, the boy's parents apologized, but the damage was done.

Although the injury was minor, it was an embarrassing moment. Her dignity suffered more than her body. For me, it was an opportunity to be the hero.

"Let me look at it," I said, trying to calm her down as I checked her wound. A small trickle of blood pooled on her kneecap. I took a clean napkin from my pocket, and with a little water that I had in a bottle leftover from earlier, I gently wiped her wound. I held the napkin in place to stop the bleeding. She let me massage the smooth skin on her ankle and leg; I pretended it was first aid, but for me, it was a sensual experience.

"Nothing's broken," I said. "I think you will be okay."

The fall shattered Marjorie's perfect semblance. I detected a tear in her eye, more from frustration than pain. "God, I'm so clumsy," she moaned.

I consoled her. "Hey, it could happen to anyone. Let me help you up."

She wrapped her arms around my neck as I slid my arm around her waist and helped pull her to her feet. As I pulled her close. I took a deep breath, inhaling the sweet smell of her jasmine perfume. We paused, staring into each other's eyes.

My heart pounded as I realized we were holding each other far longer than necessary. Things were moving incredibly fast, but she felt wonderful in my arms. It took a second for us to regain our composure. When we separated, she whispered nervously, "Thank you. I'm okay now."

Hand in hand, we rejoined the line to wait for our ride.

We queued in line, waiting as the drivers picked up their riders, some angry that the home team lost, others happy that the Phillies won. Like a schoolboy on a first date, I squeezed her hand anxiously while we waited.

When our turn came, I helped her into the back seat of a compact SUV, then I walked around and climbed in behind the driver.

The moment I was waiting for had arrived. Nine innings of anticipation are far too long for someone as smitten as I had become. I took a chance. Leaning in, I closed my eyes and kissed her tenderly. Thankfully, she kissed me back, rewarding me with a gentle sigh. I couldn't believe how quickly this all was happening. It's what happens when busy people take the time to stop and smell the roses.

"I hope you know what you're getting into. This will not be easy. Getting involved with me is going to change your life, more than you can ever imagine," she said.

If she was referring to the fact that I was white and she was black, I understood. Even in these educated times, racially mixed couples still experience negative attitudes. They still get disapproving glances from judgmental Neanderthals. Discrimination was something I had never experienced. Marjorie understood the problem very well. Nothing she said was going to scare me away from pursuing her. She was an extraordinary woman, unlike any I had ever met. That's all I needed to know.

"It can only get better. I've waited a long time for someone like you," I said.

I kissed her again, this time longer and slower. She needed to understand how I felt about her.

When our driver hit a huge pothole, the bump separated our lips.

She yelped, "Ohh."

"Sorry 'bout that," he called out.

"It's okay," I replied.

I stared into her eyes again, but the moment had passed. Trying to regain a comfortable interaction, I smiled and quietly admitted, "Before this goes any further, there's something you should know about me... I'm not a fan of baseball."

She laughed. "That's no secret. I'm surprised you knew which teams were playing."

Her comment was a bit of an exaggeration on her part. After all, I had studied my Baseball Digest. She took the baseball hat off her head and pulled it down firmly over mine. It fit perfectly. I looked at my reflection in the driver's rear-view mirror at the bright red Phillies cap adorning my crown and smiled.

"Looks like I'm a Phillies fan now."

"See," she said. "I told you getting involved with me would change your life. The change has already begun."

I wore the Phillies hat the rest of the way back home to Marjorie's house.

They say that love is blind. I don't know if that's true. Perhaps it isn't looking hard enough. That was the first time I could honestly say that I had fallen in love. Since then, I've never been the same person.

When we arrived back at Marjorie's townhouse, she invited me in. We let the driver go, and I helped her up the steps of her front porch. I waited in anticipation as she unlocked the deadbolt and opened the door. She didn't say a word, but with her hand, she urged me to come inside.

The hallway leading to her living area was dark. She had forgotten to leave a light on when she left the house. We barely had stepped inside the door when she pushed the door closed and locked the deadbolt. She wrapped her arms around me, pulling me close, and kissing me passionately. I held her as tight as I could without hurting her. Whatever was happening to us was exactly what we both wanted.

We made love three times that night. Every time I touched her soft skin, every time she looked into my eyes, my heart pounded with anticipation. I wanted that night to last forever. Just before we fell asleep, she whispered something in my ear in Spanish. Not being fluent in Spanish, I was unsure what she said. Still, I knew at that moment I wanted her to whisper in my ear every night for the rest of my life.

By the time I woke up late the next morning, Marjorie had already showered and dressed for her train ride to Philadelphia. She smiled, "Good morning, did you sleep well?"

"Yes, wonderfully."

I looked around her bedroom to see a comfortable and tastefully decorated room. The walls were a light green color, trimmed in white. A bright chrome and gold chandelier hung over the bed. Her dark wood furniture fit neatly along the walls. Like Marjorie, the décor was classy, yet unpretentious.

I lay in her bed and watched Marjorie pack her bags for her trip. I felt like a skydiver after landing safely on the ground. It felt good to be back on earth, but the freefall's excitement still coursed through my body.

Even though I knew better, I was hoping she could stay a little longer. "When do you have to leave?"

"In about an hour, I have a driver picking me up. I will board the train at Union Station. My brother will meet me this afternoon at the 30th Street Station in Philly."

She was visiting family members in Philadelphia for three days, then on to New York for a series of business meetings.

"You could come join me? You could meet me in New York. I could break away for a few hours, and we could see the city," she offered.

Her invitation excluded the days in Philadelphia, so I joked. "What, don't you want your family in Philadelphia to meet me?"

"No, nothing like that. I can't imagine you would want to get involved with them so soon. Besides, I'm staying with my mother in my childhood bedroom. Not the most romantic place."

I smiled. "No, it's okay. It will only be a week. Besides, I have a new project I need to get started on. Don't forget we have a date for next Saturday. We'll go out somewhere special for dinner. I'll make the reservations."

"I haven't forgotten. You don't consider a bag of peanuts and a beer at the ballgame an actual date, do you? I want our first proper date to be romantic," she said.

Wow, if her plans for Saturday night were more romantic than last night, I couldn't wait to see what she had planned.

As she finished packing her bag, she said. "I will go downstairs and make some coffee. If you would like to shower, there are towels under the cabinet. I left a toothbrush for you next to the sink."

She pointed toward the en-suite adjacent to her bedroom. The bath, recently remodeled, had large off-white ceramic tile, a walk-in shower, and dual sinks mounted under a dark granite countertop. It was well-lit with modern ceiling-can lighting and a full-length mirror above the sinks. Practical and luxurious.

I found a plush bath towel under the cabinet as Marjorie had instructed, showered quickly, and then met her in the kitchen, to the smell of fresh-brewed coffee.

I hadn't looked at her furnishings and decor last night. It was dark. Besides, Marjorie and I had other things on our minds. In the daylight, I observed a comfortable living room decorated with a blend of green and beige chairs and a loveseat. In stark contrast to my house, pictures of family and friends graced the sofa table and adorned the walls. I could see pictures of an older couple, probably her parents, dressed for a party, perhaps a wedding or anniversary.

Pointing to one framed picture, I called to her, "Is this your parents' picture?"

She came over and handed me a cup of coffee. "Yes, this one is from their fortieth wedding anniversary."

It was easy to see where Marjorie got her good looks. Her father was tall and handsome. Almost stately looking. Her mother was shorter, pretty, with a rounder face. Her mom's Latin heritage was quite apparent.

"My father passed away three years later. He was a great man. I miss him so much."

"I'm sure he was," I said. "How is your mom doing?"

"I have been trying to convince her to sell the house and move into something smaller. She isn't ready yet. Too many memories, I guess."

There were pictures of other members of her family, her sister, and her brother. "This is my sister Alicia and her children, Devon and Patrice".

One picture caught my eye. It was the picture of a young girl, perhaps fifteen or sixteen years old. The style of her clothing told me it was taken years ago. At first, I thought it was Marjorie's high school picture. Then I realized it was her late sister, Franchesca. Perhaps the last picture of the young girl. The resemblance to Marjorie was uncanny.

"And this is my darling sister, Franchesca. She was fifteen when they took this picture. Every day, I say a prayer for her soul."

Looking at her family pictures helped me learn more about who Marjorie Sykes was, behind the public persona. Little by little, I was getting to know more and more about this wonderful woman.

Her kitchen, recently remodeled, featured rich wood cabinets, granite counters, and newer stainless steel appliances. She had a small bistro table with four chairs in an early American style.

We sipped our coffee while we stared anxiously at each other, wishing we didn't have to part so soon. She cleaned up the kitchen just in time for her phone to chirp. Her ride to the station was out in front. "Time to go," she said.

Like a concerned boyfriend, I asked her. "Will you text me to let me know you got there safely?"

She tried not to laugh, but a chuckle escaped. "I'm a big girl; this isn't my first trip. Besides, I'm only going home. There is nothing to worry about."

I swung open the large wooden front door, but before we stepped outside, she wrapped her arms around me. She kissed me again, pressing herself to me tempestuously against the door. Her body was signaling stay, while her lips offered nothing more than a sweet "until next time".

"Will that hold you until Saturday?" she whispered.

I carried her bags down to the curb while she locked the door behind us. The driver loaded her bags into the trunk. Marjorie climbed into the back seat, and with a quick wave goodbye, they drove away.

As I watched the car turn the corner into the heavy city traffic, I stood there smugly as the morning sun shone joyously on my face.

It felt as if my whole life had been like a black-and-white film that had now suddenly turned to vivid color. If this were an old Hollywood musical, I would break into a chorus of Some Enchanted Evening, then follow up with a rendition of Singing in the Rain. I could dance down the street, nodding and bowing and smiling at every passerby that I met.

That's when I realized I was still wearing the same clothes I wore to the baseball game, with no thought about what I was doing or where I was going. I looked around and realized I was still immersed in yesterday. Today had not yet entered my mind.

How pathetic. In college, they used to call it the walk of shame. The morning after the night you threw caution to the wind and let desire control your mind. Yet, I felt no shame. It was the most glorious moment I can remember. In this great big world of seven billion people, I had somehow found the one for me. I was happy.

It was time to address the new day. Up the street was a diner where I could get some breakfast, organize my thoughts, and arrange a ride home. I took a seat in a booth, ordered a hearty breakfast, and stared out the window at the brave new world ahead of me.

For the remainder of the day, I couldn't wipe the smile from my face. Cupid's arrow had done its job. Life was resplendent. All I could think of was that Marjorie and I would meet again a week from Saturday and resume where we left off.

Chapter 11

The Usual Suspect

When I thought back on every inquiry I performed since my university days, they were always about investigating someone or some organization that was breaking the rules. I seldom wrote about the innocent parties or the positive aspects of society. I had become a glorified gumshoe, searching for proof that someone was guilty of something.

After reviewing the articles that the news media had been publishing about James Parker's murder, I felt something was wrong. It was too easy. The investigation that Lou Barnes handed me needed a twist. With some digging, my conclusion might differ from other reported articles. Rather than proving Andrew Johnson was a criminal who murdered his partner, I hoped to prove his innocence.

I was uncertain about its chance for success. At first, I asked myself. *Was I doing it to make myself feel better, or was I helping someone less fortunate?* Maybe my goal was to see the world from Marjorie's perspective.

I also debated whether I should tell Marjorie about the new investigation. I didn't want to give the impression I was helping Johnson just to score brownie points with the minority community.

However, she mentioned that she was from Philadelphia and planned to visit family there soon. Camden, New Jersey, where the crime happened, sits across the river from Philadelphia. While a separate town, Camden is a part of the larger Philadelphia metropolis.

Surely, she, or members of her family, would know about the murder of James Parker from their local news broadcasts. I didn't want her to discuss my investigation with family or friends in the area. My investigation had to remain shrouded, at least for now.

Besides, pillow talk has undercut more than one blockbuster story. Every spy novel ever written uses the slip-of-the-tongue trope as a subplot. Even something told in strict confidence to a trusted friend can somehow become public knowledge.

I also worried that contacting Marjorie too often while she was away would make me seem needy. So, I let the weekend go by without contacting her. Sunday morning, I awoke, and despite my desire to call her, I waited. Later that morning, she called me for a video chat. "I was waiting for your call. Is everything alright?"

I tried to act cool, keeping my body language relaxed. "Yes, everything is fine. I have just been busy. How are things at your mother's house?"

"Fine. I showed my mom your picture. She says she wants to meet you."

"Put her on the screen. I will introduce myself," I said.

"No, she is downstairs. I'm upstairs in my room. You will get to meet her soon enough."

"Did you get to see your brother and sister?"

"Yes, we had dinner together. They are all doing well. I'm on my way to New York early tomorrow. I have a late morning meeting," she said.

"Don't forget to text me when you get there safely," I reminded.

Once again, she laughed. "Okay, will do."

Before ending the call, she swiped her hand across her lips and blew me a kiss. "See you in a couple of days," she said.

Her warmth made my heart flutter. I returned the video kiss. "Until Saturday," I said.

I decided it was best to keep this new query to myself. Her travels to Philadelphia and New York were coincidental with my investigation in Camden. I couldn't imagine it was likely to impact her or her business. On a need-to-know basis, it seemed unnecessary to involve Marjorie.

I have always held the belief that when you decide to investigate a story, it becomes your job to research everything. Every clue matters. At first, uncertainty surrounds every investigation. I start by searching for something, anything, that appears abnormal. Strange occurrences are typically just anomalies; still, my experience told me that when something appears off, it usually is.

Since the media has covered this event as a murder and has accepted the standard line that all evidence points to Andrew Johnson, I began my investigation with the opposite hypothesis that Johnson is innocent.

I titled my report: *Andrew Johnson: The Usual Suspect*.

Establishing early on that Johnson was innocent was vital to my report. Early accounts of the murder treated Johnson as guilty even before going to trial. I wanted my readers to immediately buy into the idea that Johnson may be innocent, and the police chose him as a scapegoat instead of apprehending the actual criminals.

Once I injected a belief that they had wrongfully charged Johnson, it would give me, as a storyteller, time to prove my theory by presenting evidence that counters public opinion.

I started by collecting as many news reports and as much social media information as I could source from other media outlets. Knowing the facts the other guys were reporting created a basis for my argument. Luckily, I found a video of the Camden police press conference where they informed the public and press that they had arrested a suspect. Details were sketchy, but still a starting point.

Next, I tried to obtain a copy of the police records. When the case is a murder investigation, the police and the District Attorney share very little about the case, limiting it to dates, times, and charges. The only access to unreleased details would be through Johnson's attorney. Initially, a public defender named Edward Stivek handled Johnson's case. Like most public defenders, Stivek was an overworked, underpaid rookie. His lack of experience showed when he failed to convince the judge at the bail proceedings to grant Johnson bail. A few days after his arrest, Johnson was able to retain an experienced criminal defense attorney named Walton Freed. I found it comical that a defense attorney would have the name "Freed". For Johnson's sake, I hoped Freed would live up to his name.

After a little research on Walton Freed, I learned he was well-known and respected. He worked out of an office in nearby Trenton, New Jersey. His special skill was getting his clients off on technicalities. His clientele, most of them black or Hispanic, had a history of arrests, some with previous convictions. Their lengthy criminal histories made them prime targets for the police, and their image as bad guys convinced the public they must be guilty of something. Most times, these unfortunate souls never receive due process. They condemned even the innocent ones before they ever faced a jury. Freed had a talent for finding procedural errors. His clients, including the guilty ones, ofttimes got their charges dropped before they ever went to trial.

Despite his reputation, most of Freed's cases were for assault, drug possession, or robbery. There was no evidence to show that Freed had ever handled a murder case. Murder cases are more difficult. In cases of this nature, experience counts. It was easy for me to see why Johnson's case was being mishandled.

The first call I placed to Freed's law office went nowhere. His receptionist, who, as expected, took a message, then disconnected my call. Her flippant attitude convinced me there would be no callback. I was simply another media vulture to her, among the many calling for the latest scoop.

It took a little digging, but through social media, I finally found Walton Freed's direct mobile phone number. I called the number, not expecting too much, but to my amazement, he answered.

I spoke quickly. "Mr. Freed, my name is D.K. St. Joseph, and I want to help you clear up the Andrew Johnson murder investigation."

He nearly blew me off, giving me his practiced response. "We hold press conferences weekly to provide status to the media. My secretary should have told you the schedule."

I interrupted him. "No, Mr. Freed, you do not understand. I am not a reporter. I'm an investigative journalist." So, there would be no mistake, I stressed the next point clearly. "I'm going to help you free, Andrew Johnson. You really need to talk to me. I'm not your enemy, I am going to be your best friend."

I must have sounded convincing enough because he paused. After a few seconds of silence, he asked, "What's your name again?"

Occasionally, a bit of bluster is necessary to make a sale. I challenged Freed. "D.K. St. Joseph. Go ahead, check me out. Ask around. Then call me back when you realize you need my help."

We hung up. From the tone of our conversation, I knew I had planted a seed. It took a few hours for Freed to check me out, but later that afternoon, my phone rang. It was Walton Freed.

"D.K. St. Joseph? Walton Freed. You called earlier. You have five minutes. Convince me you aren't just another media vulture looking for a scoop."

Now he was the one trying to sound convincing with the "you have five minutes" bluff, but the fact that he called me back meant that he wanted and needed my help. I described my plan to conduct an in-depth investigation. I explained how I worked for the *Lumorist*, my process, and how it would help his case. My goal was to provide him with enough ammunition to cause reasonable doubt. Enough to counter the case the prosecution was presenting. Nothing more, nothing less.

He must have liked what he heard because he asked, "What do you need from me?"

Now I was in command. "Everything. Every document you have. The police report, any crime-scene pictures, and surveillance video. Also, send me the names and contact information of every employee at the dealership. I need it all…"

After a short pause, I gave him additional instructions, "Oh, and no more press conferences. You speak only to me. If another media outlet contacts your office, your standard reply is, 'The investigation is ongoing.' Time is of the essence. The sooner you get the information to me, the faster I can get started."

Before we hung up, we exchanged emails, and he promised to forward whatever information he had as quickly as he could. That was all I could ask. If possible, I wanted to avoid going to Camden. But unless Freed was smarter than he sounded over the phone, I realized a road trip to Camden, N.J., was in my future.

A few hours later, I received an email with a copy of the police report attached. He also included a list of names that included all the people the police suspected or had already questioned.

From the minute they discovered Parker's body in the garage area of the auto dealership that he jointly owned and operated with Johnson, the police suspected someone close to him. They quickly questioned each employee of the dealership and several recent customers.

The goal of the early questioning was to discover if any recent arguments occurred or if any bad blood from previous altercations may have triggered Parker's murder. According to police records, no one heard, saw, or witnessed anything. Only one employee, a mechanic who worked in the repair shop, made a statement. He claimed that Johnson and Parker argued often. Usually over money, but sometimes over responsibility or lack of action. There are lots of reasons business partners argue. Would a minor disagreement be enough reason for one partner to kill the other?

They also interviewed their parts suppliers, several outside contractors they used, and even their Certified Public Accountant. The most damning evidence came from Fairhill Accounting, the business that handled their accounts receivable and accounts payable. The accounting software showed unexplained cash payments going back over eighteen months.

Forensics showed someone killed Parker with two nine-millimeter bullets in the upper chest. The autopsy revealed that Parker didn't die immediately from the gunshot wounds. He bled out at the scene.

After the Camden police secured the crime scene, they immediately requested a search warrant to examine all the personal property of the employees and everything on the premises. Upon a warranted search of the dealership, they found a nine-millimeter pistol in an unassigned employee locker in a storage room. Someone recently fired the gun and then wiped it clean of any fingerprints. Ballistics tests confirmed the gun to be the murder weapon.

The weapon's registration showed the owner to be Andrew Johnson.

According to police records, no one heard or saw the shooting, a fact that disturbed me. All the evidence against Johnson was circumstantial. It was simply too easy for the police to pin this crime on Johnson, close the case, and send an innocent man to prison. I knew it was time for me to dig deeper.

As far as I could tell, the Camden police were taking the path of least resistance. They either lacked the resources or expertise to conduct a thorough investigation or simply did not care. They could dump it on the District Attorney and go back to writing traffic tickets and eating donuts.

My next phone call was to the mechanic, Gregory Supanski, who claimed that the two partners fought often. I wanted clarification on what he saw and what he knew. Supanski had only worked at the dealership for about six months. He was a skilled mechanic who enjoyed working for Johnson. He admitted to being lukewarm on James Parker.

In his phone interview, Supanski said. "Johnson was the more easy-going of the two owners. He interacted with the employees more often. Parker complained a lot and would fly off the handle for minor things that he could easily rectify. One time, I watched Parker chew out another mechanic for buying a new replacement part for a vehicle when a cheaper rebuilt part was available."

Nothing that Supanski said was in direct correlation to the incident that resulted in Parker's death. Supanski even admitted he wasn't at work the day of Parker's murder. He was unaware of the mood at the dealership or any arguments that occurred that day.

In my professional opinion, Supanski's comment about Johnson and Parker arguing often was hearsay and nothing more. It had no bearing on the case. Unless you're someone trying to paint a picture implicating Johnson.

Tuesday afternoon, I received a text from Marjorie. "I'm in New York, staying at the Marriott Marquis Hotel. Everything is going well.

I have meetings scheduled for the rest of the week. Call you when I get a chance."

I replied. "Glad to hear. I have been busy. Talk to you soon."

I made no mention to her of my latest investigation. It didn't seem important. However, I regretted my decision to pass on meeting Marjorie in New York. Her hotel was in Times Square, surrounded by fantastic restaurants and vibrant nightlife. But I had to finish this story. I had promised Lou Barnes.

It had only been a few days, but I was missing Marjorie already. Saturday evening couldn't come soon enough. I jumped online and found a wonderful Italian restaurant in the old section of Baltimore. I made a reservation for Saturday evening, specifying a special occasion. In the special request box, I wrote, "I will appreciate your most romantic table."

Working down the list of employees, my next call was to Carolyn Petty. Carolyn ran the office at Johnson's dealership. She answered phones, did the filing, arranged for the customers' financing, and handled warranty claims. Having worked in the office for a decade, she knew everything that happened at the dealership daily. She was the key to my understanding of things that happened there.

I introduced myself. "Ms. Petty, my name is D.K. St. Joseph. I'm an Investigative Journalist working on behalf of Andrew Johnson. I hope you can shed some light on what happened the evening that they killed Mr. Parker."

"I already told the police everything," she said.

"Yes, but I'm looking for evidence the police might have missed. Something that may help exonerate Mr. Johnson."

She made a statement that surely would be important testimony if this incident ever came to trial. "Mr. Johnson didn't do it," she said. "I told the police. It was those leg breakers from down the street. James Parker forgot to leave the money for them. I knew they would come looking for him."

"Could you please explain further?" I asked.

"Two of them came to the office to pick up their envelope. They come every Thursday. It wasn't in the drawer. I called Mr. Parker, but he didn't answer. They said they would be back and left. I was just locking up for the day when James came back to the office. I reminded him about the envelope, and I went home. The next morning, he was dead."

The copy of the police report I received from Freed's secretary did not include any of the information that Carolyn Petty had just relayed to me.

"Ma'am, who are the leg breakers?"

"The collectors. They make their way around the neighborhood, picking up the envelopes. Most of the time, they send school children or sometimes senior citizens. Sometimes the gang members come themselves, but they don't like to be on camera, so they hide their faces."

"Ma'am, are you telling me you have security cameras in the building?"

"Hell yes. This is Camden, New Jersey. Everybody has cameras. All over the building. We still get robbed all the time. People break in and steal tools. They steal money. They steal cars from the lot. The police never catch nobody."

"Did the police secure a copy of the camera footage?"

"Of course, I gave three discs to them. I doubt if they even bothered to look at them."

"Ms. Petty, do you still have copies of the footage from that day?"

"Yes, I keep backup copies of everything. I'm not smart with computers, but Mr. Parker showed me how to make copies. Most of the break-ins or vandalism happen at night when we are closed. I do it every morning when I get to the office. I give Mr. Parker the video, and I save a copy on a DVD. By the time I got to the office that morning, the police were already there. I made a copy for them, then I made a second copy, just in case."

This was the break I had been looking for. Carolyn Petty didn't know it, but she was about to solve a crime.

"Ms. Petty, can you provide me a copy of that security footage?"

"I need to go to the office, but the dealership is closed. It has been since they arrested Mr. Johnson. The place is surrounded by police tape and keep-out signs. I have a key, but I'm afraid to go inside."

"Ms. Petty, would you be willing to meet me at the dealership tomorrow at about eleven o'clock? I think I can arrange access."

"Okay," she replied. "I just don't want to get in trouble with the police. The Camden police are nasty."

"Perfect. Meet me there tomorrow. Just so you know, I'm a tall, white man with medium blonde hair. I will be wearing blue jeans and grey tennis shoes."

I knew that my appearance and style of dress would be easy for her to recognize. I probably will look out of place in Camden, but that will ensure she knows I'm legitimate.

"Okay, tomorrow", she said. Then we disconnected.

Although I wasn't excited about going to Camden, I couldn't ignore the chance to collect evidence to support Johnson's release. Would there be enough to break the case open?

Chapter 12

Car 54 Where Are You?

Whenever I travel for business, I prefer to rent a car rather than use my personal vehicle. I don't enjoy having the people that I'm surveilling recognize my car and license information. It's more discreet, and it's a tax write-off.

It is just about a three-hour drive from my home outside of Washington to Camden, New Jersey. Three hours of pondering all the wild ideas streaming through my brain. I called a local car rental company and secured an inexpensive plain sedan. I don't need anything fancy. It's fine as long as it runs well and doesn't smell like the previous occupant. Listening to old songs on my iPod helps me kill time and keeps me awake. If the car doesn't have a Bluetooth radio, I use headphones. Using headphones while driving is illegal in most states, but heck, even D. K. St. Joseph sheds his good guy persona once in a while and becomes a rebel.

There was plenty to think about: Johnson's case, my upcoming trip to Brussels, and how I might format this story should I find myself ready to publish. But mostly I thought about my beautiful Marjorie. I couldn't wait until Saturday to be holding her hand again. No woman has ever evoked the emotion I felt toward Marjorie. Someday, I planned to write a movie script about our love affair.

I rolled into Camden at about ten-thirty that morning. My GPS guided me to the dealership, which was little more than a used car lot on a busy corner. The building appeared to be a former grocery store that the new owners converted into a showroom housing two cars and several small offices. In the rear, they had converted the delivery receiving area to a garage with lifts for four cars and a stockroom full of supplies and tools.

The lot held about fifty cars, all used, most of them late-model sedans that were the type that came off-leases from new car dealers or rental car companies.

As Carolyn mentioned, the dealership was closed, with a sign showing "Crime Scene Do Not Enter". The front door had yellow warning tape crisscrossed from the threshold to the header, forming a big X. The wind had already taken liberties with the tape, which now flapped loosely in the breeze.

Carolyn was there early, which didn't surprise me. When I pulled up behind her white minivan, she approached wearing black slacks and a pink blouse. A ten-year employee, she had a good work ethic and likely cared for her job and her employers. Seeing an institution that played a significant role in her life closed, possibly permanently, must be challenging.

She looked exactly as I had imagined from our phone conversation. Carolyn, a slightly overweight black woman around fifty years old, had a gentle, almost motherly demeanor. You can sense certain things about people when you first meet them. Unless the person is a talented actor, initial impressions are usually accurate. I could sense that Carolyn was as honest a person as I had ever met. When she declared, "Mr. Johnson is innocent." It told me that my hypothesis was provable.

Handing her my business card, I introduced myself as D.K. St. Joseph but immediately instructed her to call me "Joseph".

I used her first name, Carolyn, to put her at ease. I needed to establish a friendly rapport as fast as possible.

"See, it is all secure. I don't know if we can go in," she said.

The rebel in me said. "I didn't drive all this way to Camden for nothing. Unlock the door, we will squeeze under the tape."

She hesitated for a second. Then, wagging her finger like a mother scolding her child, she said. "Okay, but if I go to jail, you're paying for my lawyer."

Inside the building was just as it was the morning of Parker's murder. In Parker's office, a pile of paperwork was still on the desk. The shop area where Parker's body was found still had the lights on. Detectives left behind remnants of the crime scene investigation all around the building.

One thing that bothered me was the fact that Carolyn claimed the police were already there, securing the crime scene, when she arrived at eight o'clock. Who contacted the police if no one was in the building before she arrived? The report only stated, "The police were called to the scene." It didn't address the question of who called the police in the report. Was it the security system or a silent witness? That question, still unanswered, made me wonder if it was an inside job.

While we waited for Carolyn's computer to finish copying the surveillance footage onto three DVDs, I asked Carolyn about Andrew Johnson's gun.

"Were you aware that Mr. Johnson had a gun? The gun that was used to kill James Parker?"

"Yes, we hid the gun in a file cabinet in Mr. Johnson's office. Everyone working here was aware of the gun's location. Just in case. Sketchy people walk in off the street too often. If you call the police, you might wait twenty minutes for them to show up. You could be dead before they arrive. Come on, I will show you where he kept it."

We went to Andrew Johnson's office, where they kept the gun before the shooting. She pointed to the drawer, which was still unlocked. I used a handkerchief to open it. The gun, of course, was no longer there, but the police had failed to confiscate an extra box of ammunition. I took a picture of the box, noting the brand and caliber.

"Carolyn, when we spoke on the phone, you mentioned people you called 'the leg breakers'. Can you tell me who they are and where I can find them?"

"Most of the time, they send runners. Sometimes they are schoolchildren or senior citizens. They make the rounds, collecting from all the small businesses in the neighborhood. However, now and then, two big, mean-looking thugs come in. Black men or Mexicans. They claim to work for a security company. I think the name is Thurmond Security. They go into Mr. Parker's office and close the door to speak in private. The last time they came, James seemed a little shaken up. I asked him if everything was okay. He nodded, then went back into the shop. That was all there was to it. If you ask me, they don't provide any security that I have ever seen."

"When did that happen?"

"About two weeks ago," she said.

A few seconds later, the computer beeped. The final disc emerged from the DVD recorder.

"I'm going to take these back to my hotel to review these videos. I will call you if I need anything else."

"I hope you find something. Mr. Johnson is a good man, a good boss. I can't believe he killed Mr. Parker. The police have it wrong."

On the way back to my hotel, I phoned Walton Freed. "Mr. Freed, D.K. St. Joseph. I'm in Camden now, and I've got the surveillance video from the murder night.

"I don't think you will find anything; it is pretty inconclusive," he said.

"Nevertheless, I want to review them. Can you arrange an interview with Andrew Johnson for today or tomorrow?"

I wanted to get out of Camden and back home as soon as possible. My trip to Europe was still scheduled to leave on Monday afternoon. Time was running out, and I had a lot on my plate.

"I'll see what I can do, but it isn't easy to get these face-to-face meetings. The wheels of justice move slowly around here."

Watching surveillance videos for clues is akin to watching paint dry. It is boring, tedious work. You have to pay close attention to the time marks and insignificant movements that happen in the shadows. You seldom get a clear picture of the action.

The police report stated the time of death was approximately nine o'clock at night. Carolyn Petty claimed she closed up around eight, but Parker was still in his office. I made an educated guess and started viewing the footage from the rear of the shop where they found Parker's body. I began at the eight o'clock timestamp on the video. Nothing interesting was visible until 9:05 p.m., when the camera detected movement near the storage room.

A shadowy figure resembling James Parker, based on his stout build and brown sports jacket, appeared on the right side of the picture, his back to the storage room door. Two bodies, both sizable figures, emerged on the left side of the picture. The one closest to the camera partially obscured the other. James flailed his arms, motioning away from himself and toward the garage area. Then suddenly, Parker raised his hands in a defensive position.

The man in the forefront raised a gun and fired two shots directly into Parker's chest. He collapsed onto the hard floor while the two perps retreated from camera view. As he lay on the ground, blood seeped from his bullet-riddled body.

That was the only action visible in that video section. I noted the timestamp to be six minutes and twenty-two seconds after nine. This section of the video was clearly what the police were using as evidence against Johnson.

But there was more. Two minutes later, another camera on the west side parking lot triggered. The video showed only the shadowy figures of two men running between the cars parked in the lot. It made me wonder. *Did the police even see this additional footage?*

Immediately, two questions came to mind. *Who were the gunmen? Why weren't the police looking for the second figure who could easily be seen standing in the shooter's shadow?*

As I pondered what I had just seen on the video, I realized I hadn't eaten today. Sometimes I get so involved I forget to eat or drink. I paused the streaming video and went in search of a late lunch.

I found a local diner not too far from my hotel on the Philadelphia side of the river. Eating alone allows you a few brief minutes of quiet reflection. Carolyn Petty mentioned a security company that Parker was dealing with. She called them "leg breakers". She said the company's name was "Thurmond Security".

I used my phone to search for Thurmond Security, but nothing came up. No internet presence. I tried again using just the name Thurmond with the keyword Camden. Luckily, a link popped up that showed a business address in Camden on State Street, a few blocks away from Parker Johnson Used Cars. After lunch, I took a ride to check out Thurmond Security.

I found Thurmond Security housed in a storefront on State Street in what looked like a former real estate office. The fresh sign, Thurmond Security, partially covered the old sign, Jones Realty. No one bothered to paint over the old signage. My juices were flowing as I parked just outside the front door, which still had a welcome mat from Jones Realty in front. I peered through the dirty glass windows. Inside were several old desks, likely leftover from the previous tenant. A fluted glass partition separated the front desks from the office in the back.

Two men, seated in front, glued their eyes to their phones while talking and laughing at each other's comments. I tried the handle, but the door was locked. The men noticed me peeking in. Within seconds, a third, goliath-sized black man came to the door.

Now, I'm not a small man; at six feet tall and one hundred eighty-five pounds, I can hold my own. But Goliath wasn't just tall, at an easy six foot five, he was a broad-shouldered muscleman with a thick neck. His arms looked like tree trunks, and his gigantic hands reminded me of baseball mitts.

"What do you want?"

Thinking fast, I said. "I want to speak to Mr. Thurmond." In reality, I wasn't even sure there was a Mr. Thurmond, but I was always good at bluffing.

Without a word, he closed the door in my face, turned, and walked toward the office in the back. I stood there waiting, unsure what to do next. Seconds later, the big man came back, opened the door, and motioned toward the rear. "In the office," he said.

The two other men put down their phones, stood up, and watched me walk to the rear of the building, signaling an ominous outcome for me if I wasn't careful. I approached the office door with a cautious mind, remembering the beating I had taken in Chicago. There, a handsome young black man stood behind a desk with a relaxed demeanor. He wore dark dress pants and a neatly pressed button-down cotton shirt. Unlike his associates, he appeared to be educated and polished in the social graces. He greeted me warmly.

"Can I help you, sir?" he inquired.

Getting straight to the point. I said, "I'm here on behalf of Mr. Andrew Johnson at Parker Johnson Used Cars. I understand the dealership is a client of yours?"

"They were clients of ours. I understand they closed down. I heard what happened to Parker, an unfortunate turn of events over there. What is your capacity? Are you a lawyer?"

"Mr. Johnson's lawyer has retained me to find out what happened. Since your firm provides security for the dealership, I thought you might like to shed some light on the events of that evening."

By now, all three men were standing behind me in an intimidating fashion, effectively blocking my exit from the office. Thurmond looked at the one smaller man and nodded. The two smaller men turned and walked out of the room, leaving the larger man, Goliath, hovering next to me in case I tried anything threatening. I was in no position to get physical with either of them.

Thurmond pretended to act as if I were welcome. He sat down at his desk and motioned for me to join him.

"Have a seat. My name is Boston Thurmond. I didn't catch your name?"

Have you ever been out on a tightwire? From the moment you step onto the wire, you must ask yourself. What motivates someone to leave a safe platform and walk on a thin cable, hoping to reach another secure platform on the opposite side?

That's what I felt at that moment. I had stepped inside the spider's lair with no plan for escape. What did I hope to gain from this show of bravado?

In an uncharacteristically bold move. Not sure what I was doing or how it would benefit me. I replied. "I didn't give it."

"Then you don't deserve an answer," he said.

Still, I challenged Thurmond to explain his business model. I asked. "What type of security does your firm offer, Mr. Thurmond?"

But Thurmond wasn't going to be suckered. "The kind that makes sure our clients stay in business. Doing business in Camden is risky. The merchants here band together to keep crime down. It is much like a neighborhood watch. We watch out for them; they watch out for us. It is a mutual agreement we have."

"Andrew Johnson is an innocent man," I said. "And I aim to prove it."

"Good for you. I'm not sure how I can help you. I think you need to speak with the police."

"Mr. Thurmond, your security business is a scam. You know it, and I know it."

"Whoever you are, you made a mistake coming here. Please leave, you have no business here," he said.

He nodded to the big man beside me and instructed, "Ipolo, escort this man out."

Ipolo stepped in front of me, towering over me and blocking my view of Thurmond, still seated at his desk. I realized I had played a bad hand. I took one last stab at defiance. Speaking into Ipolo's chest, I said, "You will be hearing from me."

With discretion being the better part of valor, I turned and walked back to the front door with Ipolo as my escort. Suddenly, a terrifying image flashed into my brain as I fully expected Ipolo's enormous fist to batter the back of my cranium. I could see myself lying battered on the floor of the office as Ipolo and the other henchmen punched and kicked me into submission. Then, when they finished, they tossed me, bloodied and beaten, out onto the street like a rag doll. But nothing happened. Ipolo just paced me step after step as I strode toward the exit.

I stepped outside onto the sidewalk, and to my relief, Ipolo didn't follow. He closed the door firmly behind me, and then I heard the click of a deadbolt lock.

Relieved I had escaped unscathed, I turned to the spot where I had parked my car, only it wasn't there any longer. I couldn't believe my eyes. My rental car was nowhere in sight. The parking spot where I had left it only minutes ago was empty. I was only inside for three or four minutes, and in that brief span of time, someone had boosted my car!

I wheeled around back toward the door, but like ghosts, all the men had disappeared into the building. They had locked the door, and I was standing alone on the sidewalk. I banged on the door, screaming, "Where's my car?" It was to no avail. No one came to the door. I stood there in shock.

I was alone in one of the most crime-ridden neighborhoods in Camden with no means of transportation, completely out of my element, with no one to call. Thinking I must be crazy, I looked up, down, and across the street. How could my car have disappeared that fast?

I paced back and forth for a minute, trying to regain my composure. After calming myself, I realized I was stuck. Finally, I pulled out my cell phone to call the police when, out of nowhere, a Camden police patrol car pulled up to the curb in front of me. The police officer, a large black man, climbed out of the car.

The patrolman appeared to be in his mid-fifties. He had slightly graying hair, an enormous barrel chest, and a belly that was larger than his butt. It made you wonder what kept his pants from falling down. If not for my troubled situation, it would have been amusing that this out-of-shape old man was a police officer.

"You look like you might be lost?" he said.

"I parked my rental car here five minutes ago. I went inside to talk to Thurmond, and when I came out, it was gone."

From his badge, I could see his name was Taylor. He peered up and down the street as if I had merely forgotten where I had parked the car.

With a smirk on his face, he said. "Things happen fast in Camden, my friend. What is your business here?"

There was no chance I would share any investigation information with this glorified security guard. I evaded the question by saying, "I had business with Thurmond. I wanted to talk with him about the security business."

Shielding his eyes with his hands, he peered inside the windows of Thurmond's storefront office. "Looks like they're closed. There is no one in there. Are you sure this is the right place?"

I tried in vain to argue. "I am not crazy. I'm telling you. My rental car was right here." I motioned with my hand, indicating the spot where I had parked the car. "Right here, five minutes ago."

He attempted to humor me. "What kind of car was it?"

I was so upset that I had barely paid attention to the car. I wasn't sure about either the make or model.

"It was white, a compact coupe, a newer model," I said.

"You don't know what kind of car you drive?"

I looked at the keys, which were still in my hand. There was a tag showing the make and model. I showed him the tag. "It is a Nissan. A Versa model, white. Here is the rental car information. Someone stole my car. I want to file a report."

Shaking his head, he climbed back into his patrol car, grabbed the microphone from his radio, and said something into the device. He rummaged in his briefcase on the front seat, then promptly retrieved a clipboard and pen.

"Have you got a driver's license?"

When I handed him my license, he commented, "Maryland, huh? You're pretty far from home, aren't you?"

He reluctantly hand-wrote the incident report on the front page of a blank multi-part form. He included my name, a brief description of the car, the date and time, and my driver's license information. In an open box at the bottom, he added his own verbiage of the sad-sack tale of what happened. He pulled off a carbon copy and handed it to me.

I have never seen a police officer so unsympathetic, as if it were my fault. In some ways, it may have been. I wasn't as street-smart as I thought I was. They were sending me a message; I did not belong there.

He shrugged his shoulders. "We will do what we can. I guess you'd better call your rental car company and your insurance company and report it."

I didn't have any proof, but if you were to ask me, I would tell you that Taylor didn't just work for the Camden police department. He was on Thurmond's payroll as well.

Like Thurmond, Taylor helped keep the locals from hurting themselves by maintaining the status quo.

Then, as bizarre as the entire scene had become, as if on cue, a taxicab pulled up in front of the patrol car. I hadn't called for a taxi, and I don't recall the officer calling for a cab.

The officer smiled a wry type of smile. Like he was enjoying my bewilderment.

"You should consider yourself lucky. It's really hard to get a cab in this part of town. If I were you, I would take this taxi and go back to where you came from."

It was a veiled threat. Taylor's way of telling me to go away and don't come back. To me, it was obvious, Thurmond and this cop had an arrangement. An arrangement that benefited them both financially.

I had no choice but to leave. The police wouldn't help. I was thankful I had rented that car. Had it been my personal vehicle, I would have felt violated. Luckily, my computer and other belongings were safely left at the hotel. In hindsight, it could've been worse; I could have ended up in the trunk of that rental car, at the bottom of the river, sleeping with the fishes.

There is an old saying that says, "Quit while you're ahead". It didn't seem like I was ahead. Nonetheless, I realized it was time to quit. At least for the day.

Chapter 13

Get Out Of Town

I couldn't wait to escape from this town. I had already taken too big a risk confronting Thurmond. Earlier, Carolyn Petty and I entered the crime scene without authorization, a type of trespassing. And my stolen rental car would likely cost a five-hundred-dollar deductible, which I hoped to add to the expense voucher I gave the *Lumorist*.

The evidence Carolyn Petty had shared with me was probably sufficient to cause doubt. Despite this, I wanted more conclusive proof of Andrew's innocence.

It didn't thrill the taxi driver to drive me all the way back to my Philadelphia hotel. He was aware he couldn't get a fare back to Camden. No one took a cab from Philadelphia to Camden. They take the bus or subway. I appeased him by paying him for the return trip at double the meter rate.

By the time I got back to my hotel, my phone was ringing again. Walton Freed arranged a face-to-face visitation with Andrew Johnson at the Camden County Jail at nine o'clock on Saturday morning, and agreed to let me join him. That meant I had to stay in Camden one day more than I wanted. It wasn't optimum, but it would be worth it for a chance to speak directly with Johnson.

With my car gone and nowhere else to go, I returned to watching surveillance videos in hopes of finding something I had missed before. As so often happens, I had missed several clues. Repeatedly watching the same old movie often reveals previously unnoticed details. I already knew the shooting occurred at five minutes past nine in the repair shop. I switched my focus to the events preceding and following the shooting.

I opened the video file that contained the footage from the front office, and another important piece of the puzzle popped up on the screen. At eight-forty-seven, Parker walked into the office and opened the drawer where they stored the gun. The video didn't show a gun, but Parker bolted out of the office and beyond the camera's view. If I were to bet, I'd say he grabbed the gun from the drawer and headed towards the garage. It was hypothetical, but I'd guess that someone was in the shop, and he intended to confront them.

I went back to the video that contained the shooting footage. Again, I couldn't clearly see the faces of the two men, but then I noticed something. I expected to see Parker with a gun in his hand. Instead, Parker held up his hands, attempting to defend himself. He had no weapons. Whatever he retrieved from the office drawer, he no longer had in his hand.

Again, I watched the shooter raise his gun and pull the trigger. Then, I saw it, the proof I needed. I zoomed in to ensure my eyes weren't tricking me. The shooter had a tattoo where his hand and wrist joined. It looked like a crude version of a three-pointed devil's pitchfork. Probably a gang symbol or something he may have acquired in prison.

If Johnson didn't have the same tattoo, we could rule him out as the shooter. Saturday, I would make a point of looking closely at Johnson's hands.

Trapped in my hotel room, I spent most of Friday morning reviewing the file and writing a rough draft of my report. Running an investigation from a hotel room is not an ideal methodology.

Although I had enough evidence to question the Camden Police's investigative work, I still wanted more proof.

When the police questioned Johnson, he claimed he was at his local gym the night of the shooting. A directory search on the internet revealed two nearby gyms close to the dealership. Now, this is when an investigative journalist earns his money. I called the first gym pretending to be a private investigator working on the case. I wanted to verify Andrew Johnson's attendance on the day in question. The person who answered the phone refused to be intimidated or answer any of my questions, except one. Andrew Johnson wasn't a member of this gym.

That left me with the second facility. I needed to be on my game this time. Rather than call, I went there in person. I found a ride-booking service and within a half-hour, I was walking through the front door at East Side Fitness. It surprised me to find East Side Fitness housed in a brand-new building built on a block emptied when the previous buildings were razed for urban renewal. A small, intimate facility, surely, they could verify Johnson's presence at the gym when the shooting occurred. I handed the desk clerk my business card and explained I was working on behalf of Andrew Johnson.

"Mr. Johnson is one of our favorite clients. How can I help?"

I want to confirm he was at the gym the evening of the shooting. Do you keep a log or something?"

"Yes, we require all our members and guests to sign in. Give me a moment, and I'll try to locate the record for that day.

While the young clerk went into an office to locate the past logs, I paced around impatiently by the front desk. The manager, noticing my out-of-place appearance, came over to help. I explained again why I was there.

Before the desk clerk returned, the manager made me an offer I couldn't refuse. "We keep videotapes of everyone entering and leaving the building. Access to the front door is restricted to members. If you give me about one hour, I can view the surveillance tapes to confirm."

"That will be perfect. If you confirm Andrew was here, could you make me a copy of the video?"

I left him my card and walked down the street to a dodgy-looking diner. It wasn't classy, but the food looked good, and I was starving. About twenty minutes later, my phone chimed with a text indicator. The gym manager found the footage showing Johnson entering a few minutes after eight and not exiting until fifteen minutes after nine o'clock. He was making a copy of that segment for me. It will be ready shortly.

I had just hit a home run. In just two short days, I had amassed enough evidence to prove my hypothesis and to clear Johnson. Now I just needed to package it together and get the story to Lou Barnes. As soon as I had all the evidence in order, I would share my discovery with Walton Freed. Any halfway decent lawyer would be able to prove his client's innocence.

Minutes later, I was back at East Side Fitness. The manager handed me a disc with the video footage. With the evidence in hand, I awaited a ride back to my hotel. All I needed to do was review this latest video and confirm Johnson's presence at the correct time and date.

I woke up early on Saturday morning. Walton Freed was driving from Trenton to Camden County. After hearing about my rental car mishap, Freed went out of his way to come to Philadelphia and pick me up from my hotel.

I checked out of my hotel, put my belongings in the trunk of his car, and Freed drove back across the river to Camden County Jail.

Visiting a prisoner in jail can be a tricky endeavor. The Camden County Jail limits the number of visitors and visits allowed at its sole discretion and can change the rules at a whim. In order to avoid any impropriety, visits by the inmates' lawyers are usually the easiest to obtain.

The sign on the wall clearly stated: "Visitation is a privilege, not a right. The Camden County Correctional Facility reserves the right to deny entrance to any person who poses a threat to the safety, security, and the good order of the facility."

Just before entering the visitation room, they screen everyone. You're frisked and must pass through a metal detector. They didn't allow cell phones, beverages, food, or recording devices of any type into the visitation room. They allowed me to bring a pad of paper and a small stubby pencil similar to the type that golfers might use to keep their score.

When you walk into a prison, you know you are in a different world. There is an overpowering feeling of helplessness, and oddly enough, a strange odor accompanies that feeling. It wasn't a foul smell. The building was as clean as any I had been in. The odor I sensed was an air of desperation. One you could not escape.

The rules do not allow any physical contact in the visitation room. The room had a large metal table attached to the floor. They affixed a thick pane of glass to the tabletop to prevent us from physical contact with the inmate. Guards positioned three metal chairs, two on one side and one on the other.

Freed and I sat together on one side of the table. I held my pad of paper so that I could write easily, yet away from the prying eyes of Walton Freed. Keeping with my long-standing belief not to trust anyone, I did not want Freed to see my notes. It was too soon to trust him or anyone.

About one minute after we sat down, a guard ushered Andrew Johnson into the room. The pictures I had seen of Johnson didn't do him justice. Andrew was a tall, handsome man, every bit of 6'2". He was light-skinned, and despite being in jail for nearly a week, his hair was well-groomed, and he was clean-shaven.

They had shackled his feet and hands together with chains about twelve inches long, so he shuffled when he walked. They fettered the chains holding his hands to the chain holding his feet so he couldn't raise his hands over his chest height without raising his legs.

His face wore a frustrated, almost angry expression. As if this was all wrong. He didn't belong here.

The glass barrier separated us, but we could hear and see each other clearly. When he saw me seated next to his lawyer, Johnson barked, "Who the hell are you?"

Visitors have to be mindful of what they say during these visits. The prison records all inmate sessions, which include both video and audio. You often have to ask and respond with a conversation that only favors the inmate's situation. Inmates commonly display anger and make statements that can negatively impact the accused during trial.

Trying to calm Johnson, his lawyer spoke for me. "This is the man I was telling you about. He is working to provide evidence of your innocence. I think you should hear him out."

"Mr. Johnson, my name is D.K. St. Joseph. Under any other circumstances, I would shake your hand. I'm investigating your case and have discovered some evidence that may help you. I just need you to corroborate these facts."

"I will tell you everything that I told the police. I didn't kill James Parker. James is my friend; we have been partners for years. Yes, we argued, but it was always about business."

I started with the most damning piece of evidence. "Mr. Johnson, the police have documented weekly debits from your dealership's accounts. Someone was skimming money off the top. Was it James Parker?"

"One hundred dollars a week. Protection money. We paid it every week to Thurmond Security. Every business owner in the neighborhood pays it. They call it insurance money. We pay it to make sure that our building doesn't burn down, or one of our cars doesn't disappear one night."

"Are you saying it was extortion? Did you call the police?"

Johnson laughed, "You're not from Camden, are you? Thurmond Security is nothing more than a gang of criminals. They bribe the police to ignore the payoffs. Boston Thurmond has the police in his pocket."

"So, you are saying James Parker knew about the payments?"

"Knew about them? He was the go-between. It was James's job to make the insurance payments every Thursday."

"Mr. Johnson, the murder weapon is registered in your name. The police had ballistics tests performed. The bullets matched your gun," I said.

"I registered the gun to me. But we kept it at the dealership. Everyone knew where we kept it, in a drawer in the office. We are a used car dealer; we get quite a few undesirables on our lot. The gun was there for protection."

"Mr. Johnson, can you show me your hands?"

He raised his hands as high as he could. The chain between his hands and feet limited his movement. I could barely see them over the divider between us. "Look at this shit. I can't even scratch my nose without lifting my leg."

I clearly saw that Johnson had no tattoo on his wrist. There was no way that Andrew Johnson killed James Parker. However, the interview didn't end there.

While I had his attention, I asked. "Mr. Johnson, who do you think killed James Parker?"

"I don't know. Why hasn't anyone checked the security footage? We have cameras all over the damn building. One of them must have recorded something."

I looked at Walton Freed. He shrugged his shoulders. "The police reviewed them all. They found nothing conclusive," he said. I didn't agree. I realized Freed wasn't the expert I'd hoped he was.

"Mr. Johnson, in the police report, you claimed you were at a fitness facility at the time of Mr. Parker's murder. Can anyone else at the gym identify you?"

"That's what I told the cops. Yes, one of the personal trainers, a guy named Ricky, was there that day. We spoke several times. I was using one machine incorrectly, a machine for building up your abs. He helped me adjust the seat and the weights. He showed me how to get the most out of the machine. They don't like you giving the trainers tips because it is their job. I slipped Ricky a fiver for his help. They don't get paid much; he could use an extra buck."

He looked at his lawyer in disgust. "How come you haven't asked me these questions? This shit is important."

His lawyer replied. "I have been busy trying to get you bail. Andrew, we are doing everything possible to secure your release. That is why this man is here. He is an investigator. He knows how to discover the things that the police may have missed."

Johnson looked at me in dismay. "You some kind of P.I., or something?"

"No, sir, I'm an investigative journalist. My job is to discover all I can about your case and create an interesting argument. Then, hopefully, we cast enough doubt on the prosecution's case to create reasonable doubt. You're familiar with the O.J. Simpson trials? I'm going to make you more famous than O.J. Simpson. No court in the land will convict you."

Suddenly, Johnson's face lit up as if it had been flashed from the bulb of a Kodak Brownie camera.

"You must be Marjorie's boy? Raymond said he was gonna get a big shot investigator to help me get free. I thought he was bullshitting me," he said.

Johnson's statement confused me. I wasn't sure what he was talking about, but I recognized the name, Marjorie.

"I am sorry, but I don't know Raymond. Who is Raymond?"

"Sykes, Raymond Sykes. He is a friend of mine; he does the accounting for the dealership. Raymond said Marjorie knew a guy, a guy who could help. That's you. You're Marjorie's guy."

"Sir? Are you speaking of Marjorie Sykes, from the United Poverty League?"

"Who the hell else? Good old Marjorie, she is coming through for me, after all."

The blood in my veins turned to ice. *What the hell is going on here?*

"Mr. Johnson, Marjorie Sykes didn't send me here. I work for an internet news magazine named the *Lumorist*. I'm here on their behalf. But Marjorie is a friend of mine. May I ask why you think Marjorie sent me here?"

"I told Raymond to get me some help. I knew he would talk to Marjorie on my behalf. She knows people, important people, like lawyers. She has clout. We had our differences over the years, but I knew when it got heavy, she would help me."

I needed to be sure I was understanding what Andrew was saying. I asked again, "Mr. Johnson, why do you think Marjorie Sykes sent me here? How is Marjorie Sykes involved in your case?"

That's when Andrew Johnson said something that nearly knocked me off my chair.

"She's my wife."

His wife? Could this be true?

"We are living apart right now. She moved to D.C. for her job. When I was a young man, I wasn't a proper husband, too full of myself. I drank too much, I hung out at strip clubs, and I had affairs with other women. I'm surprised Marjorie stayed with me as long as she did. She didn't deserve the way I treated her. She's a good woman."

Squirming in his seat, Andrew declared, "About four years ago, I got sick. The doctors told me I needed to stop drinking, or I was going to die. While lying in my hospital bed, the lord visited me. I've turned over a new leaf. I've stayed sober ever since. I'm a good man now. She knows that. When I get out of here, we are going to get back together."

Stunned, my hands shook as I tried to write notes. From that moment forward, I don't think that I wrote anything comprehensible; Johnson's words drained the life from my body. The woman I love had a hidden past, one that directly relates to this case. *How was she involved? Was I being set up?*

This couldn't be happening. Yet, it couldn't possibly be a coincidence.

Like a drum pounding in my ears, Andrew kept repeating, "Good old Marjorie. Good old Marjorie."

This revelation shook me up so much I couldn't ask any additional questions. For the last few minutes, Walton Freed and Andrew went over their next course of action. To me, their conversation was a muddled jumble of words. My heart thumped so rapidly I felt as if I would pass out.

Jail policy limits in-person visits to forty minutes, and our time was nearly up. When Freed realized I wasn't going to ask any more questions, he signaled the guard that we had finished our business. We watched as they escorted Andrew Johnson out of the room. I remember he walked away smiling, almost confident he was going to get a fair shake. Win or lose, he now believed that Marjorie had come through for him.

As we left the Camden County Correctional Facility, I was in a daze. I don't remember retrieving my personal items from the guard station or leaving the secure area of the jail. I think Freed was speaking to me, but I didn't hear a word he said.

We ambled across the prison parking lot toward his car. Freed asked, "Going back to your hotel?"

"No, if you don't mind, please take me to the 30th Street Train Station. I have to get back to D.C. as quickly as I possibly can. Something important has happened. I have all I need for my investigation. Anything else I need, I can do over the phone or by email."

We were back in Freed's car and heading for the highway before I calmed down enough to grasp what I had heard. I forced myself to remember, "Things are not always as they seem".

Staring out the car window as we headed across the Benjamin Franklin Bridge, toward Philadelphia, I could sense Freed was thinking about the questions I had asked Johnson and his statements. His confidence in me and my system had grown.

It was the first time I saw Freed take any initiative. I think before my involvement in Johnson's case, he limited his defense to trying and get Johnson off on a technicality. He hoped for some sort of procedural mistake at the trial, perhaps a mistrial that would embarrass the prosecution. But things had changed. Now that he had me in his pocket and my skills as an investigator, he could detect a faint light at the end of the tunnel. Freed now looked beyond proving Johnson's innocence. He saw his reputation and the demand for his legal services would skyrocket. Making him a rich and famous attorney.

Freed broke the silence by boldly demanding, "I am going to need everything you have discovered. The only reason I let you into this case was to help free Johnson."

My retort was clear, pointing out that he hadn't done enough to help Andrew Johnson. "If you were doing your job, you wouldn't have needed my help."

"I'm a lawyer; my job is to know the law. You're the investigator. Gathering evidence is your job."

I reminded him I didn't work for him. "You will get everything I have when I finish my investigation, and I promise you that if you're any good at your job, you will have enough to prove his innocence. But you have to wait for my investigation to be completed. If you reveal the evidence too soon, my story will have no impact. Once I publish my story, you will have what you need."

He made a veiled threat, trying to intimidate me by saying, "If you withhold evidence, I will have you charged with obstruction."

Freed had no authority to charge me with anything. I admit, it seemed heartless to make Johnson wait in a jail cell, but I had to stick to my guns. Like Freed, I had a job to do.

"A few more days in jail won't hurt Johnson," I said.

"Okay, but if something happens to him in jail, it's on you. You will be the one needing a lawyer."

"Understood," I said.

Chapter 14

No Woman, No Cry

I needed to confront Marjorie. I demanded to know if what Andrew Johnson said was true. More importantly, was Marjorie, a married woman, only using me to help Johnson obtain his freedom?

As soon as Freed dropped me off at the train station, I grabbed my phone. My first attempt to call Marjorie was unsuccessful, going directly to voicemail. I texted her, "Call me important!" After a minute, I called again, and again it routed to voicemail.

She wasn't answering her phone. I considered the possibility that she was in a meeting and couldn't talk. I texted her. "Marjorie, call me!!!" I used three exclamation points to emphasize the urgency. Still, there was no response. I even sent a high-priority email, which I knew would likely go unanswered. I didn't know how else to contact her.

Waiting is the hardest thing to do. The clock seems to stop when you are waiting. I looked at my phone every ten seconds, hoping that something would change. Hoping she would call back. Nothing happened in those ten-second windows. She didn't call back. Frustrated, I tossed my phone into my bag just so I would stop looking at it every few seconds.

Train rides usually make me sleepy. The rhythmic rocking and click-clacking of wheels always seemed to drone me into a stupor. Hoping that if I slept, time would pass quicker. Maybe I would wake to find it was all a mistake, a bad dream. I couldn't find a comfortable position to ease my mind. Even when I dozed off for a few minutes, the distress of my situation kept me on edge. I was losing control of my thoughts. *How could she?*

I played the sequence of events over in my head, starting with Derek approaching me at the mixer where Marjorie and I met. It all started falling into place. First, Watting approached me, then Marjorie flirted with me, and then Lou Barnes twisted my arm. My mind churned, thinking that they were all in on it together. As I put the series of events in order, my blood began to boil. In anguish, I leaped from my seat but had nowhere to go. Other passengers stared at me, confused. To avoid looking stupid, I saved face by moving to another seat further back in the train car. Unable to stay still, I paced the train aisle, pretending to be uncomfortable with my seat. I changed seats three times.

Each time I played the sequence over in my mind, it became clearer to me that they had duped me. I convinced myself that Marjorie, like a vixen out of some cheap spy novel, was only using me. She had tricked me into getting what she needed, and I had fallen for her subterfuge.

My father once told me, "You should never let a fool kiss you, and you should never let a kiss fool you." At the time, I didn't know what he meant. I thought it was just another of his ineffectual parental advisements. Now I understand.

By the time the train arrived at the beltway, my anxiety had reached a near-panic state. We were still fifteen minutes from the station. I snapped at the conductor, "Can't this train go any faster?" He looked at me like I was crazy. Yes, I was acting crazy, but with good reason. I didn't know how else to act.

As the train pulled into the station, I stood in the vestibule of the car, waiting for the door to open and my chance to be first to exit.

The other passengers probably thought of me as rude. Then again, I needed to hurry.

I disembarked from the train, my bags in tow, and raced to the nearest taxicab stand. In ten minutes, I was pounding on the door of Marjorie's townhouse. The large wooden door, the entrance to her sanctuary, felt like an impenetrable fortress to me. Despite being strong and imposing, I was ready to break down that door if she didn't answer soon.

I finally realized no amount of pounding would bring her to the door. She wasn't home. I looked at my phone to check the status of her flight. Flights coming into D.C. were delayed. Her plane wouldn't land for another ten minutes.

I paced back and forth in front of her house, hoping she would get my messages. After a few minutes, I walked to the corner store and purchased a bottle of water and a candy bar. Five minutes later, I returned to Marjorie's and parked myself on her front step. I felt she had plenty of explaining to do.

When her car service finally pulled up to the curb, I could tell it surprised her to see me. She hadn't checked her messages and wasn't expecting me for several hours. My presence on her doorstep, along with my luggage, confused her. The angry look on my face told her something was wrong.

She tried to make a joke. "Wow, you couldn't wait until tonight?"

No, I could not. I had been waiting hours for her to return my call. I was livid.

"I spoke with Andrew Johnson this morning, your husband."

The color flushed from her skin as my words registered in her brain. The ever-present smile disappeared from her face. Her eyes opened wide, then filled with sadness.

Her shoulders slumped. "I can explain," she said.

I was in no mood to listen to her explanation. Pointing with my finger, I barked. "You went to Lou Barnes knowing that he would convince me to investigate Parker's murder. You only wanted me to free Andrew Johnson, YOUR HUSBAND." I emphasized the point. "I can't believe you did that. If you had just told me the truth, I'd have helped you."

"I am sorry Joseph, Lou assured me you would not find out. He said it was just another assignment for you. He called it, 'another notch on your belt'."

I could feel the rage building up inside me. "So, did you make love to me just to get me to write Andrew's story? How could you? I trusted you. I loved you. You used me."

"No, Joseph, please don't think that way. I didn't mean for it to happen like this. Please let me explain. We have been separated, Andrew and I, for over twelve years. We have both moved on with our lives. I was afraid if I asked you to investigate, you would think I only wanted to use you for your investigative skills."

"Well, that is exactly what happened. Twist it anyway you want."

Marjorie had broken my heart. I had risked everything, my reputation, my time and effort, and worst of all, my soul, to show her we could be a team. I wasn't sure if it was anger or hurt that dominated my emotions. How could I have been so stupid to think that this beautiful, sophisticated woman wanted me?

I had to get away from there. I wheeled around and strode away as fast as I could walk.

She called as I walked away. "Joseph, please. Hear me out."

I had to summon all my strength to look calm and collected. "Don't call me anymore. It's over between you and me," I said.

By the time I reached the sidewalk, I was ready to collapse. My eyes were filling with tears. I've never been the stereotypical macho man. A strong man would be angry. He would take a forceful stance, call her a bunch of vulgar names, and walk away. A real man never lets a pretty woman get the better of him. Marjorie had gotten the best of me.

As I turned towards the busy corner, a Yellow Taxi suddenly appeared on the street before me. I flagged the cab down. Tossing my bag into the back seat, I climbed in just in time to keep her from watching me break down. I needed to escape from there as fast as possible. She couldn't see me fall to pieces.

"Where to?" The driver asked.

"Just drive."

The poet who said, "Better to have loved and lost..." was full of crap. For a long time before I met Marjorie, I was Joseph the loner. Loneliness can be boring, but it never made me cry.

I closed my eyes as tight as I could, trying to stem the flow of tears. It didn't work.

I still don't remember telling the driver my address, but somehow, he found his way to my home. I tossed a handful of bills onto the front seat, grabbed my bag, and slammed the taxi door. Bounding up the stairs, I unlocked my front door and scurried inside. In mere seconds, I found myself back in my sanctuary. The place where I controlled the world, and it didn't control me.

By the time I turned the deadbolt on the door behind me, my phone was buzzing. First, there was a series of texts, followed by several voice calls. It was Marjorie. I had nothing more to say to her.

All I knew was that my brain ached from a day full of conflict. I went into the settings on my phone and blocked her number.

Just as quickly as it had started, our affair was over. Once again, I was a team of one.

Chapter 15

The Doctor Is IN

For most people, home is where comfort resides. The place where things make sense. Today, for me, nothing made sense. In ten days, I had gone through a lifetime of emotions. I found the woman of my dreams, fell in love, risked my life to save a stranger, wrote a story with the potential to become critically acclaimed, and watched it all crumble before me - and the day was still young.

Writing has always been my best friend, a friend that never breaks my heart. I still had a story to write. The matter of the Andrew Johnson inquiry persisted. I sat down at the computer to update my notes, but concentration eluded me. Every time the room got quiet, I could hear Andrew Johnson muttering, "Good old Marjorie. Good old Marjorie.".

Between impromptu bouts of sobbing and fits of anger, I wasted time surfing the internet, laying out my clothes for my European trip, and flipping through 150 television channels. Nothing I tried would take my mind off Marjorie. Nothing made any sense.

At one point, I drafted an email to Jacques Allard informing him I could not attend the IECO conference. I cited "unforeseen circumstances" that were preventing me from traveling. My stomach churned with the idea of leaving town. Then I realized that canceling my participation in the conference would fix none of the problems I was facing, so I stopped myself from hitting the send button and saved it as a draft. I had time. Maybe I would feel different later.

In an attempt to escape Johnson's voice, I curled up in a fetal position and covered my head with a pillow.

My head pounded with the unanswerable question. *How could I have let this happen?* I don't know if I was angrier with Marjorie for setting me up or furious with myself for letting my guard down.

As I lay there contemplating my fate, an image of Coleen O'Sheen popped into my head. I always believed Coleen was delusional to think our short dating period constituted a marital commitment. In the same way, I realized my "one-night stand" with Marjorie was only a one-sided love affair. I was the delusional one.

After a good, solid cry, I surveyed my room, looking at the bare walls and empty furniture. There were no pictures of family or friends anywhere. No mementos of earlier times. Only the poster from my youth that reminded me, "The best place to hide a tree is in the forest."

I was alone again. All I could do was pick myself up, wash my face, and brush my teeth. I needed to think about something else. Realizing I hadn't eaten today, I changed my shirt and went out to find something to eat. Ten minutes later, I found myself sitting on a barstool at Ed's Bar, a local watering hole that a lot of the D.C. journalist community frequented.

Ed's is your typical old neighborhood tavern, quiet and unpretentious. Housed in an old two-story building built in the late 1940s or early 1950s. The red brick building has blackout windows and a neon sign for a brand of beer no one has ever seen advertised on television. Patrons enter the tavern through an old, solid wood door with a small window. There are no regular hours. Depending on how robust the business is that day, Ed hangs a sign on the door indicating open or closed. Inside, it's dark. So dark, no one notices that Ed hasn't remodeled the place in forty years.

There is a long cherry wood bar with brass railings and a couple of televisions that broadcast local news and sporting events. Every kind of wine and spirit available lines the wall behind the bar. Customers sit on mismatched barstools or at a half-dozen wooden early American-style tables and chairs in the dining area opposite the bar. The atmosphere appeals to busy businesspeople who want a quick lunch and loners who need a place to think.

Ed, the proprietor, lives upstairs. He ran the first-floor tavern with his wife, at least until she died of cancer a few years before I moved to the area. I never met her, but locals who have been patrons longer than me say she was a heavy smoker. I never recall seeing Ed with a cigarette in his hand. He either never smoked or he quit after his wife got sick.

In the back, Ed has a small kitchen where he prepares sandwiches, simmers soup, and sometimes makes special desserts. During the lunch hour, reporters and copywriters from the nearby newspaper and media outlets will pack the place. By early afternoon, the regular crowd returns to work, leaving the stragglers who were suffering from writer's block to hang out, waiting for inspiration. It's the kind of place that someone could come to contemplate their existence, if that's what they needed.

I don't ever remember stopping at Ed's Bar when Ed, the owner and bartender, wasn't behind the bar pouring drinks or in the kitchen cooking. Since his wife's death, Ed, like me, has been a loner. Ed, approximately fifty years old, balding, and slightly overweight, has no life outside the bar. In some ways, I could identify with him. It seemed I had no life outside of my work, and whenever I attempted to form a relationship, it failed.

Ed always knows everything that's happening in town, sometimes before it happens. Over the years, Ed and I have become fast friends. When I wanted someone to talk to, Ed was always there. Today was one of those days. More than anything, I needed someone to set me straight. By my third double Manhattan, Ed knew something was seriously bothering me.

"You drive here, Joseph?" he asked. Concerned about how much I was drinking, he stood across the bar with a worried look. He didn't want me to drive drunk. If anything happened to me, he would lose one of his best customers.

"No, I walked. I need some time to think."

Ed, a barman who also serves as a psychologist for many of his customers, asked, "Do you want to think out loud?" It was his way of saying he was ready to listen.

"No, Ed, it's too soon to talk about it. I haven't sorted things out yet."

I said I didn't want to talk. Then, as I sat there shaking my head, I started talking. "They played me, Ed. I can't believe I fell for it. You know me, I don't get suckered often."

"Joseph, we all get taken in once in a while. It is how we bounce back that counts."

Ed always knew what to say. Ed had multiple talents; he was an excellent short-order cook, an attentive listener, and a skilled salesperson. If he couldn't solve my emotional troubles, he could solve my physical ones.

"Okay then, how about a sandwich? I got some tasty pulled pork in the kitchen. I can't let you keep drinking without putting some food in your stomach."

While my primary goal was to get drunk enough to go home and pass out, I must have looked hungry. After all, a candy bar was all I had eaten since breakfast. I looked at my watch. I should have been home putting on a clean shirt and tie, readying myself for my romantic dinner at a fancy restaurant with Marjorie, but that plan got torpedoed. Instead, I would be having a leftover pulled pork sandwich from a dive bar.

"Sure, why not?" I said.

Then, as if my life couldn't get any more sad or strange, Derek Watting walked into the bar. Watting was the guy who started this whole sad sack affair in motion.

He sat down next to me. "Joseph, can I talk to you?"

Watting and I weren't what you would call friends. We were two individuals whose work brought them together from time to time. He was the person I least wanted to see.

"What the hell do you want, Derek?" I snapped.

"Nice to see you too," he replied.

Ed brought Derek a drink and hovered around as if he were part of the conversation. When he realized that Watting and I were in the midst of something serious, he backed away, pretending to be busy cleaning glasses and inventorying his booze.

"I heard what happened between you and Marjorie. I think you might be overreacting. It was just a misunderstanding."

"Why should I think that, Derek?"

"It wasn't supposed to happen this way. No one expected the two of you to connect on a personal level. No one believed you would sweep her off her feet. We thought it would be a handshake and a 'How do you do.?' moment. It would just be a casual acquaintance."

Sweep HER off her feet? What about me? What about the way I was manipulated?

"She loves you, Joseph."

I snapped back. "You forgot to say, 'Yea, Yea, Yea'."

He looked confused. "What the hell are you talking about?"

"The old Beatles song, 'She Loves You, Yea, Yea, Yea'. That's what you're talking about. Isn't it?"

"Quit being an asshole, Joseph. You know what I'm talking about. I'm talking about Marjorie."

"Why in the hell is she confiding in you about me? What the hell is your role in this drama? This doesn't concern you, or are you the mastermind behind this scam?"

"Marjorie is my friend. When I was going through my second divorce, I was drinking pretty heavily. I had lost my job and was spiraling out of control. She helped me out of a dangerous situation and got me back on my feet. That was eight years ago, but we have been best friends ever since. No one matters more to me than Marjorie Sykes. Mind if I give you some advice?"

I had my fill of Derek Watting. His advice was unnecessary and unwanted. I jumped off my barstool, ready to take my anger out on his arrogant face.

Ed shouted, "Joseph, stop! It won't help. Calm down."

My finger in his face, I taunted him. "What do you know about love, Derek? Aren't you the guy who has been through three divorces? Now you are going to give me relationship advice? You need to move along."

Watting shook his head. "I told her she was wasting her time with you. I told her from the start. It is no wonder you don't have any friends."

He threw a couple of dollars on the bar and walked out. Ed looked at me, his face displaying his concern over what had just happened.

"You okay, Joseph?"

"Wrap that sandwich up to go, Ed. There are too many busybodies in this bar. Oh, and give me another double Manhattan, to go."

As I left the bar, the sun was setting. My left hand held my sandwich in a Styrofoam container, while the right one held a double Manhattan in a plastic cup. The fresh air, combined with the alcohol, was working its magic. Upon reaching the corner, I felt the rush of alcohol in my brain. Maybe it will wipe Johnson's echo from my head? I staggered the rest of the way home and climbed up the stairs. Plopping myself at the kitchen table, I gobbled down the lukewarm pulled pork sandwich and slurped down the last Manhattan. After a few minutes, I found my way to my easy chair. Flipping through the channels, I found an old Humphrey Bogart movie on television. After my encounter with Watting, I felt a little like Bogart. A tough guy in a tough situation. I hoped the movie would distract me from all the negative thoughts racing through my head.

This day had exhausted me, and, with the help of four Manhattans; it was enough of a sedative to help me pass out. So, by the time the black and white movie ended, I had fallen asleep in the chair. My sleep wasn't restful; how could it be with all I had on my mind? I felt like a caged lion. Once free, proud, and powerful, now stuck in an emotional nightmare where I don't belong.

Tired and hungover, I slept late on Sunday, even knowing I had to finalize my article for the *Lumorist* before I left for Brussels. But the anger inside gnawed at me. How can I write objectively when I cannot think straight?

The fate of Andrew Johnson lay solely in my hands. I had discovered enough evidence to cast doubt on his involvement and also on the shoddy police work of the Camden Police. Now, it was my decision on how to proceed.

I could, as Lou Barnes requested, give him a story that he can use in the next edition of the *Lumorist*. A sensationalized article, a classic clickbait story that would entice readers with innuendo, yet draw no conclusions. As long as people read the article. It would satisfy him. He didn't care about Johnson or Marjorie. Readers, lots of them are the only thing Lou cares about, anyway.

If you remember, I began the story with the hypothesis that Andrew Johnson was innocent and a victim of bad bureaucracy. Considering the current situation, it would be easy enough to change the title and rewrite the opening paragraph to steer the reader to a different conclusion. Johnson would go to jail for murder, and I could exact my revenge on Lou Barnes, Marjorie, and her minion Derek Watting.

My anger with the underhanded trio and the whole affair was enough to justify my decision. "Screw them, screw them all," I mumbled.

In the end, my integrity and truth won out. Johnson was innocent. I proved it, and that was the story I had to tell. By late Sunday afternoon, the article was polished and ready. I corrected all the spelling and grammar mistakes and checked the language. All Lou Barnes had to do was format it for his digital magazine. Regardless of his part in this black comedy, I had kept up my end of the bargain.

With mixed emotions, I went online and checked in for my Monday afternoon flight to Brussels. My heart was no longer in making this trip. Still, the conference's activity and change of scenery were my only hope of escaping the worst days of my life. Maybe in a fortnight, the skies would clear? Then D.K. St. Joseph would again be a lonely but contented man.

Chapter 16

Screw You Lou

Without the help of four Manhattans, Sunday night resulted in more restless tossing and turning. Before I knew it, the alarm rang Monday morning. I crawled out of bed more tired than when I went to sleep. After a disastrous weekend, my self-created nightmare was almost over. I would leave for Brussels later this afternoon and put this whole Andrew Johnson thing behind me.

I always found traveling to Europe from D.C. to be exhausting. Flights to Europe typically leave in the afternoon, flying overnight and reaching their destination in the early morning. The busier hotels delay check-in until the afternoon. Either book your check-in a day early or walk around town killing time for several hours while you wait.

The secretary at IECO had arranged for my lodging to begin on Tuesday afternoon, but I arranged an early check-in at an additional cost out of my own pocket. It made sense to pay the additional fee. I had to make time for unpacking, showering, and shaving before the conference's opening ceremony. Even with early check-in, my fellow conferees will encounter a tired and crabby American. First impressions mean a lot. Hopefully, they will forgive my jet-lagged demeanor.

Still, some loose ends remained before I left for the airport. I originally had planned to spend my last few hours at home with Marjorie, but that plan had changed.

As soon as I showered and packed my toiletries, I took a rideshare over to the offices at the *Lumorist*. For most reporters, Lou demanded an appointment to grace his presence. Not for D.K. St. Joseph. I walked right into Lou Barnes' office.

Emailing the article is the normal protocol, but I wanted to bring him my story in person. I brought with me a copy of the folder containing everything I had found, including the video files. The article needed formatting, but any second-class editor would clean it up and format it to fit the *Lumorist* Internet edition. There was an important reason I wanted to meet with Lou in person. I couldn't shake the feeling that they had played me for a fool, and he played a major part in suckering me in. Call me paranoid, but I felt I was a pawn in a cruel game, and my old friend Lou had set me up.

Lou, seated at his desk, as usual, was poring over stacks of paperwork. Ironic since he was Editor-In-Chief of an internet-based magazine. You would think that by now someone would teach him to use his computer.

Not displaying any emotion, he acted as if nothing was wrong. "Joseph," he said. "What have you got for me?"

"That depends, Lou. I thought you were my friend. Now I'm finding out that with a friend like you, I don't need enemies."

He looked at me with his usual *I'm innocent* look. "What are you driving at?"

"I'm talking about the way you set me up, Lou. You told me you needed this story to save your job. You didn't tell me you were setting me up with Marjorie Sykes to bail out her husband from a murder rap."

"What's the difference? I'm getting a great story for the *Lumorist*. I help Marjorie, and you're getting paid handsomely. It's a win-win-win."

My blood was boiling. Angrily, I shouted. "You knew I was being set up. Did you know Marjorie would seduce me? Did you sell me down the river just to get a front-page story?"

"Calm down. Consider the practical aspects for a moment. This story is going to go viral. You're going to get all kinds of accolades, maybe even an award, and you got laid. Sounds like a good deal to me."

Lou's comment was boorish. To me, Marjorie wasn't just a quick score, a notch in my belt, as Lou would often say. I took a deep breath, "Lou, you are a total asshole. I don't know how we stayed friends all these years."

Lou Barnes probably never had his heart broken, because he loved nothing but a powerful story. Most people put up with his old-fashioned thinking because he got the job done. But enough is enough. It's not always about the story. Sometimes, the focus should be on individuals.

The manila folder containing a paper copy of the story, with my notes and pictures, was still in my hand. Angrily, I flung the folder onto his desk. "Here, here is your fucking story. Never ask me for a favor again." Throwing it down hard, more for dramatic effect than anything, it took a crazy bounce off the desktop, flew up, and hit Lou right in the face.

He jumped back, his reaction causing him to knock over a freshly poured cup of coffee, which flowed like mud across the paperwork on his desk and ultimately onto his lap.

"You son of a bitch," he screamed. "Get the hell out of my office and don't ever come back."

My first thought was to apologize. I didn't mean to hurt him. But my pride took over. He had used me for his personal gain. In my mind, he didn't deserve an apology.

I backed up, turned, and marched out his office door. As an extra measure of indignation, I raised my hand and gestured at him with one finger. I could hear him shouting profanities at me as I walked down the hallway. Tired of being pushed around by Lou Barnes, I was still angry but left the building with a slight feeling of redemption.

I was quickly running out of friends. It's a good thing I was leaving town for a while.

Chapter 17

It's Tuesday, This Must Be Brussels

Sleep-deprived and heartbroken, I boarded a plane from Dulles Airport on Monday afternoon, bound for Brussels, Belgium. For me, traveling east always came with a brutal case of jet lag. The overnight flight meant I would arrive at my destination in the mid-morning local time, except my body would still act as if it were the middle of the night back in Maryland. I need a few days to adapt to my new time clock.

The International Educational and Communications Organization had its headquarters in Paris, but for some reason, they were conducting this conference at their Brussels offices, the headquarters of the European Union.

My eyes stared out the window of the taxi as it shuttled me to my new temporary quarters at the Vrije Universiteit Brussel, a university in the central city. Jacques Allard had arranged for conference facilities and auditorium space at the school because the college's summer semester used only a small portion of the school's classrooms and dormitories. IECO's budget didn't allow for luxury accommodations, and the university made the space available at a discount rate.

I thought. *I'll be nothing more than a glorified college student for the next two weeks.* We had access to the college's secure network, the library, and dining facilities. They were helpful tools, although I intended to spend most of my after-work hours away from the dormitory, discovering Brussels like a tourist.

Conference members, traveling from the four corners of the world, would filter in as they arrived, taking part in an informal orientation and meet and greet. Some attendees were old friends, having worked together in the past. Others, like me, were new committee members.

As soon as I arrived, I sought out Jacques Allard to introduce myself. We had conversed via phone and email, but never met in person. Jacques was older than I had imagined, considering his liberal agenda. His youthful exuberance made Lou Barnes look even more behind the times.

It thrilled me to be one of two Yankees to represent the American contingent to the committee. The other person was someone I hadn't seen in years. My college professor, Dr. Elaine Sadeski, from Cleveland State University, was, to me, a surprise member of the committee of ten. For nearly twenty years, she had kept her interest and involvement in the project that she had introduced me to so many years ago. Now in her early sixties, she was the senior member of the committee, a titular title that in Europe represents an honor. Had the committee been based in the U.S., where age is often viewed negatively, she may not have received this honor.

She looked healthy and even more attractive than when I knew her nearly fifteen years ago. With age, she had gained a look of distinction and confidence. I was sure she would provide the committee with a guiding light in much the same way she helped me find my calling.

I immediately sought her out to reintroduce myself.

"Dr. Elaine Sadeski, I am hoping you remember me, D.K. St. Joseph."

Gone was the posture of authority that she displayed when she was the professor, and I was the student. She had replaced it with a deportment of achievement as if she was accepting credit for her influence, which led me to this point in my career.

Smiling, she extended her hand in a welcoming manner. "Of course, Mr. St. Joseph, you were one of my prize students. As you have grown into an investigative journalist, I have followed your career. I'm very proud of you and so happy that you took my advice. I look forward to working with you on this project."

Jokingly, I said, "But please be kind, I need to keep my grade point average up."

She shook her head. "As for your GPA, you are on your own. I have done all I can."

Unfortunately, they had assigned her to a separate sub-committee, not mine. Our only chance to collaborate came in the project's last phase. That's when all the teams came together to balance the publication.

We did, however, meet after hours several times. It gave us a chance to discuss our future endeavors.

The working committee of journalists from Europe, South America, and India brought perspectives from across the globe. One member, a Muslim from Iraq, brought with him stories of how the Middle East had changed post-war and the tribulations of a society torn between the picture of freedom that the Americans had brought with them and the rigid fundamentalist beliefs of the old order. His unique viewpoints became integral to how the other members viewed the volatile region.

Working side by side with my partners from across the globe helped me develop a long-term bond. A friendship that would pay dividends for me in the future. I knew one day I would have access to information in foreign countries that may not otherwise be available to Western journalists.

The Europeans, being big on pomp and circumstance, had arranged for a large gathering on Wednesday, branded as the Opening Ceremony. There were only ten working committee members, yet for the Opening Ceremony, a contingent of over forty dignitaries, translators, and technical people were present. After a brief invocation by Jacques Allard, the French leader of the committee, each member introduced themselves and offered a brief history of their involvement in what has become a global movement to lend credibility to the process of Hypothesis-Based Inquiry.

Several of the members required translators to aid them as they introduced their involvement. When it was my turn, it pleased me to learn several members were familiar with my work. Only one committee member, the Iraqi contingent, had an issue with my inclusion on the committee. I later learned of his dislike for Americans in general. His anger was spawned by his view that the Iraqi war was little more than America pressing its will on smaller, less powerful nations. While he wasn't a fundamentalist, he believed Americans persecuted Muslims for their religious beliefs. Ironically, we were both appointed to the same subcommittee. Our assignment was to choose from hundreds of well-written Hypothesis-Based articles and pare them down to one dozen. IECO would then use the articles to create a global reference document for journalists worldwide to follow.

I knew immediately we would be at odds over the nominations. He preferred works that originated from third-world countries. I preferred a sampling of works based on a wide variety of topics, regardless of their origin.

I would spend a considerable amount of energy trying to convince him we weren't enemies. Given the death and destruction his country has witnessed, I understand his distrust of the American way of life. As committee members, we would have to agree to disagree.

As the Opening Day ceremony drew to a close, they assigned us our tasks and a schedule for meetings and production deadlines. Outside of the organized meeting schedule, the time was ours. We had the freedom to come and go using the offices whenever we pleased.

It disappointed me that my involvement with Elaine Sadeski would be minimal. I wanted to work with her again. Now, with me as the master, or at least as her equal. Still, I promised to meet with her and compare notes during our free time.

The hotel that IECO had arranged for me was little more than a rooming house used by university students during the busier fall and spring semesters. They only provided a private room with a single bed and a small bureau for my belongings. I shared a community bathroom with four other rooms. While there was daily maid service, by day's end, the overused toilet smelled. If you didn't get into the shower early, you'd have to wait for your turn. Being the third or fourth person in the shower meant you had to clean the previous person's mess.

Some members, specifically those from Third World countries, found the accommodations adequate. Having been used to staying in luxury hotels, I found the rooming house to be lacking. To avoid the crowded facilities, I woke before sunup, took an early morning run, and made it to the shower before the others awoke. Had I planned better, arranging for an American-style hotel would have been in my best interest. Now, the cost of moving to an upscale hotel at this late date would be several thousand U.S. dollars, more than I wished to spend on a volunteer project. Not wanting to be viewed as the ugly

American, I accepted the meager accommodations to fit in with the group. I yielded, deciding that if it satisfied the others, it satisfied me.

At first, there wasn't much in Brussels that captivated me. I worked all day, and by evening, most museums or historic sites were closed. While there were plenty of restaurants and shops, one person can only eat and drink so much. It took a few days before I recognized the city's warm and vibrant atmosphere.

Americans always think of Paris, Rome, or London when they think of romantic places to visit. They seldom consider Brussels. Perhaps they view this city as a place where business dominates more than pleasure. Yet, Brussels has a marvelous mix of the old and new, ancient cathedrals and modern office buildings all centered around a lively city center. The Grand Palace and the inner-city parks are equal to any that the larger European cities offer.

When I was alone, I walked around the old city pondering my future, post-Brussels. Still saddened by my involvement in the Andrew Johnson case, I wondered. Am I ready to start another story? Another investigation about corruption or murder?

To tell the truth, I was burnt out on bad guys. I needed to come up with a fresh idea. At one time, I had fancied myself as a screenwriter. My writing wasn't good enough for a movie script.

Except, now my life had become the perfect script for a love story gone bad. A mystery where the protagonist falls in love, still solves the crime, but discovers his story is a fraud. It would make a great movie. Maybe with a little embellishment, I could turn it into a mini-series? Hollywood loves dark comedies. Mine was as dark as they come. All I needed was a bang-up ending.

How would my story end?

I could have the main character go off the deep end and become a mass murderer. He could buy a stash of guns and kill dozens of innocent bystanders at a county fair? Nah, too easy.

He could die a pathetic old man, alone in his rented room with a half dozen file cabinets filled full of manila folders all titled, *The Complete Story*. Afterward, his life's work will be ignored, ending up in a dumpster.

Maybe he could cut off his ear and mail it to his lost love? Then bleed to death, clutching a picture of them in happier times still in his hand.

None of those options appealed to me. I stood there, staring into space. Surely something better will come along. A tear streamed down my cheek. How had I become such a miserable, sad sack at thirty-six years old?

During the off-hours, I tried to force myself to be inspired to write something different, but my dormitory room was so noisy that I found it hard to concentrate.

Perhaps a stroll down the Rue would do me some good? I could snack on a freshly baked waffle or have a few glasses of cheap French wine. Afterward, I could return to my dorm room and pass out. Adding another pitiful scene break to my future screenplay.

Chapter 18

Free At Last

It took a few days for the *Lumorist* to publish the Andrew Johnson story, my story, the story of how easily the authorities could charge an innocent man for a crime he did not commit.

The article wasn't reported on the news in Brussels. It was just another of many violent crimes in the U.S., occurring daily in American cities. I had to browse for it on the *Lumorist* website, where it appeared on their front page.

When I read the report, my blood boiled. Lou Barnes had officially shafted me for the last time. While he kept my title, *Andrew Johnson: The Usual Suspect*, which I must say was brilliant, Lou or one of his editors changed the authorship. The byline read, "Content by D.K. St. Joseph. Editing and Production by Sherry Overton."

Sherry Overton was a recent graduate from a small college in Virginia and Barnes's daughter-in-law. It still pissed him off that I threw the file folder at him. He got his front-page story and saved his job, at least for the time being. While legally it still credited me as the author, it minimized my contribution and overstated Sherry's involvement.

But the worst part was that he removed my signature line, "The Complete Story by D.K. St. Joseph." He knew how important my signature line was to me. My first instinct was to call and confront him for the disrespectful way he handled our falling out. No one played mind games better than Lou. He enjoyed being in charge. I don't like burning bridges, especially ones we might need to use again. I didn't call; instead, I chose to let Lou have his petty victory.

Ironically, when I returned home from Brussels, in my mailbox was a paper check from the *Lumorist*, my payment for the story. The amount was double what they owed me. Despite his attempt to steal the glory for my fine work. Lou recognized I had bailed him out of a jam and rewarded me handsomely for helping him. Perhaps it was his way of waving an olive branch. A way of soothing our wounds for some future collaboration.

When the story broke, the evidence showing Andrew Johnson's innocence was irrefutable. It made the *Lumorist* the only widely read publication that had the story. Every other major media outlet scrambled to catch up and report the evidence I had uncovered. Within a few frenzied hours, Johnson's image transformed from a criminal felon to a wrongfully accused innocent man.

The press had a field day with the new information. Three days later, under pressure from the news media and several civil rights organizations, the Camden County District Attorney's office dropped all charges against Andrew Johnson. In a hurriedly called press conference, his attorney, Walton Freed, took credit for his release, citing his own "internal investigation" as the source of evidentiary work that emancipated Johnson.

I never heard from Andrew Johnson or Walton Freed. No phone calls, no emails, no thank you of any kind. While it is important to note that I got paid handsomely, and I was working on behalf of the *Lumorist*, it was an insult. Without my investigative work and risk-taking, Johnson would be in jail now. That's how the world operates sometimes. One person does the work, and someone else gets the credit.

I had to be satisfied knowing I helped tip the scales of justice back in favor of the little guy. My life wasn't perfect. I win some; I lose some. This time, I won a hollow victory. I slept better that night. It was my best sleep in a long time.

After a few days, my conference mates and I felt more confident in our abilities and ideas. They assigned my sub-committee the task of reviewing nearly one hundred contributions from journalists from across the globe. Many of the stories lacked the depth or polish that we wanted for our final document. Little by little, as we eliminated the fluff pieces, it became more difficult to choose between the better ones. My suggestion was to select a sampling of stories that had a variety of subjects as their theme. I felt the manual should be a guidebook for all future writers.

My Iraqi counterpart wanted to emphasize stories from countries that were experiencing radical change. Focusing on countries marred by corruption and persecution. He reasoned that investigations in non-Western nations could have a larger global impact than those in Germany, France, and the United States. During the voting, we frequently disagreed on which stories to eliminate. The third member of our sub-committee, an Indian named Eswar, became the swing vote.

Reading, researching, and reviewing articles doesn't sound like grueling work, but it takes a lot of concentration. Many of the submissions were from journalists whose English was a second language. That made it difficult to understand the writer's intent. They tasked us with deciding if the story could have worldwide appeal with some better editing and production. Eswar spoke multiple languages and helped interpret some of the writing.

By Friday of that first week, we were tired and ready for a break. We agreed to adjourn until Monday to allow us to rest and recharge.

My former professor, Elaine Sadeski, invited me to join her for a drink at one of the sidewalk cafes near the Grand Palace.

In school, Dr. Sadeski and I never became friends on a personal level. She was my teacher, a college professor, and I was a student. I had never thought of myself as her equal. Even today, after years of elevating my stature to an internationally recognized journalist, I still felt like her student. Except now, she remained a college professor while I surpassed her with a successful career.

I never took the time to monitor her career as she had done, observing mine with pride. My own self-centered viewpoint only included myself and people from my inner circle. I should have known she left Cleveland State University years ago. It was almost disrespectful when I asked, "How are things at Cleveland State?"

I was shocked when she informed me that she had left Cleveland State years earlier.

She went on to explain.

This time I listened intently, respectfully, as she spoke. "I stayed at CSU for about ten years after you left, because I had tenure and was a department head. Then, five years ago, they diagnosed my husband with stomach cancer. I took a sabbatical to help with his treatment and recovery. He fought hard for three years, but in the end, he succumbed.

"After some personal reflection, I chose to leave Cleveland State but continue pursuing my ambitions instead of retiring.

"Last year, I took a consulting position at the *Reporter*, a traditional news outlet, based in the Chicago area. They are trying to bring their operation into the digital age. I have been helping them restructure their entire system from editorial staff down to street reporters. It has been a massive undertaking, but the new owners have followed my recommendations, and we are almost nearing completion.

"When Jacques Allard sent his request for participation, I jumped at the chance to join this conference. It will be the culmination of my thirty-year involvement in the project. College Professors seldom receive recognition for their work outside the classroom. It is usually the students that we mentor who achieve the greatest success. I'm honored to be recognized for my contributions to the IECO.

"But enough about me. Tell me about yourself. I know your writing, but who is D.K. St. Joseph, the person?"

I often found it difficult to talk about myself. If I puffed myself too much, it would sound like bragging. If I downplay my self-worth, I sound like a loser. The only thing on my mind was my failed affair with Marjorie. Elaine Sadeski shared with me the loss of her husband and the impact it had on her life. I seized my chance to open up to a woman who might relate. Would she be willing to listen to my sad tale of a broken heart?

She listened politely, but I don't think my love life was what she wanted to talk about. Instead, she started asking me questions about how I felt about my future as an Investigative Journalist. I felt like I was at a job interview.

I told her about my past route to success. About my time in Chicago and Los Angeles before settling in D.C. for the last eight years. I explained how D.C. was fertile ground for investigators because of the high concentration of political interests and lobbying activities. Just as I was getting deep into the philosophical aspects of my work, she shifted gears. Pressing me about my plans for my future.

She leaned across the table in much the same way she leaned across her desk at Cleveland State. Suddenly, she was an advisor again. "Have you ever considered giving up your life as a lone ranger? Surely, you're growing tired of being a one-man show?"

"Yes, it is wearing on me. I suppose I have become a little jaded. I mistrust others, or at least I'm constantly on guard. Unable to discuss my ideas with a collaborator because I don't trust them," I said.

She smiled, "I've been following your work for years. While it is brilliant, it could sometimes use a little more empathy, a bit more kinship. I was wondering if you would consider a partnership. We would make a great team."

I mistakenly got the feeling that she was making a pass at me. She was attractive enough for a woman in her sixties, and certainly intelligent enough. But I had no romantic interest in her. I didn't foresee a future and wasn't interested in a brief affair with an older woman.

"I am sorry, Elaine, but I just got out of a serious relationship. The woman I loved betrayed me. I'm really not ready to become involved with another woman so soon."

Her jaw dropped, her face flushed red. At first, I thought it was anger, or I had hurt her feelings, but then laughter overcame her. She dipped her head into her hand, shaking it back and forth, trying to contain her laughter.

Obviously, I said something funny.

"You ninny, I'm not asking you for a date. I'm offering you a job."

A job? Why would I need a job?

Now a bit embarrassed by my stupidity, I said, "A job? What kind of job?"

"I told you that the *Reporter* is undergoing a total transition. They offered me the job, but I'm too old to start over. They need younger blood, someone to help them become a legitimate internet-based news outlet. Your title would be Editor-In-Chief, but it is a small company. They would charge you with doing everything from hiring and mentoring the entire staff to choosing the stories you publish. Embrace this opportunity for change, and you can earn a steady income."

I never considered a career change, if that's what you'd call it. If I took the job, it might seem like I was running away from a failed love affair. Others will think I burned my bridge with Lou Barnes, a move that would surely give me a reputation as being difficult to work with. I might become a pariah again. Based on my current situation, maybe a change would do me some good?

"I guess I would consider it," I said.

"Good, I just completed writing the job description. I will send you a copy. Update your resume to match the job requirements as much as you can. I am sure that with my recommendation and your credentials, the board of directors will look favorably at you. You will need to undergo an interview with their management team, but it's just a formality. They trust my judgment. We can consider our conversation today as your primary interview."

"Will I be able to stay in D.C.?" I asked.

"No, the job is in Chicago. That isn't negotiable. Chicago is a great town. You will fit in well. I'll be there alongside you for the coming months. We can work together. Then I plan to retire. For good this time."

There it was. Suddenly, my life was changing course. As the old doors closed behind me, a new one was opening ahead. Would I be willing to walk through? Is returning to Chicago the solution to restore my happiness? Only time will tell.

Chapter 19

Returning To Reality

It was my last week in Brussels. I'd gotten over my jet lag and felt more comfortable getting around the city center.

Still, my time here in Brussels was one of quiet reflections. Most of the IECO staff members were from countries within the European Union. Their homes and their lives were nearby, keeping them busy with family activities. It didn't offer me a lot of after-work camaraderie.

Many team members rooming with me were from the Middle East and Africa. They were practicing Muslims. They didn't partake in many of the frivolous lifestyle activities, like drinking or dining to excess, that Americans find so normal.

Elaine Sadeski and I became better friends after our conversation about the Chicago position. She was lobbying hard for my acceptance of the Editor job in Chicago. After each session, we met for a drink at her favorite cafe near the Palace. Jacques Allard joined us when he could.

When Elaine and I were alone, I poured my heart out to her about the raw deal I got from Marjorie. At times, it was hard to tell if she sympathized or simply listened. She had experienced enough of her own heartbreak at a more advanced age. It was a difficult period in her life.

Once she commented, "You are lucky you're still young, you will meet someone one of these days. For you, there is still time. I don't have that luxury."

Elaine usually retired early, leaving me alone for late dinner hours the Europeans practice. I hated the dormitory I was staying in, so I stayed away as much as possible. I spent most of my free evenings walking around, enjoying the parts of the city frequented by tourists.

There are loads of confectionery shops, outdoor dining restaurants, and historic sites in the Brussels city center. That means there are plenty of after-hours activities to keep one busy when you're not sitting in front of a computer monitor or digging through legal documents.

My last Thursday evening, I took a walk along the Rue Neuve, the prime shopping district, and stopped at a small sidewalk café to people-watch and contemplate my future. I had already thoroughly explored the city and was happy the trip was coming to an end. As I sat there nurturing a glass of the Vin de Table rose wine, a mix of red and white vintages blended at the table by the server, I pondered how my life after returning home might play out.

The workgroup was finalizing our documents for publication, which I am proud to say I played a significant role in producing. This latest version of The Hypothesis-Based Inquiry guidebook will go a long way in setting standards for investigative journalists worldwide. It will also help keep some of the less experienced writers out of court, maybe out of jail.

With time running short on this trip, I looked forward to Saturday morning, when I would board a plane back to Washington D.C. and either return to my old life, what I left of it, or move on to my next career in Chicago. I rationalized that if I stayed in D.C., it wouldn't take me long to draft a new hypothesis and begin a new investigation. I could simply resume life where I left off before the

Johnson investigation. Except I burned a few bridges back in the U.S. before I left for Europe. Getting people to talk to me and rebuilding working relationships would be the hardest part. Fortunately, a great story sells itself, and any media outlet will be happy to pay me to help scoop their competition. One blockbuster investigation and I would be back in demand.

My other option would be to accept Dr. Elaine Sadeski's challenge, give up freelancing, and start a new phase of my life as a corporate executive.

I sat at a table sipping my wine and watching people stroll past. Brussels in summer was perfect for outdoor enjoyment. There were plenty of young couples out on the street holding hands, taking pictures, and enjoying each other's affection. I enjoyed walking the streets or resting on a park bench, even if it meant sitting and watching alone.

In Brussels, I developed a habit of drinking too much wine. It was easy; the wine was cheap and quite tasty. If I got back to my dorm room drunk, I'd pass out, not bothered by my roommates' disturbances.

After a few minutes alone, the server, Julian, whom I had come to know during my brief stay in town, poured me a fresh glass of wine.

Shaking my head, I said, "I didn't order more wine, Julian."

He looked past my shoulder and nodded for me to look behind. "Compliments," he said in broken English.

I expected to see one of my conference team members or Dr. Sadeski seated behind me. Instead, I turned to find Marjorie Sykes, standing apprehensively just a few feet back.

My heart skipped a beat, as it always did when I saw her beautiful face.

"What are you doing here?" I said.

"I never got a chance to thank you for helping Andrew."

The emotions exploded inside me. Words fail to describe the conflicting thoughts flooding my mind. I felt both anger and love wrestling for control of my mind. I loved Marjorie, yet I couldn't let go of the fact that she used me. She had hurt me deeply.

"I can't believe you came to Brussels just to thank me?" Then anger took control of me. I snapped. "Was Hallmark out of cards? Why didn't you just email me your gratitude and save the airfare?"

She remained calm. "No, I wanted to meet you in person and apologize for what I did. Joseph, I made a mistake. I came to admit what I did was wrong."

By now, my heart was pounding. Never one to stumble over words, at that moment, I was tongue-tied. It took me a second to compose myself.

These last two weeks here in Brussels have felt like Chinese water torture. I wanted it to end. So much so that I considered moving away from my home to rid myself of my stupid mistake.

She could apologize for her actions, but she was still a married woman. A woman who had used her charm to take advantage of me. I wasn't ready to forgive her, but she had come a long way. The least I could do was hear her out.

I motioned for her to come closer. "How in the world did you find me?"

"It wasn't easy. You're still blocking my calls. I called the IECO conference to inquire about you. They didn't tell me much, but someone said you frequented the cafes near the palace. I asked my hotel concierge for a list of the popular sidewalk cafes near here. This is the sixth one I checked. You're not an easy person to track down. Please unblock my number so we can communicate."

I couldn't believe she followed me to Brussels. Uncertain about the next move, I wondered. Do I talk or listen? As she requested, I grabbed my phone and took the block off of her number. I guess that meant I was ready to be friends again. We sat and talked for fifteen minutes.

She started. "Joseph, before you get angry again, please hear me out. Let me try to clear the air."

"When Andrew and I were young, we fell in love. Andrew was handsome and exciting. I was young and inexperienced. My parents were against it. I couldn't see he and I weren't compatible. Our marriage didn't last long. Andrew refused to talk about a divorce. He thought of me as his property. He wanted to stay together. I knew it was a mistake, so I took back my maiden name to disassociate myself from my past. I left him and joined the United Poverty League."

She explained why she had kept her past life a secret. While she dated a few times, she avoided serious relationships with men. "I was afraid. I feared others would be like him. I couldn't accept another failure. Even the people at the United Poverty League were unaware of my marriage. After a while, it didn't seem important any longer."

Marjorie wasn't just hiding it from me; she hid her past from everyone. When they arrested Andrew, she had concerns that it would affect her career. Andrew Johnson's conviction would surely make the news. Conservative media pundits would have a field day discrediting her and her role at the United Poverty League. She would be another hypocritical Liberal with a sketchy past.

"Andrew's conviction for murder would attract extensive media attention. The headlines would read, Marjorie Sykes, United Poverty League member, married to a murderer. I couldn't let that happen. I needed help. When Derek told me you were the best investigator he knew, I sought you out."

"You could've told me. I'd have protected you," I said.

She shrugged her shoulders. "We had only just met. I didn't know you very well. I didn't know who to trust. When I spoke with

Lou Barnes, it seemed so harmless. He claimed he does this stuff all the time."

Then she said something that caught my attention. "I never thought I would fall in love again. Then, after I met you, everything changed. It all happened so fast. I tried to find a way to tell you, but the timing never seemed right. I know we got confused, but we can fix this."

Holding out her hand, she said, "I came here to tell you, Andrew and I have formally filed for divorce. It is something I should have done years ago. He reluctantly agreed not to contest it, as we have no assets to divide. The divorce isn't final yet. We have to undergo a three-month waiting period. Soon, I can move on from that chapter of my life. Then, if you will still have me, we can plan our future."

She paused for a few seconds, waiting for my reply. "D.K. St. Joseph, I know this sounds crazy, but the minute you walked into my life, I knew you were someone special. Together, we can make a wonderful team. I want to be with you."

I was ready to jump out of my chair and scream "YES". But played it cool. I had already let my emotions get the best of me once before. I would not let that happen again.

I wanted to make things right, but I learned long ago to be skeptical of people. My pain from being used was real. Was Marjorie sincere, or was she merely flattering me for some other purpose? Despite only knowing each other for a few weeks, a lot occurred during that time. We still barely knew each other.

I think she was waiting for me to respond and say, "Okay, I forgive you." I didn't.

Rather than continuing to debate over who did what, I changed the subject. I still didn't understand her relationship with Derek

Watting. Why was he always hanging around our periphery? What was his role in this charade?

"Marjorie, what's your relationship with Derek Watting?"

"Derek and I are friends. When I first moved to D.C., we met at a conference. I didn't know anyone or how to solicit donations. Derek introduced me to several corporate executives, and those introductions helped me establish grants for quite a few charities."

"At first, I'm sure he wanted to date me, but I had just gotten out of that awful marriage. I wasn't ready. Derek stuck with me, and we became best friends. We still work together occasionally; he knows many corporate executives. I will forever be grateful for his help. There is nothing romantic between Derek and me, if that answers your question."

I didn't want to play twenty questions, but I couldn't think of anything else to say. We locked eyes, gazing at each other in silence, neither one adding more to the conversation.

After nearly a minute, she caved in. Again, changing the subject, she tried to lighten the mood by saying. "Besides, we never had that romantic dinner you promised me. Brussels seems like a good place. Are you hungry?"

On that point, we agreed. Brussels is a wonderful place for a romantic dinner. Having already drunk too much wine, we left the sidewalk cafe and walked down the Rue de la Montagne to a small bistro called Le Rabassier, a place I had passed a dozen times on my strolls. It seemed to be the perfect spot for a romantic dinner and a chance to continue our discussion. We found a private table along the wall near the rear of the dining room. A place to laugh, talk, and reconnect undisturbed.

When the waiter came to the table, I ordered a bottle of Champagne and caviar canapes.

As he popped the cork, he asked in French, "Special occasion?"

Once again, Marjorie surprised me with her sophistication. Besides being fluent in Spanish, she also speaks French confidently. She laughingly replied to the waiter. "C'est notre premier rendez-vous."

He smiled and tapped his heart with approval. "Votre premier rencard! Bonne chance."

Even after spending nearly two weeks in Belgium, my French was still poor at best. I glanced at her with a confused look. "You speak French?"

"There is still a lot you don't know about me, D.K. St. Joseph. He asked if we were celebrating a special occasion. I said it was our first date. Was I wrong?"

"Well, technically, we had the baseball game," I said.

She laughed. "Yeah, a bag of peanuts. I don't consider that a first date."

"What did he say?"

"I don't think he believed it was our first date. He wished us good luck."

It was semantics. After the baseball game, we spent the night together. Some people would consider that a date. I never considered my jungle encounter with Melinda Donne as a date, so maybe Marjorie was right. The more we talked, the more my anger subsided. How could anyone stay angry at her for long?

We had a quiet dinner of Salmon and sparkling wine. We were both carefully trying not to pretend that all was forgiven. Our feelings toward each other were undeniable, but our future together was still very much uncertain.

I have to admit that sometimes I can be a hard-ass jerk. I enjoyed making her plead her case for reconciliation. We were still two people who put our careers ahead of our personal lives. That mindset doesn't bode well for a long-term relationship.

She raised the stakes. "After my return from Chicago next week, I plan to take some time off. My schedule has been brutal these last few months, and I need some time for myself. I have reservations at a resort in Florida. The weather is usually nice now. Know anyone who'd want to spend two weeks in Florida?"

She was tempting me; she knew I had no immediate plans, having burned my bridges with most of my friends in Washington. A trip to Florida sounded wonderful. I could envision myself walking the sands of a pristine beach, hand in hand with the girl of my dreams. We could party all night, sleep late the next day, and then relax by the pool with a Piña Colada.

Only a moron would turn down the invitation she had just offered me.

Then, like a dummy, I blurted out my alternate plan. "They have offered me a job as the Chief Editor at the *Reporter*, a news media company. They are looking for someone to bring their magazine into the twenty-first century. I would be hiring and mentoring a group of young journalists, as well as carving out a niche in an already crowded field of mass media outlets. I'm going to visit them next week."

"It sounds like an enormous challenge, but I'm sure you are up to the task."

"I haven't negotiated my contract yet, but they have assured me it is just a formality. The job is mine if I want it. I will relocate to Chicago as soon as I can sell my home."

I could see my words hit her like a wave crashing on the shore. It must have hurt because, for the second time, her face went flush as her rich dark skin turned colorless.

"Oh," she said. Her eyes, which always had a straight-ahead stare, dropped toward the table as she processed what I had just told her. Her head dipped into her hand as she tried to shield her disappointment. She refolded her napkin several times, then fumbled with her fork, trying to regain her composure.

I had tried to hurt her as she hurt me, but Marjorie was strong; she didn't accept rejection easily. A few seconds later, her back stiffened. She raised her head, and her gaze returned across the table toward me. I saw moisture in her eyes, but she forced a smile anyway.

With what we had left of our wine, she raised her glass to toast my future success. "How wonderful for you. I know you will be successful. They are incredibly lucky."

There was not much else to say. Our careers were always our top priority. We will always be subject to an ever-present battle raging between our hearts and our minds. Right now, our minds appear to be winning. We had no reason to believe we'd change.

I paid the check, which came out to about one hundred forty Euros. For good measure, I took one more mean shot at Marjorie. "Now we're even for the cost of the baseball tickets." She said nothing.

We bid our waiter goodbye. I think he sensed our date hadn't gone as well as it could have. He nodded, tapped his chest again, then folded his hands in a praying motion, as if to say, "I'm praying for you."

We were going to need his prayers, lots of them.

Chapter 20

Zing Went My Chordae Tendineae

The weather was perfect, a balmy evening with only a slight breeze to keep the air filled with the aromas emanating from the chocolate shops and bakeries along the side streets. We strolled down the Rue Leopold, gazing at the Brussels skyline. The streets around the Grand Palace teemed with pedestrians. It was a popular spot for locals and tourists to enjoy drinks and observe passersby. If we rekindled our love, we'd seamlessly blend in with others.

While our path seemed aimless, after walking a few minutes, we unknowingly found ourselves standing in front of her hotel.

I thought our evening was ending until she turned toward me with an inviting expression.

"Come upstairs with me. No strings attached, I promise," she said.

But there were strings attached. All of them fastened to my heart, and she was gently tugging on them. She knew what she was doing. Like a mouse smelling the cheese used as bait, I couldn't resist. I could only hope that it wasn't another trap. She took my hand and guided me toward the hotel entrance.

We turned toward the entranceway as the doorman nodded and pulled open the giant glass door.

Her hotel was magnificent. The ornate ceiling towered thirty feet in the air, the anteroom lighted by enormous crystal chandeliers. The floor was polished marble, gleaming like a giant pearl. I was almost afraid to step inside, not wanting to leave footprints on the sparkling tile. It didn't matter; I don't think my feet touched the ground as we floated, hand in hand, across the lobby toward the lift. Even though it was late, the hall was abuzz with activity. Bellhops were scurrying about with carts full of luggage, a line queued at the reservations desk, while a group of tourists seated on the lobby's leather couches spoke Farsi and were arguing over something trivial.

Her two-room hotel suite, on the twentieth-level concierge floor, was head and shoulders above my room at the rooming house where I was staying.

They furnished the suite area with a couch, a desk, and a large-screen television. All high-end furniture. I glanced inside the bathroom to see marble floors, dual sinks, a walk-in shower, and a spa tub. The room was brightly lit with overhead lighting and a large mirror.

The bedroom area offered a comfortable-looking king-sized bed, a dresser, two nightstands, and a plush chair. Earlier, the maid had turned down the bed and left two foil-wrapped mints strategically placed on the fluffed white pillows.

"Wow, very impressive," I commented.

"I travel so often that this hotel chain always upgrades me. It is one of the small perks I get from trading my personal life for my career."

Then casually, as if it were an invitation to lunch, she upped the ante. "You're welcome to stay the night."

I didn't respond. I wanted nothing more than to stay with her. Except, there was probably still a little apprehension inside me that scared me. I had already started this relationship with my eyes closed. I suppose I was unsure of my words or actions. I just stood there.

"Make yourself comfortable," she said. "I will be right back."

Marjorie disappeared into the bathroom, leaving me alone to contemplate my surroundings. I thought of turning on the TV, but the programming in Brussels was awful. It consisted mostly of poorly directed soap operas in French or Dutch or reruns of American sitcoms dubbed in French or German with French-sounding laugh tracks. Yes, the laugh tracks were dubbed, as if American laughter wasn't as funny as French laughter.

I peeked around the closed curtains to see a splendid view overlooking the market square and the Grand Palace just beyond. It was dark, but the city was sparkling with lights from the cafes and shops below.

A few minutes later, Marjorie stepped back into the bedroom. When I turned toward her, my knees buckled. She stood before me in a silky blue negligee. It had a deep V-neckline plunging nearly to her waist, revealing her perfect breasts and subtle waistline. Thin spaghetti straps held it in place. The hem broke at her thighs, striking the perfect balance between sexy and classy. It overwhelmed my brain with the image of this stunningly beautiful woman.

"I bought it for you. I was planning to wear it after our romantic dinner last Saturday. Do you like it?"

Did I like it? I don't think I ever witnessed something more beautiful in my life.

There was only one thing. Did she honestly believe we could just pick up where we left off? Would simply having sex with me remove the knife from my back and make my wounds heal? Yet she held some sort of power over me. When she was near me, all I could see were her dark eyes and bright smile. I could feel myself losing control of my common sense.

"Please, stay with me tonight. Let's not worry about tomorrow," she said.

She slipped onto the bed, beckoning me to join her. I knew I couldn't resist her proposal. I loved her more than anything or anyone I had ever met. She flew all the way to Brussels, searching the city, to find me. I told myself. *She must feel the same way. She must.*

Can you picture a more romantic setting than a luxury hotel room in Brussels with the one you love? There was no resisting her advancement. I undressed and followed her into bed. Holding her in my arms made me feel powerful again. Once again, I was the whole man I wished to become. Somehow, Marjorie completed me.

I lay there, my head on a soft pillow, my arm wrapped around her, her head tucked softly in the nape of my neck. Could life be any more perfect?

Nevertheless, our future together remained doubtful. I recalled the first time we made love. I whispered. "When we were together last time, you said something to me in Spanish. What did you say?"

"I asked you a question," she said.

She touched her lips to my temple, offering a soft kiss. Then she whispered in my ear. "Te quedarás conmigo para siempre?"

This time, I listened to every syllable she breathed. I still didn't get what she said, but I'll always remember her words. I repeated her words in my head. They sounded romantic. That was all I needed to hear.

Then she whispered. "You do not have to answer yet. Think about it. Right now, just hold me for tonight."

She turned over, pressing her backside to me. I spooned her, wrapping my arm around her, pulling her close, and kissing the back of her neck. She sighed approvingly.

Whatever she was asking, I wanted the answer to be an unquestionable yes. I closed my eyes and breathed in the scent of her jasmine perfume. In a few seconds, we were both sound asleep.

◆ ◆ ◆

The sound of my phone receiving a new text message woke me from a sound sleep. Thanks to the well-designed blackout curtains, the hotel room was still dark. I looked around the room. Marjorie was nowhere in sight. A few seconds later, the phone sounded its second alert. I climbed from the bed to see what was so important. It was a text from Marjorie.

"Thank you for staying with me last night. When you read this message, I'll be at the airport, heading to Atlanta. I thought it would be best if we made a clean break. I don't think a long-distance relationship will work for either of us. For what it's worth, I am sorry things got so messed up. Good luck with your new career in Chicago."

A minute later, there was a second text that puzzled me. The first one was so heartfelt, the second was a confusing afterthought.

"Leave the key at the front desk. I love you."

I sat on the edge of the bed in disbelief. In just one month, I found the woman of my dreams, lost her, found her again, only to lose my dream a second time.

How could two highly educated and reasonably intelligent adults screw up their love lives so badly?

My first inspiration was to jump in a taxi, run through the airport, and make a dramatic pitch for Marjorie's heart. Like in some sort of romantic comedy, she would throw her arms around me, the music would play, and we would live happily ever after.

I looked at the clock. She was boarding her plane in twenty minutes. There's no chance I'll make it to the airport in time to catch her. I started typing a text to say, "Don't go. Stay here with me. I love you too."

I don't know why I didn't hit the send button. Perhaps I was afraid. Maybe she was right? A clean break made the most sense. I rationalized that there was no way she would cancel her trip to

Atlanta; she had a responsibility to all the people who relied upon her. Our careers would make it impossible to have a normal life as a couple.

I also had responsibilities. Today it was to my fellow committee members and the closing ceremonies of the conference. It was already getting late. I had to hurry; they would start the ceremonies in two hours. I still needed to shower, shave, and change my clothes. The shower in Marjorie's hotel room felt wonderful, but I still had yesterday's clothes. I took a taxi to my dormitory room, where I donned a fresh outfit of clothing. I packed my bag and checked out of the dormitory. When I got to the IECO offices, a few minutes late, the ceremony was already in full swing.

I listened as Jacques summarized the progress we had made and thanked each participant for their contributions. He then declared the conference closed. We spent the last hour shaking hands, bowing, or hugging each other. Despite the sometimes-contentious atmosphere, we made many new friendships. The conference was a tremendous success. Future generations of journalists will have a new and modern reference document to help them succeed.

Chapter 21

The Reporter

While the IECO conference became an important event in my business career, my personal life wasn't faring as well. My failed second encounter with Marjorie, as wonderful as it was, boxed me in regarding my plans for the future. The job interview in Chicago seemed like the only logical next step. I returned to my Bethesda home just long enough to adjust to the jet lag. I did laundry, got caught up on my bills, and watched some good old American television. By Thursday, I was heading for Chicago and my job interview.

I met with the owner, Ted Jerome, and the business manager, Elise Carter, of the *Reporter*. They were both younger than me. Ted is in his early thirties, and Elise is a recent college graduate in her early twenties. Together, they held a vision of this old newspaper becoming an international news agency with trending stories that didn't just scoop the competition; they would outsell them. They were hoping I could merge my research skills with their technological savvy and youthful enthusiasm.

Despite assuming the role of the old sage, the interview went well. They introduced me to the staff, most of whom were junior reporters fresh out of college. Some would make the cut and become famous journalists; others would move on to different places or different jobs.

Ted and Elise both agreed the job of Editor-in-Chief was mine if I wanted it.

Moving across the country, even for a minimalist like me, is a big deal. It would mean dozens of changes. I must choose which possessions to bring, and what to leave behind. Do I sell my current home, or wait to see how the new career works out? Where will I live in my new city? It meant meeting new friends, finding new restaurants, shopping at new grocery stores, basically new everything.

As I left the offices of the *Reporter*, I found myself at a crossroads. Should I return to my previous life in D.C., or continue forward to a new career in Chicago? I had big decisions to make. At thirty-six, I had already accomplished more than people twenty years older. From a career perspective, I had achieved the success I sought.

Yet, my life wasn't complete. Something was still missing. In a nutshell, my life can be described in two words: "I'm satisfied". I had everything I needed, except the most important thing. Happiness. Happiness had somehow eluded me.

For the past decade, I was a loner. Avoiding meaningful relationships because it was easier. It was time to embrace adulthood and become a true man. I was in love with Marjorie Sykes. I let the woman of my dreams slip away due to my stubborn attitude. There was no doubt in my mind. I knew what I had to do. I had to get Marjorie back. I had to try one more time.

Across the street from the *Reporter's* office building, I found a pleasant coffee shop called Intelligentsia Coffee. As I sat sipping a dark roast coffee, I wondered if real happiness remained a possibility. I got on the phone and started making phone calls. It's not easy to get someone to answer a voice call nowadays. After several attempts, I connected with someone who could help me. It was Marjorie's secretary, May Stiles.

At first, she was reluctant to give a stranger any information over the phone. It took a lot of convincing, begging if you will, to win her over.

"Marjorie must have spoken about me?" I implored her, "May please, this is important. I need to find Marjorie. I have to talk to her, face to face."

The timidness in her voice told me she was uncertain, but she must have felt sorry for me because she finally relented. "Marjorie is still in Chicago; she will be there one more night."

I convinced May to help me find her and, above all, be discreet.

"Let me make a few calls. I'll get back to you," she said.

I squirmed in the Intelligentsia's corner booth, waiting for May's response. About twenty minutes later, she called me, laughing. "You're in luck. Marjorie will be at the baseball game with one of her business associates. The Phillies are playing the Cubs at Wrigley Field tonight."

That was no surprise. Marjorie never passed up a chance to attend a Phillies game. "Can you tell me where she will be sitting?"

Marjorie once flew halfway across the world to locate me in a busy city. The least I could do was find her in the baseball stadium. I told May Stiles my plan.

"Find out where her seats are. I want to surprise her. And please don't let on, okay?"

I think May was enjoying the vision of me surprising Marjorie. It was like an episode from a cheap situation comedy.

"I'll try, but she is going to get suspicious."

While I waited, my mind ran wild. I needed to make this encounter somehow memorable.

I got on the phone with the front office of the Chicago Cubs. On a busy game day, finding the right person to speak with was challenging. After a half dozen calls and several transfers, I connected with the stadium's advertising manager.

I explained what I wished to do, "I want to make a public service announcement at the game tonight." She informed me that what I wanted couldn't be a public service announcement. It didn't meet their advertising guidelines. I begged, "I have to get a message to Marjorie Sykes."

I must have sounded really pathetic because she finally offered me an announcement under the guise of an emergency contact request. Similar to a "Paging Doctor Marcus Welby, please call your office."

"I will probably get fired for this," she said. "I'll try to squeeze this in after the seventh-inning stretch. No promises."

The announcement would be simple: "Attention Marjorie Sykes, you have an emergency announcement from D.K. St. Joseph. The answer is YES!" That was all the announcement would say.

She went one step further. Along with the voice announcement, the video screen in center field would flash "Y.E.S."

I had to hope that Marjorie would hear it or see it and understand what I was saying.

A short while later, May Stiles called back.

"I told her I was going to watch the game and was going to look for her on television. Marjorie Sykes will be in box one hundred, right behind home plate."

"May you're amazing. I don't know how to thank you."

There was still one hole in my plan that I had forgotten. I needed a ticket to the game. I found a scalper online who had two seats a few rows behind Marjorie's box. They wouldn't sell me only one ticket. Despite the outrageous price, if my plan worked, buying two seats was worthwhile.

I snuck into the stadium after the start of the second inning and slipped into my seat behind Marjorie's box, hoping she wouldn't see me until she heard the announcement. I sat nervously waiting long past the seventh-inning stretch. But the announcement didn't come. By the ninth inning, I was losing hope that my gambit would work. I needed a Plan B.

I didn't expect the announcement to come during such a crucial moment in the game. The Phillies trailed by three runs with bases loaded. The manager sent in his pinch hitter, a little-used first baseman with a long history of heroic at-bats. As he stepped to the plate, a hush came over the crowd. You could hear a pin drop in the stadium except for Marjorie shouting encouragement to the pinch hitter.

The stadium announcer broke the silence with my pre-written plea. "Attention Marjorie Sykes: Marjorie Sykes, please listen; I have an important announcement." The last-second announcement confused the hometown fans. Why would they interrupt the game at this critical juncture?

He continued. "Marjorie, Sykes, I have a message from D.K. St. Joseph."

"The answer to your question is YES!"

The scoreboard in center field flashed a big, "Y" "E" "S" one letter at a time.

Marjorie looked around. Something crazy was happening, but she wasn't sure what it meant. She spun around until her eyes locked on me, standing a few rows back. Her dark eyes were at first unsure. Then she flashed that bright smile. Just two people mattered in the stadium.

For a moment, we stood and stared. In the background, I heard a bat crack and the crowd moaning in disgust. Were they commenting on our announcement or what happened on the field? They tell me it was a home run. I didn't see the play. I was staring at Marjorie.

Above the din of the crowd, I shouted. "I'm not moving to Chicago. I want to be with you, if you will still have me."

Among thousands, Margie's smile was all I saw, confirming with a nod, "Yes!"

I climbed over three rows of seats to get to Marjorie. As I wrapped my arms around her, I promised myself I would never let her get away again. The crowd clapped in an approving ovation.

As the crowd settled down, she introduced me to her business associate, Janice Stalle. I apologized for stealing Marjorie away in such an unexpected fashion. Janice smiled. She seemed happy to meet me and happy for Marjorie as well. I think she would have preferred a Cub victory, but that's baseball.

We stopped at a local watering hole near Wrigley Field for a drink. We tried to include Janice, but she knew we had important things to discuss. After a quick drink, she bid Marjorie farewell with the promise to catch up in the next few days.

Marjorie had a room at a hotel near my old alma mater, the downtown campus of Northwestern University. We departed the bar to be alone once more. It was a quick cab ride from Wrigleyville. As usual, it was a luxury hotel with a plush king-sized bed.

"How did you figure it out?" she asked.

"What, where you were sitting?"

"No, the question I asked you in Spanish. I had to ask you twice. You finally got the right answer."

"I remembered the words, and the answer is yes. Just in case the scoreboard didn't get my message across. I will say it again and again. Yes, I want to hold you forever."

She smiled and wrapped her arms around me. "Then you can start right now."

I lay there, staring at the ceiling. Our love brought us together once more.

"Is your invitation to join you in Florida still open?" I asked.

I fully expected her to say, "Of course it is." Instead, she said, "Well, maybe?"

"What do you mean, maybe?"

"Are we officially a couple again? This isn't another one-night stand, is it?"

"Marjorie, I never wanted our relationship to be a series of one-night stands. I want us to be together, always."

"Well, when we separated, I didn't know when I would see you again. I asked my mother to accompany me for part of the time. I had already booked the reservations, and I didn't want to waste the money. We are meeting at her house in Philadelphia tomorrow. We are flying to St. Petersburg the next day."

"Gee, that's too bad. Looks like I messed up again," I said.

"I am sorry. Everything got so confusing. I mean, I just didn't know what was going to happen," she said.

Then she hedged a little. "She is only coming for a couple of days. You could meet us down there. We could have the whole second week together, just the two of us?"

Just days ago, we were in love but broken up, and I was considering a move to Chicago. Being back together and looking forward to a week in Florida sounded wonderful.

The next morning, I called Elise Carter at the *Reporter*, then placed a second call to Dr. Elaine Sadeski, and informed them I had other plans for my future. It disappointed them, but I think they understood it was personal, not business.

Chapter 22

In The Presence Of Wisdom

It was strange. We were back together in a relationship, yet we flew home separately. Marjorie went ahead to Philadelphia to rendezvous with her mother for their flight down to Florida. I went home to wait a requisite couple of days before I flew down to meet them.

I met Marjorie and her mother, Sofia, in St. Petersburg on Thursday, the evening before Sofia's return home. Marjorie wanted me to meet her mother without being too pushy. She was unsure if Sofia would accept me, as I differed from anyone she had dated before. Since Marjorie was sharing a room with her mom, I booked a separate room in the same hotel for myself.

Hoping to make a good impression on Sofia, I made a reservation at an upscale restaurant with outdoor dining that served Caribbean food. We met for dinner at 7:00 p.m., and the anticipation was killing me. It would be my first taste of Sanocho and Tostones, two traditional dishes popular in the Dominican Republic. My choice of this restaurant was spot on. We sat under the stars while strolling musicians serenaded us with soft Calypso music.

It wasn't only the atmosphere that I remember. The moment Marjorie introduced us, Sofia captured my heart. She was the warmest, most genteel person I had ever met. Marjorie received her statuesque build and confident demeanor from her father, but she had inherited her mother's facial beauty. Sofia had soft, dark skin and ruby-red lips. Sofia, like Marjorie, possessed a heartwarming smile. It was easy to see where Marjorie learned to be so graceful.

Sofia and I bonded quickly, without a hint of apprehension. She had prepared herself for our meeting and wanted to keep an open mind about Marjorie's new suitor. I found Sofia easy to talk to and surprisingly well-versed in current events.

Sofia asked me thoughtful questions about my work. Questions that were more than small talk. I think she was trying to dig down and learn the type of person Marjorie was dating. She asked where I grew up and where I went to school. She asked about my family. You could say she was measuring me. For what I did not know.

We avoided any serious discussion until Marjorie excused herself to use the restroom. In an instant, it was just Sofia and me, alone without a chaperone. I tried keeping the conversation light by asking her opinion of the food, St. Petersburg, and the weather. All safe topics.

Marjorie was gone for only a few seconds when Sofia changed the subject. Her directness caught me off guard. She asked, "Joseph, have you considered children?"

Children? I hadn't given the idea of children or marriage any thought. The days Marjorie and I spent together were few and mostly consumed by attempts to seduce one another. We never paused to discuss our future together.

Sofia stated her viewpoint. "I don't understand young people today. By the time I was your age, I had three children. You shouldn't wait too long to start a family. Life is too short. There's plenty of time for you to make money."

It wasn't only about money. Marjorie and I felt our work to be an important component of who we are.

"We haven't been together long enough to consider those things," I mentioned.

"She isn't getting any younger, neither are you. If she doesn't have children soon, she'll be too old. I see her eyes sparkle when she looks at you. She flew to Europe to get you back.

"I've been watching you. You look at her the same way."

One minute later, Marjorie returned to the table. Sofia winked at me and nodded, silently implying, "We'll talk again later."

I felt like an elephant had landed on my chest. It was a strange feeling, but oddly enough, I liked it. Single people seldom worry about what their partner's parents think of them. Sofia's curiosity about where I fit into Marjorie's life was exciting. Her attention made me feel a part of something bigger than myself.

After dinner, we took our time walking back to our hotel. I escorted them back to their room. Before saying goodnight, Sofia smiled and pinched my face. Then she said something to me in Spanish, "Piensa en lo que dije". Turning, she went into her hotel room. These little Spanish sayings were starting to bother me. I wasn't sure what she said, but I knew what she was saying.

"What was that all about?" Marjorie asked.

"Oh, nothing. Your mom gave me some advice."

"She is always giving someone advice. It's part of motherhood. It's something you need to get used to hearing. Don't worry, I'll take her to the airport in the morning, then meet you tomorrow afterward.

She kissed me goodnight and followed her mother into the hotel room. It was early, and I wanted to spend some time alone with Marjorie. We hadn't been alone together since Chicago, but I let her go with her mother because it had already been a glorious night. I think I passed the first test with Sofia. I was walking on a cloud.

The first few days of our Florida visit were some of the most enjoyable of my life. We took moonlight walks on the beach. Drank cocktails by the pool. We slept late, having breakfast in bed. Holding each other, solely for the joy it brought. The same electricity we felt the day we met was still apparent.

We devoted our time to getting to know each other better. Before Florida, our conversations focused on work. Marjorie talked about her charity and her experiences with the quirky philanthropists she met with regularly. I spoke about my research or my next planned article.

It wasn't just about work and our careers. We wanted to use the time to create new memories, ones that revolve around us as a couple. We'd photograph each other daily, whether on the beach or at dinner. We went shopping at the local tourist traps, making jokes about the gaudy T-shirts and ashtrays they sold to first-time tourists. We held hands everywhere we went.

One day for lunch, we had Gelato at a famous Italian bakery on Beach Drive.

It was paradise, until the afternoon we drove up the coast for a sightseeing adventure. We wanted to see some old-time Florida sights before rapid development changed them. We drove for an hour, then decided to turn away from the coast inland toward the interstate. We would make a big loop as we headed south back to our resort. Taking the back roads, we drove through a series of small farm towns. Everywhere we looked, we could see old Florida disappearing. Replacing the quaint little towns were modern age-restricted communities built to house the endless migration of retirees from New Jersey, Pennsylvania, and my home state of Ohio.

As we passed through one little hamlet, we came across a ramshackle restaurant alongside some abandoned railroad tracks. Likely, it began as a beanery for railroad workers around the turn of the century. From the outside, it looked like a strong wind could blow it down. It wasn't fancy, but it had character.

Parked in the lot were a couple of pickup trucks, odors of home cooking seeped from inside, and the door had a welcoming "open" neon sign. It looked like fun, so we decided to be adventurous. When we stepped inside, we weren't disappointed. The interior was nearly as dilapidated as the exterior.

The room's center held a small bar, similar in height to a midwestern diner's counter. Several old wooden tables ringed the counter. At the back of the building, they added one of those overhead garage doors, which opened to an outside patio with four additional tables.

A young Hispanic boy was cleaning the plates off a table left by an earlier patron. Seated at the bar were two stereotypical good old boys. I try not to be judgmental, but if you used the term "rednecks" to describe these two characters, you would not be wrong. Neither one was very big. You might even call them skinny, except for their prominent bellies, which pressed against the bar each time they reached for their drink. They each had a beer in front of them and an empty shot glass, which told me they were drinking hard liquor as well. They both wore jeans, dirty T-shirts, and work boots. The guy on the left wore a red, white, and blue cap styled like an American flag. On the right, his partner wore a red baseball cap with a logo from a local feed store. The patriotic drinker smoked a cigarette, which I thought was odd because Florida law didn't allow smoking inside restaurants.

Opting for a patio table to avoid the cigarette smoke, we sat and patiently waited for someone to take our order. With no one coming to serve us, I scanned the dining room for help. I noticed a woman, likely our server, speaking with the cook by the kitchen door. She was smoking as well.

The other two red-neck patrons were apparently not happy with our presence. Only twenty feet away, we could clearly hear their banter. The guy on the left lamented about the good old days, "when we all kept to our own kind." They made several off-color remarks about our being there. "White boy" was one of them, "dark meat" was another. We ignored them as best we could while we waited. They clowned it up at our expense until one of them said, "nigger lover". That threw me over the top. I jumped up and headed straight for the bar. It wasn't right to make such abusive comments.

Marjorie screamed, "Joseph, No!" But it was too late. I was about to teach them a lesson in manners. Except when I was halfway to the bar, out of nowhere, a tall and muscular man about my age suddenly appeared in front of me.

"Hold on there, Chief," he said. "We don't want any trouble here today. The diner is closed. The busboy should've told you we are closed."

"The sign said open when we came in," I said.

"This is my place. When I say it's closed, it's closed."

"This isn't about food. Someone needs to talk to these two."

By now, Marjorie stood right behind me. "Come on, let's get out of here. We don't want to be here, anyway.

The big guy agreed. "Take your friend's advice and move along."

It wasn't right, but it was reality. I could hear the two cavemen snickering as we walked toward the exit.

As we stepped outside, I was in a rage. While I ranted about the ignorance of the two oafs at the bar and how the owner defended them, Marjorie stayed calm. She acted as cool as a cucumber, or so it seemed. We pulled out of the parking lot and headed back toward the interstate. I continued to rant about how I should have set those two idiots straight. Marjorie said nothing.

"How can you be so calm about this?" I asked.

That's when I realized Marjorie wasn't calm; she was petrified. She screamed at the top of her lungs. "He had a gun!"

"Who? What gun?"

"The guy with the flag hat. He had a gun. He might have killed you."

I hadn't seen the gun. Perhaps the owner did me a favor. Still, what they did wasn't right.

By the time we reached the interstate, Marjorie was in tears. I had never seen her so shaken up. I couldn't stop the car on the interstate, so I reached for her hand and said, "It will be okay. Let's go back to the resort."

We drove in silence for about twenty minutes. As I pulled up to the valet station, Marjorie, still upset, jumped from the car and bolted into the hotel. I removed our belongings from the car and handed the valet the key.

By the time I made it upstairs to our hotel room, Marjorie was sitting on the balcony overlooking the pool and the lush hotel grounds.

"Are you okay?"

She wasn't. Her voice trembled, "I'm leaving tomorrow. I need to get back home."

Our reservation had three days remaining. I didn't want to leave.

"We still have three days. Why should we leave?" I asked.

"No, I am leaving. You can stay. This isn't going to work. I should have known better. It will always be the same. Everywhere we go. The same blatant stares, the same hurtful comments, the same threats."

I couldn't believe what I heard. It sounded like she was talking about ending our relationship. I couldn't allow that to happen. I don't think she wanted to break up. Frustration had taken over her mind.

She was dedicating her life to making a better world. A world that was refusing to change.

I knelt next to her and took her hand. I rubbed the skin on the top of her hand.

"Hey, this is your outside."

Pointing to my hand, I said, "This is my outside."

I placed her hand over my heart. "It's what's in here that counts."

"Marjorie, God brought us together for a reason. He knows what he is doing."

I'm not sure why I called upon God's name. I was never very religious. Under other circumstances, I might have said Karma brought us together, or fate intervened. Considering the situation, God seemed appropriate.

I slipped my arm around her and gently pulled her to me. She pressed her head to my shoulder. I held her close for five minutes, waiting for her to calm down. When her breathing returned to normal, I whispered, "Marjorie, I love you. Stay with me."

I kissed the top of her head and repeated. "It is going to be okay."

Holding her close finally settled her down. As we pondered what I said, she pulled away and looked back at me. I knew she calmed down because she corrected my statement, "You said HE knows what he is doing. Don't you mean SHE knows what she is doing?"

We had this discussion before. Why was God always portrayed as male? Why couldn't God be a female? How each of us views the supreme being wasn't important; our relationship was.

"Marjorie, as long as we are together, that is all that counts. You and I, we are a team."

We looked out over the hotel grounds. It was still early. Our resort had a world-class pool and an outdoor bar.

"Why don't we go for a swim and put all this behind us?" I said.

She agreed and said, "Give me a few minutes to get ready."

She walked back inside our hotel room, withdrew some items from the dresser, and then disappeared into the bathroom.

After a few minutes, I changed into my swimming trunks and put on a loose-fitting Hawaiian-style shirt.

Minutes later, she emerged wearing a bright yellow one-piece bathing suit. A classic style that would make the movie star Esther Williams proud. The suit was cut just low enough on top to reveal a little cleavage and high enough at the bottom to showcase her shapely buttocks. She had fixed her hair with a part down the middle and had tied it up into two round buns that made it look like she was wearing Minnie Mouse ears. Marjorie possessed a natural ability to appear both young and mature simultaneously.

"You look beautiful," I said.

"Well, thank you. You realize that's the first time you have complimented my style?"

I couldn't believe that was true. Every time I laid eyes on Marjorie, she appeared as the most beautiful woman I'd ever met. "If that's true, I'm sorry. I promise to tell you daily from now on."

She reached into a dresser drawer and pulled out a white cover-up, which she slipped over her bathing suit. She grabbed her room key, slipped on a pair of sandals, and we were off to the pool.

The pool was crowded with guests who had similar ideas. It took a minute before we found two seats together. Putting towels and coverups on chairs, we eagerly jumped into the water. The cool water helped wash away some of the day's early anguish. We started out swimming laps, then played catch with a ball found in the water.

I ordered two drinks from the pool bar. The house specialty is a slushy drink called a Lava Flow, a twist on a Pina Colada made with raspberry compote. They were sweet enough to make you slurp them down, giving you a brain freeze if you weren't careful. And potent enough to wipe away your inhibitions.

After about an hour, we returned to our room. The Lava Flow had worked its magic because Marjorie was her relaxed self again. Before I knew it, she was kissing me passionately. We made love with the desire I hadn't felt since our first night together. Our hate-filled encounter from earlier in the day seemed like a million years ago.

Leaving the racist incident behind, we never looked back. She stayed with me in Florida for the remaining three days. Together, we weathered another unforgettable experience. We were finally a couple in every sense of the word.

Chapter 23

Bliss Is Ignorance

Our time in Florida, like all good things, ended too quickly. Marjorie was soon back on the road, traveling from city to city. Airports, hotels, business meetings, fundraisers. A new town daily. With the help of her secretary, May Stiles, she somehow kept it all straight.

Alone again, I returned to my home office, sitting by my computer, reading through reams of documents, parsing through facts and figures, and plotting various hypotheses out on a whiteboard. Somewhere in my ramblings, I hoped to find my next big story.

With the Andrew Johnson caper in my rear-view mirror, my only regret was that even though they dropped the charges against Johnson, they never arrested the actual shooter. The case remained open, another unsolved mystery in a long list of cold cases that never get closed.

On the bright side, the Andrew Johnson case called attention to the protection scheme run by Thurmond Security. The local business owners in the Camden neighborhood where Thurmond operated realized they were not alone, and collectively they had power. They banded together to help elect a new District Attorney. The Camden County DA's office could no longer ignore the mounting political pressure. A month later, they filed an indictment against Boston Thurmond for racketeering charges. A few days after the indictment came down, they arrested Thurmond at Newark Airport, attempting to board a plane for Belize with a suitcase full of cash. Inadvertently, my investigation helped tilt the scale of justice just a little toward the good guys.

Each day she was away, Marjorie and I would video chat. If we couldn't be together, at least I could see her irrepressible smile. I always asked her about her day and the city she visited. It was nice. Our lives were going well. We seemed to be satisfied. Or at least contented.

Oddly enough, happiness can impede the inspiration to begin any new investigations. Bliss allows you to look past minor irritations that otherwise make you want to change the world. I was feeling satisfied and didn't feel like picking a fight with anyone. Even the trending news stories on social media weren't enough to rile me up to start a new inquiry. I needed to continue my work, but I had no desire.

I spent a lot of time surfing the web and perusing social media. Then, one morning, it surprised me when I received an email from Melinda Donne. You'll remember Melinda Donne as the Irish war correspondent I had a brief relationship with a few years out of college. Melinda guided me through the jungles of India, seeking to connect with Islamic freedom fighters moving between Pakistan and India. Though I bailed on her early, she completed her mission and documented her encounter. Her completed story was an in-depth, award-winning account of terrorism. In her article, she acknowledged several of the people who helped her fulfill the operation, but there was no mention of D.K. St. Joseph in her report.

When Melinda and I separated, the split was not amicable. I never expected to hear from her again. Instead, I followed her career loosely as she became widely respected in Europe.

A few years after we parted ways, Melinda, while on another undertaking along the India-Pakistan border, was captured by insurgents and held for several days until government troops intervened and secured her release. Melinda never resumed reporting. Instead, she returned to her hometown in Northern Ireland to recover and, supposedly, to write her memoir about her years in the field.

The book was planned to chronicle her experiences as a journalist in the world's most volatile environments. In Melinda's email, something of a peace offering, she was asking for my help with completing and publishing her book. She was struggling to complete the project.

I was uncertain at first, having split on bad terms and not spoken for a decade. I barely knew her.

Besides, nothing I had written before was so comprehensive as a biography, yet the idea intrigued me. I had nothing else going, so I replied that I would be interested in discussing her idea, with no promises of a partnership. I asked her to forward an outline of her biography and her thesis. It would allow me to speak intelligently about her project.

We set up a time for a video conference to narrow down her vision and how she envisioned my role in the production of her life story. To adjust for the five-hour time difference between Washington, D.C., and Belfast, we scheduled our meeting for late morning; it would be late afternoon in Belfast.

Before the call, I reviewed her outline and found it lacking. Considering that it had been years since she suspended her career and supposedly had started her journal, the outline was terrible. She had no organizational skills. Her transcripts, which contained many interesting reports, were a jumbled mess of factoids. Her notes were out of sequence and, sometimes, incoherent. I recognized the potential but knew it would require significant effort to produce a readable product.

I allowed her to initiate the video call from her home in Carryduff, a suburb of Belfast. I waited at my desk, with her notes in front of me. When the application on my computer flashed the signal for an incoming session, I clicked accept and adjusted my camera so she could see me clearly.

At first, I thought it was a poor signal or a low-quality phone camera. I tapped on my computer screen as if that would somehow improve the signal. Melinda looked totally different from the robust young woman I remembered from ten years ago. When we trekked through the forest in India, she was a healthy, one-hundred-sixty pounds of muscle, with a masculine physique. The Melinda Donne I saw on the screen today looked thin, delicate, and in poor health. Her short dark hair and black horned-rimmed glasses were replaced by washed-out gray hair and rimless glasses. Her hair, parted in the middle and much longer, made her formerly round face seem more elongated.

It shocked me to see her looking so frail. I barely recognized her.

"Hello, Melinda." I chirped, trying to take an upbeat stance to our first meeting in years. I stopped short of saying, "You look well." She did not. Instead, I said, "Thank you for calling."

"Hello Joseph," she replied. "I bet you thought you would never hear from me again."

"Yes, it has been a while. But we are both busy people. Time gets away from us."

I got right to the point. "I have been going over some notes you sent me. There are some interesting transcripts. Plenty of material to work with. With better organization, your work will make a positive impression on any publisher."

"That's the reason for my call. I have been trying to organize my thoughts. All I have done is make bags of it. Some years back, I contracted with a ghostwriter to help me write this book. He turned out to be a chiseler. He took all my money and gave me back nothing useful. I should have been smarter. I'm scundered. I need help."

Melinda's candidness surprised me. She had always been a bulldog; it was her way or no way. Now she sounded defeated.

"How can I be of help?"

"I don't have a lot of money, and I have already spent my life savings trying to get this manuscript written before they take me. I'm just trying to keep 'er lit. You are the best writer I have known. You can make my story come alive. I can't pay you much. I am hoping you will accept a royalty split instead of a fee up front?"

Her proposal concerned me. Creating a story like this requires significant effort. Writing a memoir or a non-fiction treatise for many writers is a life's work. I had hoped someday I would write my own biography. Taking on a complex biography like hers would be a challenge I wasn't prepared for.

"Wow, Melinda, I will have to think about it. This type of project never crossed my radar screen."

"Don't think too long. I don't want your pity, but they have numbered my days. I have a bad case; the doctors say I only have months, maybe a year."

I didn't ask about her illness; it wasn't my business. Melinda was approximately forty years old. Such a young age to face a terrible prognosis.

She made her last pitch. "I can give you five thousand U.S. upfront for expenses. I would like you to fly here and meet with me. We'll discuss what I've accomplished and evaluate my outline. Give me your best consideration."

Still unsure, I could only respond with. "I will get back to you quickly."

We signed off on the call. I think you could call it shocking, but her revelation stunned and saddened me by her predicament.

I must be getting soft because I was considering her proposal. It made no sense for me to do it; financially, it would be a bust. Melinda and I weren't close, so guilt wasn't a factor. Then again, I remembered the fun we had those four weeks we spent together, hanging around together, and touring the East Coast. I also vividly remember our encounter in the tent when she practically overpowered me, a night that both scared me and bolstered my ego as a man. I had to decide, and quickly.

Before the day's end, I made my decision. I was at least going to give Melinda's story a go. The five thousand would barely cover the initial expenses for travel and assembling her story. I would need to validate any portions of the story that involved third parties. That meant face-to-face interviews and verifying everything they told me. I couldn't afford to combat lawsuits from people or organizations harmed or perceived to be harmed by the book. If Melinda were truly dying, I would be the one responsible for the contents of a co-authored book.

Then there was one other important consideration, Marjorie. How would Marjorie react if I devoted all my time to this project? Marjorie wasn't the jealous type, at least she never displayed any jealousy. How would she feel about me working closely with a woman I had a previous sexual relationship with?

That evening, I met Marjorie for dinner. I took every opportunity, when we were available, to meet with Marjorie. The Andrew Johnson debacle taught me not to hide anything from her. We told each other everything, even if it didn't seem important.

"There is something I need to discuss with you. I received a request to work with an old friend, Melinda Donne, to help her with her biography. It's going to be an enormous project. I thought I should run it by you before I said yes."

Marjorie thought it was odd that I would ask permission. I had never sought counseling from her before regarding my chosen investigations.

"Are we entering a new chapter in our relationship where we need to ask? You have to work, don't you?"

"Yes, it's just that this project will be different. I have written nothing this big or involved."

"Can I ask why you have never spoken about Melinda Donne before? How do you know her?"

Explaining my past relationship with Melinda was a minefield. No one knew about my panicked escape from danger in India. Leaving Melinda in the middle of a hostile situation wasn't my finest hour. I stumbled through the story, trying to keep it short and to the point. She grimaced when I told her about the incident with the leopard. No matter how I tried to explain it, Marjorie saw through my admission.

Tilting her head in a thinking motion, she said. "So, Melinda's an old girlfriend. Someone you abandoned in the jungle in a foreign country, and she is back asking for more? Do I have that right?"

"Well, it sounds terrible the way you say it," I said.

"Were you and Melinda in a sexual relationship?"

"Only once. She wasn't my type."

"But now she is?" Marjorie asked.

"No, nothing like that. She is ill, and she asked for my help. I think it is the least I can do to help a dying woman. Besides, I think the book can be a bestseller."

"So, if I say 'no', I become the monster that kept you from helping a dying woman. If I say 'yes', my boyfriend spends the next few months working side by side with his old girlfriend." She sarcastically added, "Thank you for including me in your decision."

She was playing devil's advocate. Possibly to gauge my sincerity. Maybe it was her subtle warning not to start up with an old girlfriend. In reality, I was madly in love with Marjorie. I would give up everything I had to make her happy. She knew it; she didn't have to ask.

"Joseph, I will never stand in your way. Your happiness is important to our relationship. If this project is something you want to do, then you must. If I can help you, just ask. I will be your girl Friday. When do I get to meet Melinda?"

I hadn't even considered introducing Marjorie to Melinda. At some point, it would be inevitable. I had to make myself look like a superhero in both women's eyes. Not an enviable task. I didn't answer her last question.

The next morning, I video-chatted with Melinda. "Okay, Melinda, I'm on board. Let's give it a go and see where we take this thing."

She took her phone and, using the camera, scanned her office. Her desk and an adjacent table had stacks of notebooks, binders, and documents galore. Next to the desk, she had stacked several boxes, almost five feet high, with more documents and mementos. It shocked me that she never digitized her notes.

"Here are all my notes. Where should we start?"

What had I gotten myself into? I hadn't even started, and my first look at the project already overwhelmed me.

"Can you scan any of this stuff in and send it to me electronically?"

"If you show me how, I will do what I can."

I couldn't believe she didn't know how to use modern technology. It was no wonder her ghostwriter dumped her. He couldn't charge her enough to justify the amount of work transcribing her notes would take. I had to rethink my approach. My only reply was, "I will call you back."

Thank goodness for e-commerce. I jumped online and found an inexpensive scanner at an electronics store in Belfast. It would allow Melinda to send me documents as needed quickly and easily. Within hours, I had a digital scanner on its way to Melinda's house and a plane ticket to Belfast in my hand. There was work to be done and no time to waste.

Chapter 24

If It's Tuesday, It Must Be Belfast

It was my first visit to Belfast and an experience I will never forget. The city of Belfast is one of the most interesting places in the world. It's an old manufacturing city with a long history of political unrest and violence. Yet at the same time, it's a charming seaside town filled with friendly people, an up-and-coming economy, and distinguished historical sights.

Fortunately, they welcome Americans, so I encountered no problem finding a taxi to take me to Melinda's house in Carryduff. My taxi driver routed me from the airport directly into the heart of Belfast, where you can still see the remains of the political conflict known as "The Troubles". It was a period of civil war between Irish-leaning Catholics and the British-leaning Protestants. Even today, barriers called peace walls divide the city into enclaves, not by race but by religious belief. In many parts of the city, the two adversaries cover the peace walls with murals of freedom fighters or political messages reminding residents of their struggle against the enemy on the other side of the wall.

The taxi driver gladly offered me a sightseeing tour of the city, which included a carefully worded commentary on some of the history of Belfast. The Catholics aligned themselves with the Republic of Ireland. The Protestants who controlled the government allied with the U.K. government. My driver tried to remain apolitical, as he pointed out Catholic neighborhoods flying the Irish flag, and the Protestant neighborhoods flying the flag of the U.K..

Their differences seemed minor, yet, like all political conflicts, the root of the problem is the same. It was the status of the "Haves" versus the "Have Nots" that divided the people.

That was different than in America, where most of the division between people is along racial or ethnic lines. In the U.S., you can identify someone as Black, Asian, or Hispanic by their skin color or speech pattern. In Belfast, it's more difficult to tell a Protestant from a Catholic by looking at them. It's only by knowing which side of the line they live on; you can tell if they are your friend or enemy.

Melinda's residence was in Carryduff, a suburb a few kilometers south of Belfast. It is a peaceful hamlet that has expanded outward with development as the population of Belfast has grown. While the town has developed into a modern suburb, Melinda's house was near the old City Centre, characterized by narrow streets lined with quaint cottages, small shops, and pubs.

Arriving at Melinda's opened another chapter in this incredible story. She lived in a small turn-of-the-century stone and brick English cottage surrounded by a white picket fence. The building couldn't be over eight hundred square feet. Typical size in this community, but diminutive when compared to residential homes in America. It was likely built over one hundred years ago. Sometime in the last fifty years, after they built the country house, Melinda or a previous owner added modern plumbing and electricity, as evidenced by the pipes running along the exterior walls of the building. They had remodeled the exterior with a cream-colored stucco finish. Bright blue painted shutters and a greying shake shingle wood roof gave the cottage an old-world charm.

When the taxi rolled up in front of her house, the driver
noticed the placard on the wall near the door with the name "Donne".
He immediately recognized the name.

"Aye," he said. "This is a famous one. We know well the name
Donne around these parts. She's a daring one."

"Yes, quite a woman," I replied.

For me, Brexit has made it confusing between using Euros,
which the Irish use, and British pounds, which Northern Ireland uses.
I wasn't sure how much of each currency to bring with me on my trip.
So, I brought a little of each one. To conserve on cash, I paid him in
U.S. dollars, which he was happy to accept. American dollars seemed
like a good middle ground, as he could exchange them for his
preferred currency without judgment.

A stone walkway led through the gate to an imposing, brightly
blue-painted, solid wood half door. I rolled my bags up to the stoop
and rapped on the welcoming front door using an ancient
doorknocker. It took a minute, but Melinda finally pulled open the
door.

It stunned me to see Melinda looking frail. She appeared old,
well beyond her actual age, which should be about forty. She smiled at
first. I think she remembered me as the youthful boy that she seduced
in that two-man pup tent years ago, then her face turned sad as if she
realized that she no longer possessed the youthful appearance that I
would remember from our last encounter.

She held her hand out, offering me a friendly handshake.
"Welcome, thank you for coming. You look lovely, just as I remember.
I'm sorry to appear an old hag. I've had my troubles."

When I stepped inside, it shocked me to see how she lived. She
appointed her house with a minimal number of furnishings. Straight
ahead, I could see a small kitchenette with a stove and refrigerator, a

bistro table and two chairs, and a window bringing light into the room from the rear yard.

On the left side wall, she had created her office space. It included the same desk and table, and the stack of papers that she had shown me on the video chat. There was a sofa the size of a loveseat under the front window. I didn't see any television or entertainment center, any elaborate wall hangings, or any personal memorabilia.

But the strangest thing was in the middle of the main room. There she had set up a two-man camouflage pup tent that looked remarkably like the one where we slept in India. At first, I thought she had done it as a joke for my visit, then I realized it was a permanent fixture.

She motioned towards a doorway to the right of the kitchen. "Put your bags in the other room. I'll make some tea, then we can get to work," she said.

The other room was a small bedroom, not too much bigger than an American closet, again starkly furnished with only an end table and a mattress and box spring on the floor. I immediately wondered. *Where do I sleep? Perhaps I should have asked about a hotel?* She soon answered my question. As we sat down to reintroduce ourselves over a cup of freshly brewed tea, Melinda opened up about her situation.

"I wanted you to come here to see how I live. It wasn't always this way, but I have had a lot of trauma. I know you remember me as being bold and fearless, and in the old days, I was unafraid of almost anything. When I was captured by a group of Islamic terrorists, everything changed."

I remember hearing about her encounter, but her version of what happened was much more vivid than the news reports. She told me about how the fundamentalist group that held her captive had no regard for women, especially Western women.

They stripped her naked and locked her in a cage about the size of a dog kennel. They fed her dead animals, and she drank dirty water left over from when they cleaned themselves. Every day her captors held a mock trial, accusing her of being infidel and harlot. They would not let her explain her mission or defend herself. Each time they pronounced her guilty, after which they beat her and raped her repeatedly.

After a while, one of the young conscripts felt sorry for her. He tried to convince her to plead guilty and beg for a merciful death. She didn't know what she was guilty of doing. One evening, after bringing her a meal of rancid leftovers, he made her a promise. He said if tomorrow she would let him plead guilty on her behalf, he would cut her head off, and her torture would end. Her spirit broken, she nodded her head in agreement. That was the last thing she remembered until she woke up in a hospital with needles in her arms, a feeding tube through her nose, and bandages on her head.

She was in recovery for several weeks while they helped her learn to eat, speak, and walk again. When she was well enough to eat and walk on her own, the Indian government flew her home in a military jet to Belfast.

Melinda was a survivor, but she paid a mighty price for her bravery. By the time she returned home, she suffered from a severe case of Post-Traumatic Stress Disorder. Even after years of treatment, crowded public places terrified her. She couldn't go to stores or crowded restaurants. Daytime was better than nighttime. At least she could see what was happening during the day. At night, she had trouble sleeping; the tent was the only place she felt safe, explaining why she had her tent pitched in her living room. Her state of continuous fear played havoc with her health. Making matters worse, she had contracted a rare form of bacterial infection that the Western doctors were treating with poor results. The infection was ravaging her body. She suffered from sporadic fever and uncontrolled weight loss. She surprised her doctors by living longer than most of them believed was possible, but with no reliable treatment, her prognosis for recovery was negative.

"This life of mine has not been good," she complained. "I can't concentrate on writing; everything I try comes out as gibberish. I have tried to get others to help with no success. Joseph, you are my last hope to tell my story."

Her candor left me without a reply. I hadn't realized how bad her life had become. Rather than feign understanding, I said nothing.

"You can sleep in the spare room; I sleep in the tent when I sleep," she said.

Then somehow, through all the anguish she had experienced, a glint of the old Melinda shone in her eye. A smile popped across her face. She remembered our last night together in the jungle.

"Don't worry, you're safe. I won't climb into bed with you tonight. Sadly, those days are over for me," she said.

She refilled my tea, and we talked at length about my career. I told her about my relationship with Marjorie. I showed her pictures of Marjorie, to which she approved. Melinda gave me the impression she was genuinely happy that I had found love and a successful career.

"Is she a writer also?" she asked.

"No, she works for a charity that raises money and supports social programs for underprivileged communities in the States."

"Aye, an admirable calling. Our world needs more like her."

Sitting and talking with Melinda reminded me of why we had become friends so many years ago. She made me comfortable, even in a less-than-perfect situation. I was happy I took on the challenge of writing her life story. We finished our tea and went to work, designing a plan for her memoir.

The digital scanner I ordered had arrived a few hours before I did. I unpacked the device, set it up, and showed her how to use it. It would be a valuable tool in the future, as it would be impossible for me to take all her notes and photographs with me. I had brought several USB storage drives with me from home that I could use to make digital copies of her notes. Later, she could email me additional items. She caught on quickly.

She showed me her first draft of the book she had tried to produce herself. While it wasn't all bad for a first draft, the main missing element was her hypothesis. It was page after page of dates and facts. Her writing didn't have a goal, one that would endear the reader or make them want to see the world through her eyes.

She knew it needed work. A well-known publisher in the U.K. had advanced her several thousand pounds. She used that money to hire the ghostwriter. She thought he would help her turn her experiences into a gripping novel. The ghostwriter ripped her off, taking her money and producing nothing in return. The project was well behind schedule and overdue for publication. Her publishers demanded a completed manuscript, but she had nothing to give them, and she didn't have enough money to return the advance.

I knew the manuscript would take care of itself in time. She had more than enough stories to write several books. I put the manuscript aside, grabbed a pencil and paper, and asked her to tell me, in her own words, her life story. I wanted to add the human element to her story. After a few hours of listening to Melinda relate some of her adventures, accompanied by lots of note-taking or scanning photographs and travel documents, we were famished. I was pushing her pretty hard, and we needed a break.

"There is a little pub up the street. They know me well. It is a bit flat, but they have the black stuff. Would you mind if we went there?" she asked.

Our dinner comprised a pint of Guinness and a hearty bowl of local Irish stew. She was right; the pub was low-key, and the proprietor, an older gentleman named Aidan, seemed to know Melinda didn't do well in rousing environments. He served us quietly, keeping an eye open for anything we should need. If the other customers got too boisterous, he calmed them on Melinda's behalf.

By the time we returned to her cottage, Melinda was exhausted. It was clear she no longer had the stamina to work long hours. She could never complete this project on her own.

"Why don't you lie down for a while? Let me keep working. I will be quiet. I will just read and take notes. Okay?" I said.

She agreed and quickly changed into her pajamas. It shocked me to see how fragile she had become. As a young woman, she was sizeable, solid, muscular, and tough. Now it was all she could do to crawl into her tent and repose.

I read quietly, amazed at the adventures this woman had experienced. Her escapades were so interesting, I thought that any halfway proficient writer could make this book a bestseller. The more I read, the more I realized how blessed I was that she chose me to help write her story. She had truly led an amazing life. While some of us get to be old and grey, she wouldn't have that privilege. I vowed her life of adventure will endure long after she departs from this world.

Her sleep was restless. I was sitting only a few feet away from her tent, and I could hear her stirring. She grunted as if she were fighting with an attacker. Several times she screamed, then whimpered as she fell back asleep. I don't know how the poor girl got any rest. Over and over, I could hear her mumble, trying to console herself that she was safe.

Her restlessness distracted me, making it hard to concentrate. I worked as long as I could until I was finally tired. My long day of travel had worn me down, and I needed to rest. I retired to the bedroom alone. Even through a closed bedroom door, I could hear Melinda crying out into the night.

Chapter 25

The Blitzkrieg

The next morning was a blitzkrieg of scanning, copying, and emailing. With only two days in Northern Ireland, my time was short. I had a flight out of Belfast the next day, and I needed to gather as many notes and documents as I could carry before I returned home. We worked side-by-side reading, scanning, and transcribing. In one day, Melinda and I became closer than we were before. I even had her laughing occasionally. She hadn't been doing much laughing as of late.

I enjoyed my time in Belfast, but this was a job. I had to remain as objective as possible. The subject of the book had to focus on Melinda as a brilliant journalist. A war correspondent who helped reveal war's misery and tragedy to the world. I aimed to avoid writing a book about a dying young woman's final days. That would be too easy. A trap to solicit pity from the reader would make our book just another sad story that comes and goes. This book had to be timeless, a historical epic.

Melinda worked until tired, then resumed working after a brief break. We were both reading, making notes, and trying to sort out the best of her journal entries.

By late morning, the silence was deafening. The only sounds we heard were the scanner busily buzzing and copying documents to a USB drive, and our two voices debating the order of stories and the identities of people in the picture.

When her tea kettle whistled, signaling time for a break, I pulled out my phone and opened a music app. I spun up a song by musical artist Van Morrison, a popular rocker from Northern Ireland. Music filled the room, and soon we were both singing along. I think the music, in combination with our success, took Melinda's mind away from her troubles. She was smiling again; the color returned to her face.

Shortly after noon, I took a walk outside to let Melinda take a quick nap. I walked up the street to a quaint intersection of small businesses. There was a car park that served a chemist and a doctor's office. A few cars passed slowly up the street and out of the city center. Around the corner, I found a bakery and next to that, a resale shop. In the resale shop's window, I noticed a nifty jigsaw puzzle. A thousand-piece mountain scene, with snowcapped peaks and blue skies. The serene image had subtle shades of white, green, and blue, and presented a bit of a challenge. I always found puzzles to be therapeutic. I offered eighty pence, a fair price for a used puzzle. Then I bought a half dozen lovely blueberry scones at the bakery and returned to Melinda's house.

I handed her the puzzle box. "For me?" she smiled.

"I want you to promise me you will spend thirty minutes a day on the puzzle. And for goodness' sake, put on some music or a movie once in a while, okay? It will help take your mind off your stress."

We had our afternoon tea along with a blueberry scone. It seemed to please Melinda. My presence and these simple pleasures were helping to reduce her anxiety.

It was odd to sit at her desk and read or write while Melinda was only a few steps away, trying to sleep safely inside her tent. Her whimpers would break my concentration, causing me to lose track of my place. Finally, I found my headphones in my bag, and listening to soft background music helped me keep my concentration.

Melinda would retire early, usually by the time darkness set in. Her sleep was always restless, sometimes fitful. Shortly before midnight, she scurried out of the tent to go to the toilet. I think it surprised her to see me still awake and reading by the light of one small lamp. At first, she looked frightened.

"I am sorry. I'm trying to get as much done as possible before I leave. Will you be alright if I keep working?" I asked.

"It is okay, I'm having a bit of an episode," she said. "It will pass in a little while."

She sat across from me on the sofa, shivering. I hadn't noticed, but the night air had turned cold.

"Are you cold?" I asked.

"A little." She nodded across the room. "Could you hand me that blanket?"

A neatly folded blanket lay on the chair beside me. I took the blanket and wrapped it around her. "Better," she whispered.

She appeared fragile, like a lost little girl with no way home. I had to do something.

"Melinda? Would it be alright if I held you?"

She responded like a saddened child. Nodding her head, a welcoming, "Yes".

I slid over next to her, pulling the blanket tighter around her, then I slipped my arm around her, drawing her closer to me. She dipped her head onto my shoulder, and I let her close her eyes to return to sleep.

It delighted me that she felt comfortable enough to let me hold her. It wasn't sexual, just two old friends supporting each other. In a few minutes, she was sound asleep in my arms.

We couldn't spend the night sleeping on that little sofa, so I took a chance. I slid my arm under her legs and carried her into the bedroom; she was light as a feather, only skin and bones. I laid her down on the bed, tucked a pillow under her head, then covered her with the blanket. Then I fluffed a pillow for myself and lay down on the floor opposite her. She remained in a deep sleep for several hours. I made no further progress on our work that evening. That was fine, it made me happy, because I somehow knew that this was the best sleep Melinda had experienced in a long while.

We woke on Thursday morning; the house was calm, and our task was fulfilled. After a quick cup of tea and a scone, I packed up for my trip home. I packed as much as I could cram into my suitcase. I stuffed a couple of manila envelopes full of photographs that I would mail to myself at the airport. The rest she would have to send to me as needed. Melinda called for a taxi to shuttle me to the airport. We walked outside to a bench in front of her house while we waited for my ride.

"Thank you for coming. I know it was a lot to ask to travel all this way," she said.

"It is okay, we accomplished a lot. I'm surprised you contacted me, considering what I did to you in the jungle. I was a coward. I was only thinking of myself."

"Can I tell you something?" she asked without waiting for an answer. "When we were together in the States, I really liked you. I kept waiting for you to make your move, but you never did. When you left me in India, I was angrier about your shunning me than the impact on the mission. I was hoping we would become chums."

"Melinda, I liked you as well. The timing was wrong. I just wasn't looking for a girlfriend. I am so sorry I hurt you."

She stared at the ground, still unsure of her future. "Now I'm the scared one. Sometimes these things just happen. It's called life."

A few minutes later, my taxi arrived to take me to the airport.

She stiffened her back as if our short time together gave her renewed hope.

I hugged Melinda goodbye, hoping that I would see her again before her health issues worsened.

"Ring me up next week so we stay on task," she said. "Safe travels."

Chapter 26

We Don't Talk Anymore

I used the last of my frequent flyer miles to upgrade my airplane seat to business class. The added comfort and space gave me a chance to work on Melinda's book without interruptions from the coach passengers. I withdrew the rough manuscript that Melinda's ghostwriter had bungled from my bag and highlighted paragraphs I hoped would be reusable segments.

Melinda and her ghostwriter titled the manuscript, *The World as Seen by Melinda Donne*. I disliked the way they started this book. It didn't hook the reader. Maybe it was just a working title? I wanted something that would catch a prospective reader's attention. With my pencil, I scratched a line through the title. There had to be a better identity for this story.

I was flipping through the first few pages, making notes and occasionally staring into space, hoping for inspiration, when the woman seated next to me interrupted. Bored, she wanted to start a conversation.

"I'm sorry to bother you. I couldn't help but notice your paper. Are you a writer?"

"Technically, I'm an Investigative Journalist. My name is D.K. St. Joseph," I said proudly. "You may have heard of me?"

She smiled and shook her head. "No, sorry, I don't watch the news much."

"Actually, today I am a writer. I'm helping write a friend's memoir," I said.

"I'm working on this book as her partner. She was an International War Correspondent who traveled the world reporting on political conflicts, genocide, and corruption. She is an amazing woman. The book is about her experiences and encounters."

"I always find people like that to be remarkable. It seems some people know no fear," she said.

As soon as the words came out of her mouth, I knew that was the new title. It was a fitting way to describe Melinda. She was fearless.

I scribbled in big capital letters across the front page, *FEARLESS*, the new title for the book. I followed it up with a smaller subtitle, *The Melinda Donne Story*.

I asked the woman if she liked to read non-fiction books. I showed her the new title and told her to watch the bookstores in the coming months. She agreed she would buy a copy as soon as it hit the stores. Success! I'm not a salesperson, but I made our first book pre-sale.

After my return home from Belfast, I was even more invested in this project to help Melinda tell her story. Being a war correspondent is a dangerous job, and Melinda never shied away from the danger. It likely cost her a long and healthy life. She had gathered so much information in her notes and experiences that if her story wasn't told, the world would suffer a major loss.

I placed myself under a self-imposed deadline to finish the manuscript in eight weeks. It was a tremendous undertaking, but I was up for the task.

In the beginning, it was daily video chats with Melinda. I wanted to make sure that I interpreted her transcripts correctly. Occasionally, she would correct me; other times, she would explain in greater detail what she was experiencing at the time she wrote the journal entry. I had one issue with her writing. She would write her notes from the perspective of a Western reporter. At the time she wrote them, her reports were going to be picked up by United Press International or the British Broadcasting Company. Their policy mandated the tone of the reports must align with the thinking of their subscribers. Expressing an unpopular opinion that contradicts the broadcaster's view requires, at a minimum, a disclaimer from the author, something she preferred to avoid. Occasionally, the publication would edit out the controversial wording, watering down a dynamic account of the situation. In Melinda's memoir, there would be no need to "spout the company line".

One example I recall was a report she filed from a battle in Syria. She not only interviewed the Syrian government military forces, but she also had significant contact with fighters from the Syrian National Coalition, whose forces opposed the government troops. She was also able to spend time with and interview the international aid volunteers whose task it was to save lives with food and healthcare for those affected by the fighting.

Contrary to the notes in her journal account, the report the BBC ultimately published downplayed the terror and misery that the local citizens experienced. I wanted to round out the report, restoring the balance to both viewpoints. Melinda agreed and helped me. Through a review of her cryptic notes, we added back a lot of depth to the storyline.

It amazed me when she recalled the boldness of her actions when interviewing fighters in the heat of battle, with bombs exploding overhead and bullets zipping past as she wrote. She was truly fearless, maybe even a bit crazy.

My international contacts through the IECO Journalism organization also proved to be an invaluable resource. During my discovery, I made a point of contacting several other reporters, local

Syrian correspondents, and journalists from Iraq and Israel who covered the same events. They, like Melinda, had reported on the battles with their facts and perspectives. Their input helped me verify Melinda's facts and clarify the events as they happened in real-time.

The video chats and time spent reviewing her notes seemed to have a cathartic effect on Melinda. After the second week, she was looking stronger. She no longer looked like death warmed over, but still a long way from her former healthy self.

Due to the time difference, I would arrange video chats in the late morning in Belfast. This meant I would be online very early, sometimes at three or four o'clock.

One day, about three weeks into our chats, an excited Melinda had a surprise for me.

"I want to show you something," she said.

She used the camera on her laptop to scan the room where she had her office set up. At first, I noticed nothing different, then I realized she had removed the tent from her living room.

"I took it down yesterday. I have a new bed, and I'm sleeping in the bedroom again. This project has helped occupy my mind. I have you to thank for my progress." Then she laughed. "And I bought four new puzzles since I last saw you. They have really helped me relax."

"Congratulations," I said. "Welcome back to the land of the living."

"I still have my episodes, but they are not as frequent or as bad. Next week I am going to London. I found a doctor who thinks he can help with my treatment; I'm going to give it a lash. So next Tuesday I am going across the pond. My parents are going to help me with the travel. London gets a bit overwhelming."

After a few weeks, Melinda and I had made substantial progress. The first group of chapters we sent to the publisher met with a positive response. The editors requested a minimum number of changes, some of which I agreed to allow. Often it was over language, but if it meant changing Melinda's own words, I refused to change. We met in the middle and stayed on task toward our new publishing deadline. Melinda's emotional attitude improved notably with each minor victory. The effort we made together brought a sense of accomplishment I hadn't felt in quite a while. The deeper I dug into the project, the more convinced I was that this book would become a bestseller.

What I didn't notice was the effect it was having on my personal life.

I remember that for those few weeks into transcribing Melinda's notes, my relationship with Marjorie sank into what I would call an uncomfortable period.

I became obsessed with the manuscript. I needed to get the last changes of Melinda's story to the publisher before she became so ill, she wouldn't be able to enjoy her triumph. I moved my desk back to my townhouse and began working sixteen-hour days. A self-imposed burden, leaving little time for other things.

Marjorie was back at work, traveling from city to city, her schedule daunting even for her. Since I was working, she visited her mother more often.

I started missing my daily video chat with Marjorie. The time difference between Belfast, D.C., and whatever city Marjorie was in played havoc with our schedules. I didn't realize that we were growing apart.

Whenever we were together, it was always the same. We had dinner, with our conversation focusing on my work and Melinda. If we had the energy for sex, it was uninspired. We were both tired; we often fell asleep, too exhausted to even talk. Some nights, we were too tired to care.

As the weeks flew by, I was losing track of what day it was. It didn't matter. Every day mirrored the last. In the mornings, I transcribed Melinda's cryptic notes into cognitive episodes. In the evenings, I made edits to meet the publisher's demands. All day, my hours consisted of emailing, faxing, and video chats.

I was never sure what city Marjorie was visiting. To me, they were all the same. I was tired; Marjorie was irritable. We began arguing over little things like the weather in D.C. or Marjorie's flight delay.

Marjorie started referring to Melinda as "my other girlfriend", which over the course of a couple of weeks degenerated into "my girlfriend". She said she didn't harbor animosity toward Melinda, only the time I was spending on her memoir. Marjorie felt unloved and unappreciated.

I just didn't see it.

Late one evening, I showed up at Marjorie's house unannounced, intending to spend the night. Marjorie wasn't in a good mood. She was sitting on the deck in her backyard, drinking wine with Derek Watting. I knew they were friends, but I never understood why he always showed up at inopportune times. I tried to play nice, but I was too tired. I asked her to send Watting away so we could be alone.

I said, "I'm going to take a shower. Why don't you get rid of Derek, climb into bed, and I will meet you in a few minutes?"

Her body language should have been a clue. "Don't bother, I have an early flight in the morning, and I'm tired. You shouldn't have come. Just go back home, please."

It was the first time Marjorie denied me anything. Sadly, I was too consumed with my own work to feel bad about it. I said goodbye and went back home to my townhouse. Without interruption, I could continue working for a few more hours.

Consumed with myself, I was unaware that Marjorie was struggling at her work. Political ideals in America were changing, and there was a lot of pushback from corporate sponsors. Large companies were straddling the fence, trying not to side with the wrong political movement. Angering the wrong politician would have consequences affecting the organization's earnings for years to come.

The grassroots organizations that relied so heavily on the United Poverty League were falling apart. The shelves at local food pantries were bare. Neighborhood clinics couldn't get drugs or supplies.

In typical Marjorie fashion, she tried to make up the shortfall by working even harder. Practically begging wealthy benefactors for help.

She needed someone to talk to and, unlike me, Watting was ready to listen.

Lack of communication and lack of empathy can kill a relationship faster than anything else. Our relationship was breaking apart as quickly as it had formed.

Chapter 27

They Set Melinda Up

The weeks flew past, and we were nearing the end of our project. We were rewriting the final chapters, aiming for a dramatic ending to the book.

I knew how I wanted to end the book. Melinda had told me everything she knew about her capture and torture in India. In her original report, she tried to show the world the horror of war, but her details were sketchy. I suspected I hadn't gotten the full story of her kidnapping. I wanted more details.

I refused to let political correctness whitewash away the pain she endured. Finding an unbiased account of what happened would make the story come alive. It was time to dig deeper into the events surrounding her capture.

Finding the desired information was another challenge. The bureaucracy in India makes the bureaucrats in the U.S. and Europe seem like amateurs. India not only has layers upon layers of government, but its Islamic territories have quasi-governments. Factions that operate outside the jurisdiction of the central government.

Being a respected member in good standing with the international journalists at IECO has its benefits. Especially when trying to perform research on events that happen in a foreign country.

I emailed Jacques Allard at the IECO offices in Paris, requesting help. I was seeking contact details for journalists knowledgeable about Kashmir's officialdom and the place where they had held Melinda captive. His response yielded the names and contact information of two highly respected reporters. I emailed both explaining my position and how I was working with Melinda Donne. I requested any help they could offer regarding the details surrounding her capture and subsequent rescue.

Both responded within hours of my request. Patella Ram, a recognized Indian war correspondent, was able to find a print copy of the original government statement. The paper detailed the timeline of the events as they had been publicly divulged. He emailed me a copy. It helped fill in a few holes of the days following her rescue, days for which Melinda had no memory.

Amrita Chitria, an award-winning journalist, took my request one step further. She had spent several months investigating the raid that freed Melinda. She had uncovered details that were not released by the Indian government bureaucrats. She also contacted Ramesh Signa, the former head of the Administrative Council for the State of Jammu and Kashmir, asking for his help. Signa, who was now retired, agreed to speak about the incident on the condition of anonymity. After a series of emails, we arranged for a video conference between me, Chitria, and Signa.

I discovered that at the time of Melinda's capture, Signa had the responsibility to oversee the loose autonomy of the Jammu and Kashmir state in India. Primarily a Muslim population, the state's political leadership is often at odds with the Hindu central government of India.

Signa revealed a political motivation for Melinda's capture. During the years in question, India was still receiving financial aid from the United Kingdom. They intended the aid to assist the poorest of the poor with programs to provide food, clean water, and health care. That aid, amounting to millions of British pounds, never reached the people it intended to help.

Melinda Donne had learned of a local warlord who was siphoning the money off for personal gain and maintaining power by bribing insurgents in the area.

Signa admitted that the central government knew about the graft but was powerless to stop it. Under further questioning, he admitted that certain members of the bureaucracy were concerned about Melinda's exposé. They felt the British would view the whole thing with such outrage that the U.K. would terminate the financial aid program. The program was already unpopular in Great Britain as British taxpayers couldn't understand why they were supporting a country, India, whose economy had eclipsed that of the United Kingdom years earlier.

Someone in the central government warned the local warlord, Haafiz al Abdalla, of Melinda's mission to the region to research the problem and unmask the corruption. Abdalla, in turn, alerted the terrorist group. It was no surprise when the radical group took her into custody. Melinda had always believed it was just bad luck that she encountered the Islamic group. She wasn't aware that they had set her up.

Signa affirmed that it took several days to obtain permission to deploy a Black Cat team trained in hostage rescue to the area to rescue her and remove the insurgency, including Abdalla. By the time they defined the Black Cat's mission, planned the risky operation, and could execute her rescue, it was too late. The terrorists had already tortured Melinda, and she was near death. One more day, and she would not survive.

The rescue team airlifted her to a military hospital in Jammu, where she was hospitalized in a near comatose state. They treated her for bruises, lacerations, malnutrition, and severe dehydration. She received several weeks of physical therapy.

The Indian government downplayed both her capture and the subsequent rescue. They treated it as nothing more than a routine military exercise.

They never fully briefed her on the details of her rescue.

After her return to Northern Ireland, she withdrew from the public eye, struggling only to stay alive and return to some form of normal life.

I grappled with whether to share the information I had discovered with Melinda. The years had passed; It concerned me that reopening her wounds would hamper her recovery. There was no turning the clock back. But Signa's revelation would be sure to cause international outrage, catapulting her book onto bestseller lists worldwide. Still, I was unsure if, considering her fragile mental state, it might be better to leave this chapter of her life unfinished. In the end, I decided it was too important to leave it out of the book. Melinda reluctantly agreed.

We added another important piece to the manuscript. One that would capture the attention of readers. A shocking chapter that would stun the world.

The book was complete. Although we missed her original timetable, our manuscript satisfied Melinda's publisher. They released the book immediately in the U.K. and then followed it up with a release a few weeks later in the U.S. It was there that my next adventure began.

Chapter 28

An Honest Woman

Then it happened. I screwed up again. Marjorie and I had a date scheduled for Saturday night. I was in New York taping a promotional interview for a popular podcast before the U.S. release of Melinda's book. My flight home would have me home in plenty of time for our dinner reservation.

Except the producers of a national Sunday morning news magazine asked me to stay one more day and appear on their show. It offered me the prospect of putting Melinda's biography solidly out there in front of millions of viewers. How could I turn down a chance for free advertising?

When I called to cancel our dinner plans, Marjorie was unhappy. The strain on our relationship was becoming too much for her. I could hear defeat in her voice as we quarreled over my involvement in this project.

"Joseph, I cannot take this anymore. I think we need to take some time."

I didn't immediately understand what she was saying, because I replied with my usual assuaging promise. "Once the book is launched, we'll have plenty of time for ourselves."

Her voice cracked as she repeated, "No, I mean you and me. We need some time away from each other. I've waited too long. You need to grow up. Goodbye."

Then she hung up the phone. I don't know what I was thinking, but it suddenly dawned on me that she was breaking up with me. Our love affair was coming apart at the seams. This time, it was my fault. *Can this be happening again?*

But it was happening. I tried calling her over and over, but each time she rejected my call. She refused to speak to me.

I still hadn't grasped the enormity of the situation because I stayed in New York. The next morning, I did a guest spot on the news magazine before heading to the airport.

When I arrived home, I went straight to Marjorie's house. I naively thought that by showing up and asking for absolution, all would be forgiven. Everything would be right again. I rang the doorbell several times, but there was no answer. Frustrated, I banged on the door until my fist hurt. The commotion I caused disturbed her next-door neighbor, an elderly lady, who opened her door and informed me. "She's not home. She left to visit her mother in Philadelphia."

Once again, I found myself on a barstool at Ed's Bar, and as always, Ed sensed trouble. I don't know how he does it, but Ed always knows everything about everyone in the city.

"Trouble with your girlfriend, Marjorie?" he asked.

"Yeah, I screwed up again. This time, I think she has had enough of my crap. I'm in trouble, Ed."

Ed had the perfect solution. "How about a sandwich? I still have some tasty chicken salad from lunch. I won't even charge you."

"*Why not?* At least I can think on a full stomach."

Ed disappeared into the kitchen to make my sandwich while I waited.

Anyone following this story would expect it's time for Derek Watting to reappear. That's exactly what happened. Watting walked into the bar and sat two stools down from me. We almost came to blows the last time he showed up unannounced. This time, he said nothing to me.

When Ed returned with my sandwich, Watting ordered a beer and sat there with a wry smile on his face. I knew he was here about Marjorie.

Why the hell every time Marjorie and I argue, this f_ing guy shows up?

Derek knew I needed help, but he waited for me to ask.

After a few minutes, I yielded. "Don't you ever get tired of playing Cupid?"

"Don't you ever get tired of being stupid? The most wonderful woman in the world loves you, and you can't seem to get a grip on the situation."

"I wouldn't be acting stupid if I knew what I did wrong?"

Derek shook his head. "You have been so busy ballyhooing the new book, you have neglected her. You forgot that Marjorie's divorce was finalized two days ago."

He was right. In my zeal to complete the book before Melinda's health failed, the date of her divorce had completely slipped my mind. We had planned our dinner date to celebrate her freedom and plan our future together. No wonder she was in a foul mood.

"Shit, I can't believe I forgot. I'm such an idiot," I said.

I couldn't believe I was asking Derek for advice. "What do you think I should do?"

"Well, if it were me, I would make an honest woman out of her."

Watting was right. Marjorie was now a free woman. We didn't have to pretend we were just dating any longer. We could move forward. I knew what I had to do.

I grabbed my phone and looked online for a jewelry store that specialized in engagement rings. When it came to jewelry, I knew nothing. The store named Daban Jewelry had loads of great customer reviews, and it was only a few miles away. If I hurried, I could get there before they closed. Bouncing off the barstool, I waved goodbye to Ed and bolted out the door.

Daban Jewelry was one of those family-owned and operated places. It was a high-class joint with well-dressed salespeople and expensive jewelry. Since it was late, I was the only customer in the shop. The salesperson, a woman about fifty years old, greeted me eagerly. She seemed knowledgeable and friendly. Inquiring about Marjorie's tastes, she asked, "What does she like?"

"White gold. She likes white gold." Marjorie liked white gold because it glistened against her dark skin.

"At present, white gold isn't popular. I only have a few." She showed me several rings that were in the glass case, the ones in my price range. None of them screamed Marjorie.

Disappointed, I said. "I think I need to look elsewhere."

"Wait, just a minute. I have one more." She walked over to another counter and returned with a classic setting holding a huge marquise-cut diamond flanked by several smaller square baguettes.

"We purchased this at an estate sale. The previous owner wore the original band out, so we recreated a new band from platinum and reset the diamonds. It is essentially a replica of the original. These are old-world diamonds from Namibia. They are flawless. You won't find a better-quality piece anywhere today."

It was magnificent. The only problem was the price. It exceeded my budget by three times the amount. The saleswoman mistook me for a wealthy person. *Hey, I am from Cleveland, not Scarsdale.*

But then again, this was for Marjorie. She was like no one I had ever met. Marjorie deserved the best.

I asked nervously. "Can you make me a deal?"

"We don't sell rings of this quality too often. The best I can do is offer you a ten percent markdown, and only if you also buy the matching wedding band."

I felt trapped. I was counting on royalties from Melinda's book. If it doesn't become a bestseller, I am screwed. I couldn't afford the ring. If I don't buy this beautiful ring for Marjorie, I may never be screwed again.

I had no choice. Exhaling deeply, I said. "I'll take them."

While I waited for the rings to be boxed, a moment of panic struck. *What if she says no to my proposal?*

As she handed me the package. I mumbled. "God, I hope she says yes."

Chapter 29

La Familia

Sleeping was tough for me that night. The clock couldn't spin fast enough. Even before the alarm buzzed, I woke up, packed a bag, and headed for the train station. Marjorie was refusing to answer my calls or texts. She was hiding out at her mother's house as if she thought that would keep me away. She was wrong.

By early afternoon, my ride-booking service was pulling up in front of Sofia's house in Philadelphia. It was my first visit there. The neighborhood was a mixed bag of established businesses, single-family homes, and apartments. Graffiti adorned the walls of many of the old fences and garages. An old church and school occupied the corner about a block away from Sofia's house.

I recognized the Sykes house from a picture Marjorie had shared with me. It was a typical brick-and-mortar 1940s bungalow with a large dormer in the front and a second-story addition added to the back sometime later. Probably in the 1950s or 1960s. The well-maintained front yard had a large maple tree and colorful flower beds bordering a brick walkway that led to a welcoming front porch. Nothing fancy, just the type of home where you might comfortably raise a family.

I marched up the front steps and rang the doorbell. The bell alerted the occupants. I could hear two voices inside. It sounded as if an argument was ensuing. No one answered the doorbell. I waited briefly, then opened the screen door and knocked firmly on the big wooden inner door. I had no intention of leaving.

Inside, the argument went quiet. After a pause, the door cracked open, and I caught a glimpse of Sofia peeking out. Marjorie was nowhere in sight. Upon recognizing me, Sofia opened the door wider and, speaking in a voice loud enough for anyone standing nearby to hear, she feigned surprise.

"Oh, Joseph, it is you."

"Sofia, I need to see Marjorie. It's important," I said.

She winked at me, then placed her finger over her lips, signaling me to keep silent.

Without speaking, she pushed the screen door open and motioned for me to come inside.

Keeping up the ruse, she said, "She told me she doesn't want to see you. You will have to leave."

I stepped inside and scanned the room, but I couldn't see Marjorie anywhere. For effect, Sofia slammed the door shut loudly enough so Marjorie would hear the door close, leaving me standing in the vestibule. From her hiding spot in a back room, Marjorie stepped out.

"Is he gone?" she asked Sofia.

Then she saw me. Anger flashed across her face. "What are you doing here? I don't want you here."

Sofia quietly retreated to the kitchen, leaving us to resolve our differences face-to-face.

I held out my hand. "Marjorie, please, we have to stop doing this to each other. We are not children. We have to stop hurting each other."

She didn't take my hand. "I thought you were busy with your girlfriend, Melinda. Is she tired of using you to write her story?"

"No, I realized you were more important. I know I screwed up. Publishing this book project got the better of me. But I promise you my work will never come before you again."

She stood fast. "Why should I believe you? Your career has always been more important."

I got down on my knee, removed the jewelry box from my pocket, and said, "Because I want you to be my wife. I love you. Please don't make me live without you."

It is cliché to say, "The silence was deafening." But that's how it felt. The entire world went quiet. The birds outside stopped chirping, and the noise from the kitchen abated as Sofia eavesdropped, waiting for Marjorie's answer. My heart pounded in my ears as I envisioned her saying, "No". It felt like an eternity before she answered.

Then the warmth returned to her face. Her eyes lit up like stars in the night sky. She stuck out her left hand as if to say, "Put the ring on my finger."

I pulled the ring from the box and slid it onto her finger, repeating, "Marjorie Sykes, will you marry me?"

As I gazed back up at her, she responded with a smile. A wave of relief flooded through my body.

"Yes, of course," she said.

Within seconds, Sofia joyfully charged back into the living room with her arms outstretched. She hugged me, then Marjorie, then both of us at once. Her tears of joy told the story. We were going to be family.

"We have to call Alicia and Raymond," she exclaimed.

Within the hour, Sofia was hard at work in the kitchen. She prepared a celebratory meal of Pollo Guisado, a traditional Dominican chicken dish, and Tostones, fried plantains.

By five o'clock, Alicia and her two children, Devon and Patrice, were walking through the front door. It was the first time I had met

Alicia. She looked quite different from Marjorie. With a shorter stature and a round, soft face, she more closely resembled Sofia's Hispanic features.

Alicia's husband, Jay, joined us a little later. Jay, a Mexican-born man of substantial girth, looked imposing, with a shaved head and dark beard, but he welcomed me with open arms. He seemed to welcome the idea of another outsider joining the family. Jay owned a string of auto repair shops in the Philadelphia metro. He started as a mechanic, bought the shop he worked at, and eventually parlayed it into several successful stores. Like any celebration, hugs and handshakes were plentiful and welcome.

Shortly after six, Marjorie's brother, Raymond Sykes, walked through the door. Raymond, like Marjorie, looked more like their father. Raymond II was the spitting image of the picture I saw of Raymond Sr, sitting on the mantel at Marjorie's house. Only the clothes were different.

Marjorie introduced us to one another. Raymond didn't seem pleased with the announcement of our engagement. He knew about me from the Andrew Johnson case, but we never met. I helped his friend, so he stayed silent, but he was the only person present without a smile.

I hadn't taken part in a big family dinner in years. It was a bit of a change for me. Everyone was talking at once, laughing, arguing, piling the food onto their plates. When we were all seated, Jay interrupted the group's chat to propose a toast.

"To Marjorie and Joseph, may you share many long and loving years."

Sofia smiled, the children laughed, and Raymond scowled. Soon, everyone was stuffing their mouths. Sofia had prepared a feast fit for kings.

The party broke up a little after nine o'clock. Alicia and Jay wanted the kids home early to prepare for the next school day. While Sofia and Marjorie cleaned up the dishes, Raymond pulled me aside and asked to speak with me in private. We went outside for what I thought would be friendly, brotherly advice.

It wasn't brotherly advice he offered. His unhappiness with my marriage proposal burst from his lips.

"What's in this for you?" His question echoed with disdain.

"I don't know what you mean. I love Marjorie."

Black people often view white people with a mistrustful eye. Raymond was obviously not happy that someone like me, a white man with blond hair, several years younger than his sister, a person Marjorie had met only a few weeks ago, had invaded his family. He somehow had gotten the impression that I was using Marjorie to create a trending story. That an interracial relationship would be nothing more than a newsworthy story to further my career.

"What's a hot-shot reporter like you want with my sister? Aren't there any women like you who can satisfy your ambition?" He protested.

"Raymond, I know you have faced discrimination throughout your entire life." You're wary of our relationship, but this isn't a career move."

"People have hurt Marjorie before. I don't want it to happen again. Andrew abused Marjorie; in those days, he was a bad guy. She doesn't always make the best choices when it comes to men. She deserves better than what she gets. I'm just watching out for my little sister."

I thought his comment was self-espousing. He was pretending to be the family guardian. To me, it felt like he was more concerned about his own image. Perhaps he should have directed his concern towards Franchesca, his other little sister, rather than Marjorie. I almost shot back, "Maybe you should've watched out for Franchesca." Opening old wounds wouldn't change the past. Besides, I didn't know the entire story about Franchesca's death. Raymond and I didn't see eye to eye. It didn't appear we would ever be.

"I don't know how to reassure you, but I won't hurt her," I said.

"Just remember, she is my little sister. I watch out for my family. I know people, too."

It was a veiled threat, meant to intimidate me. Yet somehow, I knew it was more of a desperate attempt to reassure himself. Raymond was an accountant, not an inner-city gang banger. He didn't strike me as someone who would resort to violence.

I extended my hand. Reluctantly, he shook my hand, and I assured him I would dedicate myself to making her happy. It was then that I noticed something that I hadn't observed during dinner. Raymond had a tattoo on his wrist just above his right hand. I wasn't sure, but it looked eerily like that same devil's pitchfork tattoo I had seen on the wrist of James Parker's assassin.

It probably meant nothing. Lots of people have tattoos, and besides, Raymond grew up in Philadelphia, not Camden. But being the cynic that I am makes me question everything. Just another little coincidence, one that makes you wonder.

Initially, I considered asking Marjorie about the tattoo, but ultimately decided against it. I'm sure sometime down the road she will explain. No sense spoiling our engagement celebration.

When everyone had left, I realized that in my haste to get to Philadelphia, I hadn't made a hotel reservation or even discussed our sleeping arrangements. I had visions of being alone again with Marjorie. After all, she had accepted my marriage proposal.

I grabbed my phone and opened up the travel app. I asked Marjorie, "Should I get us a room downtown?"

"No, save your money. We can stay here tonight. I have all my clothes unpacked."

"What about your mom? Will she be okay with it?"

"Oh, she won't mind," she laughed.

I was a little apprehensive about sleeping in Sofia's house with her daughter. But much to my chagrin, my apprehension was quickly alleviated. A few minutes later, Sofia came downstairs, her arms filled with a blanket, sheets, and a pillow. Sofia had old-fashioned values and strict rules about her daughters. She decreed, "When you are married, you can sleep together."

I slept that night on the couch in the living room, alone.

The next day, Marjorie packed her bags for our return trip home. I could hear Sofia singing a cheerful-sounding song in Spanish as she prepared breakfast in the kitchen. She wouldn't let us leave without a scrumptious meal to sustain us for the three-hour trip home. You can imagine that I was looking forward to getting back to normal. Meeting her family was enjoyable, but I wanted to focus on rekindling our relationship.

"Good, we can go to the City Hall tomorrow for our marriage license," I said.

We hadn't discussed it, but Marjorie had other ideas. "Ugh, excuse me, you're not getting off that easy. If you want to marry me, you are going to have to do better than City Hall. I want a real wedding. I want a gown, a reverend, a celebration with my family and friends, the whole enchilada."

Of course, she did. I had just spent half of my life's savings on a set of wedding rings. Now she wants to spend the other half hosting a big party. Who knew proposing could be so expensive?

She had a grin from ear to ear. Her pitch-black eyes, rich dark skin, and bright smile melted my heart. The sight of her, the most beautiful woman I'd seen, made me feel like the luckiest man alive. She knew whatever she wanted; she would have.

I conceded. "Okay, let's have the biggest wedding ever," I said.

Chapter 30

The Tie In

After the success of Melinda Donne's memoir, my bank account was growing again, royalty payments were adding up, at least for the time being. Having promised Marjorie that work would no longer dominate my life, I cut back on my work schedule. I kept busy writing articles for a group of internet-based magazines that enjoyed having a big name on their front page. Once you become a best-selling author, they will purchase anything you write. They may not pay a lot, but enough so that I was doing okay, at least financially.

One magazine that I started sending articles to was *The Reporter*. Yes, that same periodical in Chicago that previously offered me the job as editor. After I begged off, the management, at the recommendation of my former professor, Elaine Sadeski, hired a young go-getter named James Crowder. Crowder had fresh ideas on how to perform investigations in the twenty-first century. James was brilliant, but still, his journalism skills were a little raw. He liked my articles because they were more professional and better researched than the young writers on his staff. One thing he worried about was inaccuracy or plagiarism. With my articles, inaccuracy was never a problem.

One afternoon, I was sitting in my makeshift office at Marjorie's townhouse, a converted closet, researching a potential target for a story on the effect of low wages on the economy. It was a very different storyline for me. I wasn't chasing any specific bad guy or corporation; it was more about government policy and how it has affected the class structure in America. It was a boring subject that I had to make interesting somehow.

I took a break to check my email and noticed an entry with a letterhead from *The Reporter*. At first, I assumed it was spam or a sales pitch, but upon reading further, it turned out to be a message from James Crowder. He was asking for my help with implementing a new training program. Most of his staff were young and inexperienced. He wanted them to learn from someone with a good pedigree. James asked me to call him to discuss his plan and my availability.

I wasn't busy. The only commitment I had was a minor event called a wedding. Marjorie had the wedding schedule well in order. Being smart enough not to upset her plans, I waited to discuss the project with her before committing to James.

Still, training wasn't exactly my forte. I needed more details, so I called *The Reporter* and asked for James Crowder. He answered quickly. I introduced myself.

"Yes, Mr. St. Joseph, I'm implementing a training program for some of the newer members of my staff, all recent graduates, and I could use help from someone with your expertise."

"James, while I appreciate your consideration, I think that Dr. Elaine Sadeski would be a better choice to help you get this program started. You know that education is her specialty, and she has a good relationship with your board members. Have you contacted her?"

"Yes, sir, I have. Dr. Sadeski is living in Paris now. She recommended I contact you."

It had only been a couple of months since I last spoke with Elaine. I wasn't aware she had relocated to Paris. I understood what the philosophers meant when they said, the world goes by in a flash.

Surprised, I asked him for more information. "Okay, James, tell me how you envision this training program will work."

"Dr. Sadeski and I have been discussing a program based on the IECO Hypothesis-Based Inquiry model. She's advocated this writing style for years. She claimed your understanding of the process surpassed that of most people. I would like you to compile five or six cases that exemplify the type of work these young journalists will encounter. Then, guide the students through the casework, analyzing the article's structure and highlighting the finer points. You can use your own stories if it makes you comfortable."

I must admit, the whole idea intrigued me. Still, I needed to confirm the timeline with Marjorie to avoid any conflicts with the wedding schedule. There will be plenty of work opportunities, but only one wedding, I hope.

"How soon would you need me there?" I asked.

"The sooner the better, but I recognize you are busy. Please think it over and make me a proposal. I will do my best to adjust to your schedule."

I replied, "Okay, I won't leave you hanging. I'll reach out to you by tomorrow."

We signed off, agreeing to formalize a plan. Seconds later, I was texting Marjorie. She was somewhere between St. Louis and New Orleans. I waited.

About twenty minutes later, she called. She had just deplaned in New Orleans and was heading to a taxi stand. She had a meeting with the Louisiana Humanitarian Foundation in two hours. I swear I don't know how she does it. I could never keep up with her schedule. A nervous breakdown is what I would experience.

She was in a good mood. "Hi sweetheart, how are you today?"

"I'm good. I have something I want to run by you before I commit."

I think she could hear the excitement in my voice as I explained *The Reporter's* proposal. She already planned to work for two more weeks before the wedding. She agreed that if I could put the class together and present it within the next two weeks, she wouldn't oppose the idea. That was all I needed to hear. It was all systems go!

I was eager to call James Crowder back, but I tempered my enthusiasm long enough to sit down and draft a plan, including a course outline that I could send him in response to his request. I also thought about my fee, although, truth be told, I was so excited I would have done it for free.

While I worked up a plan, I thought about Elaine Sadeski. I looked at my watch. *Was it too late to call?* It would be late evening in Paris, but the Parisians are night people. I dialed her number. She answered quickly.

"Hello, D.K. St. Joseph, I thought I would be hearing from you. You must have received a call from James Crowder at *The Reporter*."

"Yes, I did. No agreement yet, but a hopeful outcome. But that isn't why I called. I recently learned you're now a resident of Paris. Is this true?"

She laughed. "Yes, after the conference, Jacques Allard asked me to join him here. I agreed."

It was something of a surprise, considering Elaine was at least ten years older than Jacques. While Elaine was still an attractive woman, tall and stately, whereas Jacques was a smallish, balding man with a nerdy persona, they were an unlikely couple. It seems all that matters is being good friends.

She laughed again. "I tell everyone I'm Jacques' mistress. He calls me his muse. At my age, it's simply a pleasure to have someone who wants to take me to dinner or buy me a drink at a sidewalk café."

Americans might look suspiciously at their age difference and wonder why a younger man might choose an older woman. But French men differ from Americans. Jacques was likely happy to have an attractive woman at his side. Her age wasn't important. Still, I sensed their affair went deeper than mere meals and beverages.

"I understand you're planning a wedding. Is this perchance the same young lady you were pining over in Brussels?" she said.

How she would know about my marriage plans to Marjorie is a mystery. I didn't think other people kept tabs on me. Apparently, I was wrong.

"Yes, we reconciled shortly after the conference," I said.

"You should come to Paris for your honeymoon. It is the city of love and romance, you know? Jacques and I would love to show you around."

"I appreciate the invitation, perhaps another time. We have plans for a honeymoon in the Dominican Republic. Marjorie has a family history there. We plan to research her roots."

Then she asked me a question that made me pause. "Have you solved the James Parker murder yet?"

What the hell? How could she possibly know about my murder mystery dilemma? Did she know about Raymond Sykes and the tattoo? *Was she reading my mind?*

"How could you know about that?" I asked.

She must have thought I sounded paranoid.

"Relax, I'm not spying on you. I knew the minute I read your article published in the *Lumorist* that proved Andrew Johnson was innocent that you wouldn't stop there. You are so transparent. When I heard the police hadn't charged anyone else with the crime, I figured you wouldn't let it rest. Now you just confirmed my suspicions. Just be careful. You may wind up trading your journalism credentials for a detective badge."

"No, that will not happen, I promise. After this, no more murder mysteries. I am going back to exposing political corruption."

Still, Elaine Sadeski was on target. Raymond Sykes, James Parker, and that damned tattoo were eating away at me. I avoided the subject around Marjorie and her family because I didn't want them to think I was investigating her brother, Raymond. Every time I pushed it to the back of my mind, it resurfaced.

I knew it wasn't going to be long before it came again to the forefront.

Chapter 31

Learning From Teaching

When I arrived at the Chicago offices of *The Reporter*, I was amazed by what I saw. I was used to seeing newspaper and magazine editorial offices set up in a traditional fishbowl style. In a typical office, writers and support staff sit in rows of desks, sometimes facing each other, across open aisles. Telephones ring, news broadcasts blare, and people try to outshout each other for attention. Along the walls are conference rooms or the somewhat quiet offices of the senior writers. The editor's office, like a king's throne, sits at the hallway's end, away from the hubbub. Crowder instead set up their offices to resemble a war room modeled after the FBI or NSA cyber analysts. He sat in the middle, observing the teams and keeping tabs on their progress.

His operation differed in other ways as well. Instead of competing for a scoop, his journalists worked together in teams researching news articles, scouring the internet, and exploring the dark web. He was using trained cybersecurity experts to hack into databases that contained personal and financial records of the people they were investigating. Using the dark web and financial databases was a risky way to do business, but he was willing to risk publishing a story that used shady sources if it outpaced his competitors.

Some of the software applications his cyber specialists had created used a rudimentary form of Artificial Intelligence, allowing his people to find answers quickly. They could perform research that would take me weeks in a matter of minutes. I immediately recognized he was creating a new model for investigative journalism.

He knew once his young reporters learned how to present their arguments professionally, his publication would be the envy of the news media. I set up shop in a conference room. From there, I conducted a three-day class, which was a short version of Dr. Sadeski's college course. It was enough to show his reporters how to use my storyline method for Hypothesis-Based Inquiry. His group of young, enthusiastic journalists absorbed the concept like a dry sponge absorbs water. The class was a rousing success. I felt good knowing I had helped create a whole new group of forward-thinking journalists.

As a bonus, my visit turned out to be a learning experience for me. While I was in their offices, I received an education on how to use their software applications to cut my research time down from weeks to hours. I was there to teach, but I also learned a new skill set. My new skills proved handy sooner than expected.

With our wedding approaching, Marjorie hinted at my asking Raymond to be a groomsman for the ceremony. She had already chosen her best friend, Derek Watting, to be her Man of Honor and her sister Alicia as her bridesmaid. My brother William had already agreed to join me as my best man. My brother James stayed in Singapore with his pregnant wife, so he would not be attending the wedding. I needed another groomsman. I tossed around the idea of having my sister, Katherine, stand up on my side of the church. She wasn't warm to the idea, so I let her off the hook.

I had no other close friends I could ask. No one in the D.C. area. With no other choice, I asked Raymond. He reluctantly agreed.

Raymond and I always appeared to be at odds. He refused to warm up to me. No matter how hard I tried, he always seemed guarded. And then there was the issue with the tattoo on his wrist. Every time I saw Raymond, my mind would not stop thinking about that tattoo, and James Parker's murder.

A couple of days later, at Marjorie's request, I drove up to Philly to meet Raymond. Together, we visited a tailor to get fitted for new suits for the wedding. It provided me with an opportunity to observe the tattoo more closely. I emblazoned it in my mind. After the fitting, I offered to buy lunch. He was initially hesitant; he insisted he needed to return to his office, but after a little pressure, he agreed to a sandwich and a drink. We stopped at a tavern near his old neighborhood named The Top Hat.

I learned this was Raymond's version of Ed's Bar, the place he came to hide from the world. Only to me, Ed's Bar seemed modern compared to this place. The Top Hat looked to be a Depression era building with a large stone and wood front, and small, dark-tinted windows. The rundown building looked as if the depression hadn't ended.

The bartender recognized Raymond the moment he walked in the door. Raymond flashed two fingers at the bartender. Syd, the owner, drew two beers from the tap and two shots of the house brand of whiskey.

"Anything to eat?" Syd asked.

"Two specials," replied Raymond."

The "specials" turned out to be a hamburger atop a hoagie-style bun with Swiss cheese and sauteed onions. The cook dumped a pile of curly fries on top of the melted cheese. It was easier to eat it with a knife and fork than to pick it up.

Raymond sat quietly at first. To break the silence, I kept asking him questions about his business, his family, and, of course, Marjorie. Most of the talking was done by me, making it feel like an interrogation instead of a conversation.

When Syd poured Raymond a second shot, he looked at my empty glass. I declined. "I can't. I'm driving back to D.C. in a little while," I said.

I wanted to learn the history of the tattoo without spooking him. I asked casually, "What does that tattoo mean?"

He responded with, "Nothing anymore. When we were young, James Parker, myself, and three other boys got tattoos. It wasn't intended as a gang symbol, just a dare. My mother wasn't too pleased, but in those days, you couldn't get a tattoo removed. I was stuck with it. She got over it."

After downing the second shot of whiskey, Raymond's tongue loosened up. He seemed burdened with something to share, and it was time to unburden himself. I let him talk.

"We used to hang out at the schoolyard down the street from our house. Two of the older boys, Javier and Solomon, took the whole thing too seriously. They thought of themselves as hard-ass gansta types. They started selling drugs and burglarizing local businesses. James and I pulled back from the group. Then one day, the other guy, Rufus Brown, got caught in a robbery attempt. The business owner shot him, and he died on his way to the hospital."

Defending his past, he said, "We were good kids. We were in over our heads. Javier and Solomon wouldn't give up the gang. They said, 'Once a member, always a member.' Javier started recruiting newer members, and the gang grew. They threatened us if we tried to get out of the gang. A short time later, James moved out of the neighborhood. He eventually ended up in Camden. He thought he was far enough away to safely stay out of the gang. James would sometimes come back to the old neighborhood to visit me. One weekend, he brought his new friend Andrew Johnson with him. Andrew was a couple of years older than us. Handsome and smart,

Andrew was a player. He started flirting with Marjorie, who immediately fell head over heels for him."

Shaking his head, he said, "My father didn't like Andrew, but he was powerless to stop them. If he tried to force her to stop seeing Andrew, she would only rebel. He hoped that when Marjorie went to college, she would forget about Andrew, but Marjorie was in love. The summer before Marjorie's final year, they went to the courthouse and got married. I think she thought Andrew would settle down, but Andrew didn't. When Marjorie was away at school, he would go out carousing every night."

Shrugging, he said, "She tried to make it work, so after graduation, they got an apartment, but Andrew never stayed home. They would argue all the time. One Saturday night, Andrew came home drunk. They had a big fight. Andrew slapped Marjorie around pretty good. She called the police, but they just treated it as a domestic squabble and did nothing. Marjorie had enough. She packed her bags and left him. Later, she joined the United Poverty League and moved to Washington. Andrew didn't follow her. We all thought that was the end."

After signaling Syd for another drink, he finished his story. "About five or six years ago, Andrew found religion. He turned his life around and started helping people. He tried to reconcile with Marjorie, but by then she had moved on. She was no longer attracted to Andrew."

Andrew Johnson shared parts of his story during our jail visit. Except he left out the part about his mistreating Marjorie. Now Raymond was filling in a lot of the blanks. I didn't know that James Parker was Raymond's friend before he knew Andrew Johnson, a revelation that added an element to my thoughts on who killed Parker.

Javier, Solomon, and Raymond were the only three people alive who still had the tattoo. Three people of interest. That's when Raymond dropped a bombshell.

"I think I know who killed Franchesca," he said.

I knew little about Franchesca's death other than it was a gang-related shooting. I let Raymond continue to talk.

"One day, James and I were down on the corner hanging out when I saw a car coming down the street toward us. It was Javier's car, with Solomon in the passenger seat. I figured it was going to be trouble, so I told James to run. I ran the opposite way. Then I heard shots. Franchesca was hanging out nearby, and a bullet hit her. James saw the whole thing, but he was afraid. I think that was the last time he came back to the neighborhood. He thought they would come after us again. He made me promise not to tell. I told no one."

I could not believe what he had just revealed. "We need to go to the police," I said. "They murdered Franchesca. There is no statute of limitations on murder."

Raymond was reluctant, resistant if you will, to reopen both the case involving Franchesca's death and the hurt it caused her family.

"I don't want to reopen this case. It has taken us twenty years to move past it," he said.

I stood fast. It would be hurtful, but justice must be done. I threatened Raymond. "Either we do it together, or I will do it alone. Your choice."

"I don't know what to do. If you help me, we can do it together," he said.

Returning to Raymond's office, I dialed the non-emergency line of the Philadelphia police. I explained the reason for the call and asked for assistance. It took a little time. Raymond and I sat there, staring at each other in an uncomfortable truce. But about twenty minutes later, I received a call from a Philadelphia police homicide investigator. We explained who we were, identified the case, and stated that we had new information.

Officer Mick Garson was none too happy to reopen a twenty-year-old case. But he took our information and promised to return our call as soon as he could open the archived file.

With nothing left for me to do in Philly, I drove back to Bethesda. I was learning a lot about my new future family.

I also realized how little I knew about the woman I was marrying. She never confided in me about the abuse she experienced in her first marriage. It shook me up to hear another side of Marjorie's story. I promised myself no one would ever hurt her again.

It was two days later when Garson called back. That meant another trip back to the Philadelphia offices where his homicide unit worked. After a brief introduction, I let Raymond tell his version of the events leading to Franchesca's death. Garson listened politely.

When Raymond finished, he asked. "Raymond, did you see Solomon or Javier shoot the gun that killed your sister?"

Unfortunately, Raymond was running away at the time. He wasn't positive if it was Solomon, Javier, or someone else who pulled the trigger.

Then Garson explained. "The detective they assigned this case to has long retired. We'll add the information to the file, but without a clear eyewitness, the charges won't stick. The District Attorney will never take this to trial. I'm sorry."

Raymond looked at me in disgust. He never wanted to reopen these wounds. Fortunately, Garson agreed with me. "The information you shared today is important. If we can find another witness to corroborate what you told me, we can reopen the case. There is always a chance, it's just not today."

Raymond cooled down on his way back to his office. I think he came to realize I was trying to help.

I headed home after we met with Garson. Three hours of driving, ample time to think. And think I did; I learned a lot in my short time with Raymond. Information Raymond never shared with anyone else.

Families, even the closest ones, keep unshared secrets.

Chapter 32

If The Shoe Fits

When Lou Barnes first asked me to write Andrew Johnson's story, I set out to prove Andrew was innocent. I hypothesized he was being falsely accused. My concentration wasn't on solving the crime. That was the job of the police.

The new information that Raymond Sykes had shared had me rethinking the entire investigation. I decided to re-look at the crime footage.

When I got home, I sat down to review the old video files that Carolyn Petty had given me of the James Parker shooting. I suspected something was wrong. The video files weren't clear, not ideal for an investigation of this type. Scouring the web, I found a software application that would improve the images a little. After enhancing the images, I could see that the shooter's hand tattoo and the one on Raymond Sykes' hand matched perfectly. I was in a real pickle. If the crime involved Raymond, continuing with my research would surely cause a rift between me and the Sykes family. Even worse, it would harm my relationship with Marjorie. My marriage could be in jeopardy. But I always lived with the mantra, "The truth is the truth." Something had to be done.

I kept playing it over in my mind, trying to sort it out, when an idea came to me. Raymond's accounting firm handled the auto dealership accounts for Andrew Johnson and James Parker. *What other details did I overlook in this story?* I already knew Johnson didn't have any tattoos, a fact that helped free him from prison. But what about Parker? Maybe Parker's murder wasn't just about the protection money? Maybe there was another reason they killed him?

Carolyn Petty included copies of security footage for several days before and after the shooting. My original focus hovered around the time of the event. I asked myself, *What might I find studying the video in the time slots preceding and following the shooting? Would I find any additional evidence?*

It was time-consuming, but using a fast-forward option, I could scan hours of footage in just minutes. That's when I caught something on camera that piqued my interest. Just before 9:00 a.m., the morning of the shooting, the camera caught James Parker reviewing the cars in the lot. His likely intention was to open the business and assess any potential overnight vandalism.

A large, imposing man whom I didn't recognize approached him. The bigger man stood with his body away from the camera, but James smartly maneuvered himself until they were both visible in camera range. The two men appeared to be arguing. James tried defending himself, waving his hands, as the other man menacingly pointed a gun towards him. Finally, the larger intruder lowered the gun and turned away, kicking the bumper of one car in the lot as he left.

Luckily, a few seconds of clear footage captured the man's face and clothing. The clothes he wore were nondescript dark pants, a gray shirt, and a New Jersey Nets basketball cap. I searched for any images or logos that stood out. The only thing I saw was his shoes, bright blue sneakers with a brand insignia. I didn't recognize the symbol; it wasn't any popular brand like Nike or Adidas.

I scoured numerous websites for shoe brands with an emblem matching his shoes. I even printed a picture of the shoe, hoping to match it with online images. Luck wasn't with me. I didn't recognize the insignia.

Around dinnertime, I took a break to grab a sandwich at Ed's bar. While enjoying a beer and a pulled pork sandwich, I asked Ed if he recognized the brand. I showed him the picture I had printed out from my computer. Ed, who always seemed to know everything about everything, held up his foot and pointed to his shoe. "You mean like this?" Incredibly, he wore the same brand of shoe that the guy on the camera was wearing.

I almost fell off my barstool. Hours of searching the internet yielded nothing. Five minutes at Ed's bar and I had the answer. "Where did you get those?" I asked.

"They are good shoes for people with wide feet. But they're hard to find. A local department store is the only store in this area that carries them. None of the big box stores carry them. They are a brand from Australia. You can't even get them on the internet."

I wrote down the brand name and took a picture to identify the logo's marks. As soon as I got back to my office, I searched for stores in Camden that carry that brand. Sure enough, there was an independent department store in Camden, named CNJ Dry Goods, that sold those same shoes. Remarkably, I now had a lead.

I vowed to Marjorie to be honest and prioritize our relationship over my work. That's why I felt terrible about my next move. Against my better judgment, I planned to solve Parker's murder, even if it meant working twenty-four hours a day and involving her family.

Chapter 33

I Did, I Will, I Do

When Marjorie first described her ideal wedding, I had visions of a huge cathedral filled with family, friends, and business associates from across the country. I imagined a ceremony led by a covey of priests and ministers representing every Christian faith on the planet, all there to witness what would surely be the most talked-about nuptials trending worldwide on the internet.

A huge reception would follow the ceremony at a ballroom filled with people from every walk of life, clamoring for free booze and expensive hors d'oeuvres, all at my expense.

I loved Marjorie, but enough is enough. Every time she talked about her wedding, my imagination went wild. I could only grit my teeth and close my eyes.

I should have known that Marjorie was far more sensible than she pretended. In reality, the ceremony Marjorie planned was quite practical. She wanted a family affair. The Sykes family, the St. Joseph family, and a few close friends and associates. It was intimate, but it satisfied her that all of her loved ones and close friends could be with her on our special day.

We invited fewer than one hundred people, with many being her business associates in other cities. Most would RSVP their regrets; they wouldn't be attending. That meant the crowd was quite reasonable.

My parents, William Sr. and Nadine St. Joseph, represented the St. Joseph family along with my brother William, his wife Barbara, and his two children. My aunt Cecilia, my mom's sister, who attends every family function whether or not you invite her, would be there. Cecilia's son, my cousin Rich, rounded out our group.

My family drove down from Cleveland the day before. I reserved rooms for them in an upscale hotel near Sofia's house. The evening before the wedding, we all met for dinner. My mom greeted me with the warmest hug we had shared in years. "My little D.K., we have waited so long for you to settle down," she said.

I wanted my parents to like my new relatives, and I wanted Marjorie's family to trust my family. The two families bonded well. Even Raymond, who typically wore a scowl, was in a positive mood.

Marjorie's family was a little larger with her sister Alicia, her husband Jay, and their children, Devon and Patrice. Raymond and his significant other, Nicola, who wore a dress so revealing it made you wonder if she was just stopping by the wedding on her way to a nightclub. Nicola's son from a previous marriage would also attend.

Marjorie also invited her secretary, May Stiles, and fellow board member Charles Napier and his wife, both from the United Poverty League.

It was intimate, but it satisfied her that all of her loved ones and close friends could be with her on our special day.

We held the wedding at the Baptist church in her old neighborhood, in Philadelphia. The minister, an old friend of Marjorie's father, conducted the ceremony. The Catholic parish, where she attended parochial school and worshiped as a child, refused to marry us. Marjorie's previous marriage and recent divorce from Andrew Johnson stood in the way. The Catholic Church teaches that marriage is a sacred bond that a civil divorce cannot undo. I always thought that rule was a silly tenet. Why shouldn't the church bless the union of two loving individuals who desire to live as partners?

It was a beautiful early fall day, and the calm, cool temperatures outside kept everyone in a chipper mood. The florist filled the chapel with white, red, and blue flowers, the colors of the American and Dominican flags. The guests came dressed, the men in their finest suits, the women in their fashionable dresses. Nothing could spoil our perfect wedding. Once we were all present, the ceremony began.

William and I stood poised at the front of the chapel. My sometimes friend and often nemesis, Derek Watting, Marjorie's best friend, stood opposite William on the other side of the aisle. Alicia, in a lovely off-white gown, joined Derek as a member of the wedding party, as did Raymond on my side.

The organist signaled the ceremony's start, and two beautiful women emerged at the back of the church. Sofia, in a chic royal blue gown, her hair pulled back away from her face, beamed with pride as she walked Marjorie down the aisle.

Marjorie was a vision in white lace. Her long, silky gown flattered her tall, shapely figure. Her hair pulled back in a braided cornrow style allowed her ebony face to beam with joy. It was the church wedding she had dreamed of since she was a young girl, especially since her first marriage to Andrew was a courthouse affair. She walked gracefully up the aisle, a bouquet of white roses and blue hydrangea grasped tightly in her hand, Sofia at her side.

As she approached the altar, she smiled at Alicia, then winked triumphantly at Derek, as if to say, "We did it.".

Sofia guided her to me, then, as before, pinched my cheek. "I'm so happy for both of you," she said. Then she turned and walked back toward her seat in a pew next to Devon and Patrice.

I took Marjorie's hand while she took my heart away. Somehow, Marjorie Sykes had transformed this workaholic cynic who thought of nothing but his work and turned him into a family member.

We spoke our pre-written vows to each other. Then I slid the matching band I had purchased with the engagement ring onto her finger. When it was my turn to say, "I do.", I spoke as clearly and as proudly as I could make two words sound. My heart pounded in my chest waiting for the minister to say, "You may kiss the bride.". When he gave his last instruction, I was ready. I kissed her like there was no tomorrow. Yet, there would be countless tomorrows. Marjorie was finally mine, for all time.

The reception was held at a restaurant near the church. It was a joyous occasion with all of our loved ones in attendance. The intimacy of the small group allowed both families to feel comfortable while getting to know each other better. The Sykes and St. Joseph's families were now intertwined, hopefully forever. Apprehensive at first, I should have realized it wouldn't be a problem. Despite their own preferences, both families, who were good people, accepted and respected their differences.

To my surprise, my father, who normally maintained a low-key approach toward life, made the most heartfelt speech. He pledged to the Sykes family to become partners in one larger family. He thanked Marjorie for corralling his wayward son. It thrilled my parents that I had finally found the one person who would make me happy.

After dinner, my dad pulled me aside and hugged me. "I don't think I ever told you how proud I am of you. You have become someone important, a man with purpose and family. Good luck, son."

He was right. Having importance solely to strangers results in a hollow existence. The two virtues that give life meaning are loving others and being loved.

◆◆◆

Several of the guests brought presents, and most of the friends and family who couldn't attend simply sent cards offering their congratulations. In the stack of cards, there was an envelope addressed solely to Marjorie Sykes. The return address had Melinda Donne's house number in Carryduff, Northern Ireland. Marjorie glanced at me with a look of uncertainty. My close relationship with Melinda was still something of a sore spot with Marjorie.

I took no responsibility for the card. "Don't look at me. She addressed it to you," I said.

She tore it open and pulled out a lovely card. It was a congratulatory wedding card with a heartfelt saying and beautiful artwork. Inside the card was a slip of paper with a handwritten note.

It read. *Dear Marjorie, Congratulations on your wedding. My Best Wishes for a long and happy life together. Thank you for letting me borrow your husband. I am sure it put a lot of strain on your relationship, but he helped me more than I could ever repay. He is a hero in my eyes. I hope he is in your eyes too. – Melinda Donne.*

She looked at me again, as if I had somehow coerced Melinda to send the card.

I held up my hands in a defensive posture. "I had nothing to do with it, I swear. Take it in the spirit in which she wrote it."

"Now I have to send her a thank-you note. Mr. Hero."

"You know what? Tomorrow, we will call her. You can thank her in person," I said.

"So let me get this straight. Tomorrow, on your honeymoon, you plan on calling your old girlfriend?"

Her question was rhetorical. I sheepishly replied. "Well, maybe we should wait. When we come back, we'll send her a Thank You card."

Marjorie smiled, "You're learning, husband. You are learning."

Marjorie was right. We agreed our honeymoon was no time to involve ourselves in other people's problems. I challenged her to take it one step further. No internet, no email, no phone calls, and especially no work-related activities. Despite initial hesitation, she ultimately agreed that this is our time. The world could survive a week without Marjorie Sykes or D.K. St. Joseph, and we could survive without the world's troubles.

We spent our wedding night at a luxury hotel in downtown Philadelphia, where we made love like two teenagers in heat. The next day, we boarded a flight out of Philly, destined for Punta Cana in the Dominican Republic. Marjorie had booked a week at the Secrets Cap Cana Resort, one of the world-class resorts where we could consummate our marriage, undisturbed by the outside world. The resort was located on Juanillo Beach, one of the most stunning beaches in the Dominican Republic. If we chose, we never had to leave the resort. It had everything a honeymooning couple needed to relax and get to know each other. We had such a whirlwind courtship; we still barely knew each other's habits. I knew I loved Marjorie that first day when our hands touched, and she smiled that irrepressible smile. Our on-and-off relationship and busy work schedules hindered our time to bond like typical couples.

It was our first visit to the Dominican Republic, both of us. For me, spending time at a tourist resort would satisfy my curiosity about the island. Except Marjorie brought with her a list of names and addresses of distant relatives, aunts, cousins, and old family friends. Sofia had instructed us to visit as many as possible so Marjorie could learn a bit more about her Dominican heritage.

Following Sofia's instructions, after breakfast at a beachfront restaurant, we set out each morning to discover other parts of the island and locate Sofia's relatives she left behind when she moved to America. I found driving in the Dominican Republic is scary, as they don't enforce the rules of the road like back home. We almost got into several collisions with impatient locals. Still, the dramatic scenery, the white sand beaches, and the dense forest were so spectacular that it was worth the risk.

Despite a growing economy, financial inequality remains a major problem in the Dominican Republic. The gap between wealthy business owners and poor peasants is alarming. In the resort areas, the world-class resorts feature an almost embarrassing level of opulence. In the country and inner cities, people live in huts with dirt floors.

We visited Marjorie's aunt Lucha, who lived along with Marjorie's cousin Fredo in a small town about thirty kilometers from our resort. Marjorie had never met her aunt in person, only seeing pictures of her and having an occasional telephone conversation.

I asked Marjorie. "How is it that your aunt did not emigrate to the U.S. with the rest of the family?"

"Lucha is the oldest of five children. She is almost ten years older than my mom. She had gotten married before the family moved. Lucha and her new husband, Raul, stayed in their native home. Raul passed away about ten years ago, and Lucha moved in with my cousin Fredo."

Fredo, a construction laborer, had a house constructed of whitewashed cement blocks and wood shingles. It seemed like one of the nicer houses in town. Many others were wooden shacks or broken-down trailer homes. Although it appeared modern, it lacked several conveniences that people in the U.S. expect in a home. Like other houses in their village, chickens roamed freely in the front yard, and Fredo tended a small garden yielding fresh vegetables.

When Lucha moved in, Fredo put an addition on the rear of the house, built from recycled and repurposed material from other construction jobs. He installed a modern plumbing system with a toilet and a bathtub. Except, the village did not have a public waste treatment facility. Fredo didn't have enough money to install a septic system, so his plumbing system released the wastewater into a nearby ditch, just a few hundred feet from the house. When we visited, a breeze coming from the backyard brought the foul smell right back into the house. When you looked out the window toward the rear of the property, you could see the vapor rising from the pit filled with raw sewage and decomposing garbage.

I pulled Marjorie aside to point out my concern. I whispered, "This is a disaster in the making. This system will make them sick if it continues."

She shook her head. "I'll talk to him. Maybe we can help?"

The lack of access to infrastructure appalled Marjorie. Even in the poorest inner cities and undeveloped rural communities in the U.S., people have waste treatment systems. Marjorie has a way of diplomatically speaking to people without embarrassing them. She tactfully asked Fredo how much it would cost to install a working septic system. To my surprise, she wrote him a check on the spot for the entire cost. Asking him only to pay it forward to someone else who might need help in his village.

With one of the lowest education spending rates per capita, the outlook for growing a middle class in the Dominican Republic is bleak. The government invests most of its money in tourist areas, its major industry.

Despite their poverty, the locals welcomed us with open arms at each place we visited. Though they had open arms, they often left me out of the conversation because I didn't speak Spanish. Call me paranoid, but I think they were talking about me. I wasn't always sure. It didn't matter. They were wonderful people.

As long as it satisfied Marjorie's desire to visit her family and learn about her heritage, she was happy. As long as we returned to our luxury resort in time to resume our lovemaking, it satisfied me.

For the first time, Marjorie and I spent a whole week not discussing work. Whenever I ran out of something to talk about, I put my arm around Marjorie and kissed her. If life were always this simple, I'd seriously consider relocating to the Dominican Republic.

It wasn't easy staying away from the internet, and the urge to post the wonderful sights we were seeing on this beautiful island on social media was compelling. We took a lot of pictures to show our friends when we returned home.

Although working was off-limits, I'm sure Marjorie was making mental notes on how the United Poverty League might expand its reach to the island, as the number of people living below the poverty level was far higher than in the States. Honestly, I couldn't stop myself from wondering how this country could support such opulence as we experienced at our resort and such poverty as we saw in the countryside villages. I hypothesized that political corruption must be rampant. Perhaps it would be a topic for an investigation sometime down the road?

We made vows to return here someday as activists, aiming to learn about the culture and help alleviate the long-standing poverty and crime.

A few weeks later, Marjorie received a text with pictures from her cousin Fredo. He stood next to a hole in the ground where he installed his new septic tank. He held up a homemade sign that read, "gracias por tu amor", or "thank you for your love."

Chapter 34

It's That Damn Tattoo

After the honeymoon, Marjorie returned to work. To compensate for her two-week absence, she filled her travel schedule with a new city or town every day. That left me at home in my temporary office researching and planning my next hypothesis with the hope that something brilliant would burst from my brain.

Except for Marjorie's continuous travel, our life together settled into a comfortable period that was more like dating than marriage. We would text and video chat when she was on the road. When she was home, we exercised together or dined as a couple.

At night, when I was alone, I thought about Marjorie and her past relationship with Andrew Johnson. I didn't doubt our love for each other, that she had moved on from her past. Yet, I couldn't shake the feeling that the Andrew Johnson story still wasn't finished. We had more to do before closing this chapter of our lives.

After hearing Raymond's version that Andrew had beaten Marjorie, it concerned me that she went to bat for him when she didn't owe him anything. Even though Johnson eventually turned over a new leaf and straightened his life out, it showed what a caring person Marjorie had become, a credit to her parents.

A variety of half-started projects covered my desk, all waiting for that moment of inspiration when one would seize my interest and create my next award-winning exposé.

Financially, I was still doing okay. The book that Melinda and I had co-authored was selling well. Even after the initial splash, it continued a steady stream of sales through online portals. Money-wise, Melinda would be doing even better than me. Just as money continued to flow into my account, she continued to receive large royalty checks. Money she could use to help her combat her illness.

It had been several weeks since I had spoken with Melinda. I emailed her several times with no response. It wasn't critical. I had nothing pressing to discuss. I simply wanted an update on how her recovery was going. When I last spoke with Melinda, she had told me she was undergoing experimental treatment in London, called Brief Eclectic Psychotherapy, for her PTSD, with the hope it would help reduce her painful episodes resulting from her capture. She also began a new medical regimen to combat the bacterial infection that was ravaging her body. Money wasn't important to Melinda. She was fighting her own private war for life.

Over the next few days, I tried to call Melinda via phone and video chat. The first few calls received no answer. I left a message asking for a return call.

On the fifth day, the calls stopped going through to her voicemail. Initially, I thought it was due to long-distance network problems from the U.S. to Northern Ireland. I was wrong. The phone system was working fine. Frustrated, I placed a call to Melinda's agent at the publishing house that handled her book distribution.

She was apologetic. "Oh, Mr. St. Joseph, I have been meaning to call you. Melinda had a relapse. It seems her new treatment wasn't successful. I understand they admitted her to the hospital on Tuesday. This morning, we received word that she has passed away. I am so sorry."

Melinda Donne's death was barely a blip on the radar in the United States. Except for a brief period after her book release, she remained out of public view for so long that no one in the U.S. paid attention. In Northern Ireland and the U.K., she had become something of a folk hero. The news media, including the *BBC*, *The Telegraph*, and *The Irish Central*, all posted articles honoring her life. Even the official website of the British Royal Family carried the news of Melinda's passing.

Funny, but I never remember Melinda telling me if she was Catholic or Protestant. It no longer mattered. Condolences for the fearless lass from Carryduff, Northern Ireland, came from both sides of those peace walls.

The details of her passing were sketchy. Even the British press, which is known for its portrayal of everything as scandalous, maintained a low-key approach toward the events surrounding her death.

Seeking more information, I contacted Thomas Kincade, a journalist at the BBC and a friend of Melinda. We had met a few years earlier at a news media conference and occasionally swapped the opposing viewpoints that Americans and British journalists sometimes offer. Thomas was privy to more details about Melinda's passing. The official report of her death in the hospital was incorrect.

Melinda had experienced a relapse as the infection that was ravaging her body once again placed her in intensive care. When the hospital determined there was nothing more they could do to treat her, they released her. They sent her home to fight her battle alone.

The next day, exhausted from her struggle, Melinda hired a car and, in the dark of night, drove it into the Knockbracken Reservoir. A fisherman found the car in ten feet of water with Melinda's body trapped inside.

A few days later, I wrote a short obituary about Melinda's passing and asked James Crowder to publish it on the *Reporter's* website. He found a spot near the lifestyle section. At least more people in the U.S. would learn of Melinda's passing.

Another soldier had died in the fight for truth and justice. I had lost another friend.

Having failed to convince the Philadelphia police to reopen the case involving Franchesca's murder, I looked at other options. Raymond and Solomon, the last two, with gang tattoos. The only two not imprisoned. That makes this crime solvable. *Pick one and run with it.* Since Raymond was my brother-in-law, I gave him the benefit of the doubt. I picked Solomon, hoping to prove he killed Parker. If Solomon Montgomery killed Parker, he must face the consequences for the crime.

I drafted my hypothesis: *The Tattooed Killer Has Returned.*

I only had two leads. The killer had a unique tattoo on their right hand and wore shoes available at a limited number of local stores. The video of James Parker's shooting was not strong enough evidence to arrest Solomon for murder. I needed more.

♦♦♦

Once again, I opened my desk drawer, pulled out the DVD discs that Carolyn had copied for me, and rolled the video. Perhaps there was more action I hadn't seen?

It is quite common for criminals who are planning a crime to scope out the job in advance. They are also prone to return to the crime scene afterward. For the first few hours, nothing noteworthy happened. Then I arrived back at the spot I had viewed earlier, where Solomon showed up and argued with Parker.

It was quite clear that Solomon and his accomplice visited the dealership the morning before the shooting. They were casing the joint to get the layout.

I watched the video footage for the remaining part of the day at Fast Forward. I hoped to catch something else that could be of interest. Occasionally, a prospective customer perusing the lot, or the auto mechanic, would trip the camera near the storage room. Nothing out of the norm for the automobile sales and maintenance business caught my eye.

At that point, it was inconsequential; I had enough footage and was able to capture a clear profile of the large black man, which I saved to a file, and then printed a copy to use in my investigation. It was time to return to Camden.

It wasn't hard to convince Marjorie to go back home to visit her family for a few days. She needed the time off. She hadn't seen Sofia in a few weeks. I also needed a reason to be in Philadelphia. The reason I fabricated was a visit to Tom Brown, a friend who worked at The Northeast Institute, a Philadelphia think tank. My cover story was that Tom needed help with an article he was working on for his organization. It was only a little white lie. I could've easily met Tom via a video chat, but I wanted to be in Camden, so I told Marjorie he had asked me to meet him.

In something of a change for us, we drove up to Philadelphia. We usually took the train, but I convinced Marjorie that it would be cheaper and faster, and a road trip along the shore might be a fun experience. It also allowed Marjorie to load the trunk up with gifts for her mother and Alicia's children.

While I was meeting with Tom Brown, Marjorie, and Sofia turned the day into a shopping trip at a nearby suburban mall and warehouse food store. I couldn't wait to see what treats Sofia would cook up in her kitchen.

I kept my meeting with Tom short, then I headed directly for CNJ Dry Goods, the department store in Camden that sold those shoes I saw on the video. The store looked more like a surplus outlet, loaded with clearance and closeout items I'd never seen in upscale stores in a shopping mall. I introduced myself to the store owner, Ralph, as the guy who called earlier.

"We carry items that other stores no longer stock. It's a brand that's popular in Europe and Canada, but not here in the States. That makes us a niche market. We get customers from all over the Eastern Seaboard. Once, a guy traveled from Ohio to buy them. The internet has cut into our business, but we still provide a service."

Ralph had no trouble recognizing the shoes, and when I showed him the picture of Solomon Montgomery, he remembered him.

"Yes, I remember him. He called me about an hour before he came in to try them on. I was the only store around that had a size fourteen triple E. He asked me to hold them for him and said his name was Solomon. It was no trouble holding them for him. I don't sell many size fourteens."

The pieces of the puzzle were coming together. I knew Solomon had the tattoo, now I also knew he wore those same shoes I saw in the video. It was likely Solomon who had the confrontation with James Parker earlier that day.

I headed straight to Raymond Sykes' office. Raymond wasn't happy to see me. He had spilled his guts to me a few weeks back when we were together before the wedding. I think he hoped it was all in the past. He knew why I was there. To reopen an old wound.

I told him I was still gathering evidence to ensure Solomon is sent to prison for a long time.

"What is the point?" He argued. "Didn't we just try this with the Philadelphia police? Why can't you just let it rest?"

"That was Philadelphia, Pennsylvania; this is Camden, New Jersey," I said. "I think we have a real good chance of getting this guy once and for all."

I showed Raymond the video footage of James Parker and the big black man who assaulted him at the dealership. He was the only one who could identify Solomon.

"Yes, that's Solomon," he confirmed. "I haven't seen him in years. He's noticeably heavier, but there's no denying it's him.

There were still several unanswered questions. It wasn't clear how Solomon found James Parker in Camden, New Jersey, or what prompted him to visit the dealership that day, yet video surveillance feeds clearly show Solomon and James speaking, arguing, in the lot the day before the shooting. Did Solomon go to the store for shoes and mistakenly wander past the dealership? Maybe he decided, since he was in the neighborhood, he would pay Parker a visit.

James Parker surely must have recognized Solomon. Parker was the only eyewitness to Franchesca's shooting. He could put Solomon back in prison. Maybe Parker threatened Solomon with going to the police? The answer to those questions lies solely with Solomon Montgomery.

One thing I learned was that it wasn't Boston Thurmond's "leg breakers" that killed Parker for the protection money, as Carolyn Petty had suggested. Solomon killed him to shut him up for Franchesca's shooting.

Raymond and I reviewed the video several times to confirm his agreement with my conclusions. The third time through, Raymond noticed something that I had missed. Approximately four minutes after the shooting, the camera in the west lot caught two people running from the scene. One was Solomon, the other an unknown figure that we couldn't identify.

"Look," he said. "That person with Solomon. It's not a man; it's a woman."

I looked closely and realized he was correct. The person was much shorter than Solomon, and more importantly, had a different physique. She had large, round buttocks and humongous breasts. Her hourglass figure was clearly the shape of a voluptuous woman. We had just found an additional clue. If we could identify the woman, we could solidify our hypothesis.

"Good," I said. "With this surveillance footage, your testimony, and the department store owner's testimony, I think we have enough to build a case against Solomon. We need to go to the Camden Police and show them what we have."

Gaining attention from the right person at Camden Police was a challenge. Nonetheless, the case stayed open despite pressure from the mayor's office to close it. It took several phone calls, but we finally connected with Detective Martin Sanchez. Sanchez was skeptical at first, but he agreed to meet with us at Raymond's office. We showed him the video footage we had compiled and, along with Raymond's testimony, agreed we had solid evidence to arrest Solomon.

"I just wish we had more," he said. "Who is that other person with Solomon?"

That's when Raymond surprised me for the second time with his astuteness.

"Don't you have fingerprints or something?" he asked.

"Of course, we dusted the entire place. We have prints from everyone who worked at the dealership. They wiped the gun clean, as were the doorknobs. We found a set of prints on the locker where we found the gun. We haven't been able to identify who they belonged to. This video helps, but it is inconclusive."

It wasn't my job to tell Sanchez what to do next, but I did anyway.

"Find Solomon, find his lady friend, and match and check her prints against the ones you haven't identified. You just might find the second person's identity. Maybe they will toss Solomon under the bus?" I said.

It was back in the hands of the Camden Police. All Raymond and I could do was wait and hope they get it right this time.

It took a few days, but Raymond finally received a phone call to come to police headquarters and identify Solomon in a lineup. This time, the Camden Police did their job. They arrested Solomon and his live-in girlfriend, Marcia Barden, at Marcia's rental apartment a few blocks from the car dealership.

Marcia's fingerprints matched a set of prints the forensic people lifted from the locker where they stashed the gun. In their haste to hide the gun, she forgot to wipe the locker clean.

Under questioning, Marcia agreed to a plea deal. Her attorney claimed she had no intent to harm Parker and was not an accomplice to murder. She admitted only to helping Solomon hide the weapon. Marcia wouldn't admit to it, but the police believe she was the one who reported the shooting.

She agreed to testify against Solomon in exchange for a short sentence at a minimum-security prison. According to the Camden County District Attorney, the case was a slam dunk. Solomon would soon enjoy years of free room and board courtesy of New Jersey.

Only one more thing remained. It was time for Raymond to come clean and close the book on Franchesca's death.

I convinced Raymond that he must clear his conscience and tell his family the entire story. There is only one problem. I was an outsider who had involved myself in the Sykes family business. They might hate me for stirring up a hurtful past.

"I'm going to need your help to explain this story to your family. I have promised Marjorie I wouldn't keep my work a secret. This is going to upset her and your mother. We need to let everyone know. No more secrets. We're in this together," I said.

We all gathered around Sofia's dining room table. On one side, it was Marjorie and me; on the other, Alicia and Jay. Sofia sat at the head of the table near the window. Raymond sat at the far end, his back to the wall.

Raymond took a deep breath, then started his confession.

"I have a secret I've never shared with anyone except James Parker. I know who killed Franchesca."

He held out his right hand, displaying his tattoo. "Remember when I was younger, James Parker, and I got these tattoos? Other boys in the neighborhood also got them. It was a gang symbol. We used to hang out on the street near the school. The other boys, Javier, Rufus, and Solomon, started getting in trouble. They were robbing stores and selling drugs. James and I told them we quit; we wanted nothing to do with them, but they wouldn't let us alone. James moved away, and I stopped going down by the schoolyard to avoid them."

It upset Sofia. "Your father told you not to get involved with those boys."

Raymond continued. "I hadn't seen Javier or Solomon for several weeks. I thought the gang problem was over. That day, we were goofing off with some guys in the church parking lot, tossing around a football. Franchesca was hanging out in front, a few steps away with her girlfriends. I saw Javier's car coming down the street, and I knew he was looking for James and me. It was Javier driving and Solomon in the shotgun seat. I yelled to James to run, but he just stood there. I ran down the alley, then around the corner, and hid under the front porch of the house on the corner. They started shooting. I'm sure James and I were the targets, but they missed. I found out later that Franchesca got hit."

Raymond was sobbing. "I never told anyone. I was the reason they killed Franchesca."

"James saw the whole thing, but he refused to talk to the police. When they questioned him. He pretended he didn't see anything. But James knew Solomon was the shooter. Solomon knew James saw him and vowed to get him. The idea of Solomon coming after him scared him. That's when James stopped coming around."

"Solomon and Javier both ended up in and out of prison for other crimes. James and I thought we were all safe. After a few years, it seemed like it didn't matter anymore. It was in the past. As far as I know, Javier is still in prison. They tell me he still runs the gang from inside. I haven't seen him or Solomon in years, but I still look over my shoulder sometimes."

Everyone at the table sat there, stunned. They didn't know what to say.

I probably should have kept my mouth shut, but I spoke up. Trying to make them realize they were finally getting closure, I said. "If they hadn't charged Andrew with James's murder, we would have never found out. It never should've happened this way."

Alicia piped in with a comment directed at Marjorie. "Daddy never liked Andrew from the day you two met. I knew Andrew would bring this family nothing but trouble."

Marjorie interjected. She tried to defend her relationship with Andrew. "This isn't about Andrew. Andrew loved me. We were just too young, too immature."

I think she was trying to ease her conscience that she had made a mistake with Andrew. As soon as she realized it wasn't smart to defend your failed first marriage in front of your new husband, she quieted down. It could only lead to dissension. Not a good way to win an argument. She stopped short of any more comments.

When I asked Marjorie to marry me, I knew of her past. This conversation wasn't about Andrew; it was about Franchesca. I didn't want the Sykes family to blame each other for Franchesca's death. I tried to bring the conversation back to the present.

"A few days ago, Raymond and I contacted the Philadelphia police about Franchesca's death. They declined to reopen the case."

"Since then, I discovered something else when I investigated the James Parker murder. The person who shot Parker had the same tattoo as Raymond. I suspected it was Solomon." Together, Raymond and I found evidence against Solomon in the Camden shooting. We knew it wouldn't bring Franchesca back, but we could at least have him arrested for Parker's murder. The Camden police arrested him yesterday. Franchesca's killer is now in prison. That has to mean something."

By now, everyone at the table was in tears. Sofia had her hands folded in prayer. I expected her to break down. To my surprise, Sofia was like a rock. She had mourned Franchesca's death for many years. Raymond's disclosure would not change history.

"We have to pray for Franchesca, for her soul to rest," she said.

We all folded our hands, and Sofia said a prayer for Franchesca.

After his arrest, they held Solomon Montgomery in the Camden County Correctional Facility. His public defender tried to convince the judge that Solomon's life was in danger because his former gang partner, Javier, still ran the gang from his current prison cell. The District Attorney, who had much more experience, convinced the judge to designate Solomon as a potential flight risk. The judge agreed, denying his bail pending a plea hearing. Javier couldn't take the chance of Solomon using his knowledge of Javier's operation to bargain down his sentence. Two days later, they found Solomon hung to death in his cell. He had ripped his prison jumpsuit into strips to create a noose, which he hung from the bars of his cell. His cellmate, whose bunk was six feet away, claimed to be asleep. He never heard or saw anything.

It wasn't the form of justice that the Sykes family had hoped for, but the man who took Franchesca's life finally paid the ultimate price for his crimes.

Chapter 35

A Team Of Three

Upon hearing the news about Solomon's death, Sofia insisted we all go to the cemetery to let Franchesca and Raymond Sr. know that they can now rest in peace.

As a rule, I never liked cemeteries. Despite the well-maintained park-like settings, the ornate headstones and mausoleums, and the freshly placed flowers, cemeteries are places of sadness. Even years after their passing, visiting the departed is always filled with lament.

Except today for the Sykes family. While they were saddened by the loss of the young Franchesca, long before she lived her life to the fullest, today brought a feeling of closure. As Sofia had put it, "Now Franchesca can rest in peace."

For me, it was a chance to meet Franchesca and Marjorie's father, Raymond Sr., who lay in the grave next to her. One privilege of being a father is to see your daughters fulfill their dreams. Raymond Sr. missed seeing Franchesca's journey into adulthood. He was never able to walk his beautiful daughter, Marjorie, down the aisle.

I knelt at the base of their graves and promised them both that I would do all I could to care for their family until we could reunite them all one day. I think they heard my pledge.

From the moment we woke up Saturday morning, I could see that Marjorie was irritable. She hadn't slept well and snapped at me for making noise when I awoke before her.

Maybe yesterday's events still upset her? I convinced her to go for a run, hoping a good workout would help her mood. We usually exercised separately, her at the exercise facilities in her hotels, and me at my local gym in Bethesda. Neither of us had hit the gym in a couple of days, and we both needed the workout.

We laid out a course from Sofia's home in the Poplar neighborhood, toward the Museum of Art in a loop just short of a five-mile route. Normally, when we ran together, I would take the lead and she would follow. Often, she required my encouragement to keep pace. Today, she took the lead, setting a blistering pace for which I was unprepared. She had something on her mind, but she wasn't sharing.

I immediately thought it was about something that occurred at her workplace. When we were first dating, she told me of how she received frequent hate mail and sporadic death threats. Occasionally, one would concern her enough that she would pass them along to the United Poverty League attorneys, who had people who would follow up and share them with the police if necessary. Some days, she went to her meetings with fear in her heart. She tried to play down the threat to her safety, not wanting to involve me or her family. Whenever we went out in public, I always kept a watchful eye for bigoted looks or comments that someone might direct our way. We had to remain vigilant due to the presence of so many unstable individuals.

As we approached the park, she was ahead of me by a good twenty feet. There was a fury in her run as if she were running from something or someone. When we turned down Kelly Drive heading south, I caught a glimpse of her face. Drops of liquid ran down her cheeks. Most people would mistake the moisture for perspiration, but to me, they looked like tears. I tried to catch her, but she paced ahead full steam. I yelled to her to slow down.

"I'll meet you at the steps," she said.

As we neared the Philadelphia Museum of Art, a popular tourist destination, an area that was crowded with sightseers, she paused briefly at the statue of Rocky, the famous fictional movie hero.

I started chanting the theme song from the movie, then turned and bounded up the museum steps, raising my arms in triumph, mimicking the celebration Rocky had done in the movie. It was enough to cheer her up as she laughed at my antics.

The run distracted her from her troubles, if only temporarily. We ran the last leg of our course back to Sofia's house together side by side at a much slower pace. When we arrived back at Sofia's house, we were both satisfied with our workout. We bounded up the steps, and before we reentered the house, she grabbed me and planted a kiss that made my toes curl. Whenever she kissed me that way, it only meant one thing: sex. I couldn't wait to get inside.

I was wrong about the sex. We showered separately. Her choice, not mine. Marjorie was quite clear that she didn't want to have sex with me at her mother's house. At night, when I reached for her playfully, she would swat my hand aside.

She would say. "No, you will just have to wait."

Marjorie showered first, as she needed more time for her post-shower routine. Finally, it was my turn. The hot shower felt good after the aggressive pace Marjorie had set for our run. As I dried myself off, I was ready for action. Marjorie was in front of the bathroom mirror with a towel wrapped around her, tending to her skin with a variety of lotions and creams. I wrapped my arm around her, pulling her close and kissing the back of her neck, a move that always seemed to turn her on. She responded with an approving sigh, but then quietly whispered. "You're just going to frustrate yourself; we are not doing anything. So put that thing away."

"Come on, nobody will know," I pleaded.

"I will know. My mom will see it all over my face. So, stop it."

I insisted. "Next time, we are getting a hotel."

I dressed and went downstairs, giving Marjorie the privacy that a woman needs to ready herself for her day. Besides, my advances were going nowhere, so why exasperate myself? Marjorie came downstairs a few minutes later and joined Sofia in the kitchen to help prepare our next meal.

While I sat in the living room watching an old movie, Marjorie and Sofia were having a heated discussion in the kitchen. I knew by the sound of their voices that they were arguing because they were speaking in Spanish. It may have been to keep me from eavesdropping, or simply because Sofia defaulted to Spanish when she got excited.

The discussion ended abruptly, with Marjorie storming out of the kitchen and heading for the stairs.

"Everything alright?" I inquired.

"Fine, just fine," Marjorie grumbled back. As she raced upstairs to the bedroom.

Now, I consider myself a pretty smart guy. Smart enough to know you don't get between a mother and daughter argument. It's crazy, I know, but for some reason, I felt I had to tempt fate.

I walked into the kitchen to find Sofia cooking. Whenever something important was happening in her life, Sofia would always cook. It helped her see the world clearly again. Today, something important happened without my knowledge. I wanted to inquire, but had to avoid escalating the argument.

Sofia had canisters, mixing bowls, and cookie trays strewn all over the kitchen counter. She just pulled some fresh pastries from the oven. They smelled heavenly.

"Everything alright?" I inquired.

I expected her to be in a grumpy mood ala, Marjorie. To my surprise, she put down her mixing spoon, then came over and pinched my cheek. It was a sign of affection reserved only for people she loved.

Smiling, she said, "Come, sit down. I want you to taste one of my Cocadas."

I sat at the table, facing the doorway, while she slid a plate containing a freshly baked coconut cupcake and a glass of milk in front of me. Then she kissed me on top of my head.

"Eat," she said.

Whatever was wrong, I wasn't the bad guy, for once.

I bit off a chunk of the Cocada. It was like a warm hug, the delightful soft cake melting in my mouth.

A minute later, Marjorie reappeared in the kitchen, her face wearing a bewildered look. She paused, looking at Sofia with uncertainty. Sofia looked back with the type of stern look a mother gives her daughter when she means business.

"Tell him," she said.

Something was happening, and I was in the dark, completely clueless.

An exasperated Marjorie turned toward me and took a seat opposite me at the table. With a serious look, she said.

"Remember how I once warned you that getting involved with me is going to change your life, in more ways than you can ever imagine?"

It took me a minute, but I remembered. "Yes, and I told you, 'It can only get better.' I meant it then, and I still mean it."

"Well, brace yourself, it is going to get a lot better..." She paused momentarily. "D.K. St. Joseph, you are going to be a father. I'm pregnant!"

I dropped my Cocada.

Sofia danced gingerly about the kitchen, thrilled that Marjorie would have her own family. She sang in Spanish as she waved her hands and swayed with joy.

"You can move back home, and I can watch the baby for you," she declared.

That was the subject they had been discussing earlier. Marjorie looked across the table at me, rolling her eyes and gently shaking her head, "No".

That's when my heart started to palpitate. I never expected to be a father so soon. Marjorie and I were again setting off on a fresh course. One we hadn't planned. There were a million decisions to make. Where will we live? Will Marjorie continue working after the baby is born? Will I become a househusband?

It was too soon to answer those questions. Regardless of what we decide, we will soon become a team of three.

Chapter 36

The Lumorist? Oui?

One revelation followed another that weekend. Becoming a member of Marjorie's family transformed my life. The St. Joseph family wasn't dysfunctional; we just had a different dynamic than Marjorie's family.

The ride home to D.C. from Philadelphia was one of quiet contemplation. Once again, our lives were changing. There was a lot to think about.

Rather than drive the interstate and rush home, we opted for a slower route through Delaware, cruising along Chesapeake Bay east of Baltimore using local roads. It allowed us time to admire the scenery, occasionally catching glimpses of the river and bay. Marjorie pointed out the quaint mom-and-pop stores and taverns in the small towns and marveled at the colorful sailboats out on the water.

While it thrilled me that we were starting a family, I realized our careers would have to change. Our child wouldn't thrive with a workaholic father and a mother who traveled five days a week.

As each mile passed, I thought more about the challenges ahead and my ability to deal with them. About halfway home, Marjorie broke the silence.

"My mom offered to sell us the house for a very reasonable price. She wants us to move back to Philly. She wants to help care for the baby. I told her you wouldn't want to do that. You don't, do you? I told her you wanted to stay in Washington."

"I guess we need to think about our future. We're going to need a bigger place to live. I think we should consider Bethesda or Rockville for our next home."

Bethesda and Rockville are both upper-class suburbs with excellent schools and low crime. The area also has a demographic of about ninety percent white. It made perfect sense to me.

Marjorie didn't share my mindset. She had lived her entire life in an inner city, urban neighborhood. She believed the future belongs to a multicultural populace. The idea of a snobby, entitled suburb didn't appeal to her.

"What if her skin is dark like mine? She'll never fit in with the snooty suburban white girls," she said.

I countered. "What if his skin is light like mine? He might get into trouble with the gangs in your old neighborhood. He'll probably get beaten up at school."

I always considered myself an open-minded person, but I had never believed raising a child in an inner-city setting was in their best interest. Our vision of the world differed; we grew up with differing ideals. It was clear; we had a lot to talk about. I had little doubt Marjorie would be a loving and attentive mother. It doesn't matter if they were a boy or a girl or the color of their skin. As parents, we need to do our best. Marjorie's family wasn't wealthy, but I wasn't born to the purple, either. It wasn't racist, or at least I didn't think it was, but my parents taught me to move up in the world. I believed moving to an upper-class suburb was part of the equation. Sometimes, we must relearn the ideals that are ingrained in us from our childhood.

I hadn't answered Marjorie's question about moving back to Philadelphia; it wasn't my first choice. While I could adapt to any city, Philadelphia wasn't my home. Still, it was too soon to exclude any options.

"Let's not overthink this. We're intelligent enough to make the right decisions. We are a team. Together, we will work this out," I said.

One thing I knew was that I couldn't wait to get back home and introduce myself to my child. I wanted to kiss Marjorie's stomach and whisper words of love to our baby through her soon-to-be burgeoning midsection. Then I wanted to kiss my wife's lips and tell her I loved her.

We had a lot of decisions to make, starting with our careers. I asked Marjorie how she planned to balance her work and motherhood.

"I intend to work as long as I'm comfortable. I still have a lot to accomplish. I also want to bring in someone to take over my board role as the fundraiser negotiator. Traveling week in and week out hasn't been healthy for our relationship. Having a baby will worsen the situation. Motherhood comes first, activism second. Long term, I think I can transition to an administrative role; I can still help those in need and stay in the D.C. area. Maybe even work from home."

Her plan sounded good to me. I added. "I'll help at home, but one of us needs to earn enough to pay the bills. Perhaps it's time to seek a career with a steadier income than that of an independent investigator. I can start a publication and write a column that's syndicated nationwide."

I dedicated the days following our conversation to refining my resume and reaching out to previous contacts for insights on media trends and potential jobs that offer stability and room for my investigations. I wanted to avoid being shoehorned into the nine-to-five drudgery that so many of us gravitate toward later in our careers.

They say that timing is everything, and to prove that theory, a few days after I began my job search, I received an email from Jacques

Allard, the Chairman of Communication and Education at IECO. Jacques was retiring at the end of the year. He and Elaine Sadeski planned to travel and see the world. He wanted to place my name under consideration to replace him. It wasn't a done deal, but his recommendation carried a lot of weight and could smooth my acceptance if I sought the position.

Had this offer come six months earlier, I probably would be wearing a beret and sitting at a sidewalk cafe along the Seine right now. Wine would accompany every meal, and I would look down my nose at the American tourists who passed by my table. With the changes, it wasn't my decision alone. I needed to discuss this offer with my new wife. I couldn't wait for her to hear the news.

That evening, Marjorie came home from a meeting with bureaucrats from the Department of Housing and Urban Development. She was trying to sell them on a new program to help low-income homebuyers finance a home. The day exhausted her. Even though her pregnancy wasn't showing yet, the growing fetus inside her was sapping her energy.

I asked her. "Tuff day?"

"No, unless you consider the sudden urge to vomit at the most inappropriate times a problem."

I tried to be sympathetic, although I knew nothing of what she was experiencing. "Sit down and relax. I will get us a snack."

She crawled onto the sofa on the deck outside, stretched her tired legs across the cushions, and gazed over the flowers in the backyard. The days were still warm enough to enjoy the fall weather. In a few weeks, the flowers would be gone and the nights would be longer than the days. I went to the kitchen and returned with two glasses of sparkling water. Marjorie had stopped drinking alcohol until the baby was born. I positioned myself at the other end of the couch, smiling at her. When I started massaging her feet, she knew something was up.

"Why the sudden attention towards me? Did you do something wrong?" she asked.

"Can't a husband be nice to his wife without doing something wrong?"

"The look on your face says something is on your mind. Spill it."

As I gently massaged her toes, I told her about the email from Jacques Allard and about the job opening in Paris.

"Paris, *ooh là là*." She laughed.

I stopped rubbing her feet. "I think we need to consider it."

"Wow, that would be a big step. Life-changing. Are we ready for such a big change?"

It was worth discussing. Paris might be the solution to where we live next and how we raise our child.

I used all the best arguments I could think of, like: "You already speak French.", "Our child would be multi-lingual, a citizen of the world.", "You wouldn't have to shave your legs any longer." That last one made her laugh again.

But a move to Paris would create several other issues. Marjorie would be thousands of miles from Sofia and her childhood home. Her brother Raymond and sister Alicia, and their family, would become strangers. It wasn't just Marjorie's family; I decided I wanted my child to know my parents and my brothers and sister as well. I realized that my family hadn't abandoned me. They never changed what they were doing. I had abandoned them. It was time for me, my parents, and my siblings to become a family once again.

Despite my interest in the Paris job, I had to decline. Family is more important than money. I know it sounds as if I was being unselfish and might someday regret it. I wasn't. The job offer wasn't guaranteed, and I had other ideas I needed to pursue. I'm someone who believes things always work out in the end. Sometimes, when one door closes, another one opens.

I decided to stick with my first love, investigative journalism. Countless untold stories, both political and criminal, remained to be discovered. If I placed my ear on the train tracks and listened, the rumble would be there. I told Marjorie about my decision to stay in D.C. She took my hand, and together we prayed for enlightenment.

Several days passed with no resolution until a rumor spread through the local media. I needed specifics, and Ed's Bar was the top spot to discover what the rumor mill was buzzing about. I arrived a little early, and the lunch crowd was still hanging about. I wanted to talk one-on-one with Ed, but he was busy pandering for tips and trying to sell today's special to a hungry throng of reporters and tourists who often came to see if they could meet a celebrity. I helped his cause by ordering a sandwich and a beer. When I ordered my second beer, Ed realized I wanted more than a sandwich. I wanted to talk. He nodded.

"Let me clean up some of these tables and cash out a couple of checks," he said.

Ed's bar was small, with only a handful of tables. Carino, the busboy, cleaned the tables while Ed rang up the tabs for the last of the lunchtime crowd. Ed made a point to personally thank each guest. He knew who buttered his bread, or at least who put money in the cash register.

After a few minutes, he walked back to the kitchen and returned with a freshly baked lemon square. Squished on the plate like a pile of scraps, he said. "This one broke coming out of the pan. I couldn't give it to the tourists; they would give me a negative review. It's on the house."

Ed always took care of his regulars.

"So, I guess you heard?" he said.

I had heard all kinds of rumors. That's why I went to Ed's. I needed the latest news, and Ed always knew the complete story.

"They sacked Lou Barnes," he said. "You probably heard. He was always at odds with the management, and his numbers were flagging. He hadn't had a breaking story since you and he divorced. the *Lumorist* had become the old news channel, and they blamed him for its collapse. They want to spice things up, bring in fresh blood."

That was it! That was my opportunity to move on to the next phase of my life. The Editor-in-Chief position at the *Lumorist* paid handsomely, well enough to support a growing family. Business travel would be minimal. Working full-time in D.C. would be an enormous help to Marjorie, and under the right circumstances, I could still contribute my own journalism work and keep my byline alive.

"I'm surprised they haven't contacted you," he said. "Ellie McCourtney, their human resources manager, was in here for lunch yesterday. I told her you might be interested."

It was a mystery how Ed, a neighborhood bartender, stayed informed about the local news. Nevertheless, I was grateful he spoke up and opened the door for me. Having Ed's recommendation was as good as any I could hope for.

That was all I needed to hear. I knew what I had to do. I chomped down my lemon bar, guzzled the last of my beer, and tossed down enough cash on the bar to cover my tab and a healthy tip for Ed.

"Thanks, Ed. See you in a couple of days." I said as I waved my way out the front door.

One thing my parents instilled in me was optimism. Believe in a brighter future with diligent work and unwavering determination. Lady Luck had smiled down on me many times in the past. I have achieved a lot since my days at Cleveland State. I knew with the right approach, I would continue to achieve great things.

In the same style, I wrote my Hypothesis-Based Inquiries; I rewrote my resume cover letter, starting with a hypothesis. The suggestion was simple. *The Lumorist*: *A Better Look at the World.*

I followed the title with a story about how the *Lumorist*, with me as their Editor, went from a stodgy old newspaper turned internet magazine into a third-millennium information superpower.

The format differed vastly from the standard introduction that most job applicants use when writing their resume cover letters. Introducing myself and listing all of my past accomplishments seemed a waste of time. They knew me well in literary circles, and although not exactly a household name, I was a best-selling author. One who had achieved international acclaim. Boasting about my past accomplishments seemed trite. Instead of dwelling on my past accomplishments, I urged their management to focus on envisioning the future of the *Lumorist* with me as Editor-in-Chief.

My proposition employed a simple three-pronged approach. Under my guidance, we would restructure the offices to resemble the war room prototype I had observed at the *Reporter*.

Second, the *Lumorist* would initiate a new training program based on the IECO Hypothesis-Based Inquiry model for all new and seasoned reporters.

Finally, they would allow for an increase in the research staff by adding a minimum of two cybersecurity agents. Agents with expertise in searching network traffic, examining financial records, and exploring the dark web. We would support our reporters by providing them with information that no other news outlet would have. Our goal would be to make their stories smarter and more reliable.

I gambled that my approach would not only demonstrate I had the expertise to run a news organization but would also intrigue the management with the possibility of future success.

I did one more unusual thing. Most candidates would be sending their resumes via email or downloading them through the company's electronic portal. Despite proposing an all-new technology-driven approach to their day-to-day operations, I went old school with my resume.

I found some high-quality stationery in Marjorie's desk drawer. I printed my cover letter and an updated copy of my resume, which I couriered directly to Ellie McCourtney, the Human Resources Manager. There was no way she would overlook my bid for the position.

The next day, Ellie called me to set up an interview. A new door was opening.

I drove a hard bargain. I insisted on full authority with the restructuring process and an adequate budget to redesign the magazines' operations. I must say it quite surprised me that they agreed to all my demands. My pay rate was to be commensurate with the additional responsibility the Editor-in-Chief position would now encompass. I also negotiated a clause for separate reimbursement for all articles and stories authored by me for use in their publication and demanded that I maintain copyright to any books or publications that I publish at some future date through outlets other than the *Lumorist*.

Finally, in lieu of a signing bonus, I asked the Lumorist management to become an annual contributor to the United Poverty League, Marjorie's charity. I wanted to make sure that Marjorie, or her replacement, if she chose to step aside, would continue to make their fundraising goals and help those living below the poverty line to enjoy a better life.

They accepted all my conditions; I could start in two weeks.

I didn't wait the full two weeks to develop my transition plans. As soon as the Human Resources personnel processed my security access, I started meeting with my staff members and began interviewing staff additions. I wanted the transition to be smooth and swift.

Sitting in my new office, where Lou Barnes had formerly reigned supreme, I gazed over the future home of a modern news media operation. My mind flashed back to the day I sat across from Professor Sadeski as she encouraged me to use my talent to change the world of investigative journalism. More than anyone else, she was responsible for my success.

I had come full circle. My first action was to write a Thank-You letter to everyone who contributed to my success. The list included Dr. Elaine Sadeski, Jacques Allard, William and Nadine St. Joseph, and James Crowder. I even included Derek Watting on my thank-you list. The fun part was signing my name, D.K. St. Joseph - Editor-in-Chief.

Only one thing remained. Locate a spot on the wall to hang my framed poster with the inscription: "The best place to hide a tree is in the forest."

Chapter 37

The Complete Story

"And that, my friends, is: The Complete Story by D.K. St. Joseph."

I looked across the table at the seating area in my office and smiled. Seated across from me were three young journalism students. They had driven down from Cleveland State University to interview one of the school's most successful alumni. It was part of a group project they were writing on Hypothesis-Based Inquiry methods. It seemed Dr. Sadeski's legacy was still alive and well at Cleveland State.

The three students, Louise Kelly, Jonathan Judge, and Tommie Cull, stared back at me as if they were in a trance. When they requested an interview with author D.K. St. Joseph, they probably thought I would give them a ten-minute summary of my career. They didn't realize it would be a three-and-a-half-hour epic tale of my life from the beginning to the present day.

Once you get D.K. St. Joseph talking, he doesn't stop until he has given you the complete story. They were too polite to stop me.

I stared back at them, expecting questions. Maybe applause?

"So, what questions do you have?" I asked.

My lengthy dissertation exhausted them. They stopped taking notes sometime after the first hour. After that, they just listened politely.

After a few seconds, more out of courtesy than interest, Jonathan looked at his notebook, then asked, "How old were you when you traveled to India for your encounter in the jungle with the Leopard? That is an amazing story."

"I don't know, maybe twenty-six?" I responded. "Haven't you read the book? It is all in the book."

Tommie, trying to appear as the leader of the group, quickly proclaimed, "I read it. It was great, riveting."

Jonathon sheepishly admitted. "The Cleveland State Library only has one copy. There is a waiting list. I'm waiting for Louise to finish. Then it will be my turn."

Louise reached into her backpack and pulled out a copy of FEARLESS, the book I had co-authored with Melinda Donne. She had a bookmark stuffed amongst the last few pages.

"I'm almost done," she exclaimed. "It's brilliant. I wanted to finish before we came for the interview today. Unfortunately, I ran out of time."

I took the book, the book Melinda and I co-authored, from her hand. It was a well-worn copy she borrowed from the school library.

"Only one copy in a college library? We can't have that. I will send them more copies tomorrow," I said.

Asking them collectively, "Are you satisfied that you got what you came for?"

They looked at each other and nodded. "Yes," said Louise. "I feel confident we'll have the best essay in the class."

I couldn't have these young, impressionable minds leaving my office empty-handed. I stood, walked to a cabinet on the other side of my office, and grabbed three hardbound copies of FEARLESS. I opened each one to the last page and just below the last words, I signed:

Good Luck with your career in Journalism

"Saint Joseph"

Epilogue

Accomplished

I bid farewell to the three anxious journalist students, satisfied that I had given them a fair look at what their lives could be like if they chose to pursue their careers in journalism.

As they left my office, a rush of emotion flooded through my veins. *Had I really achieved all those amazing accomplishments in such a short period of time?*

When, as a teenager, I told my father I wanted to be someone important and that I didn't want my journey through life to mirror his, my vision for success was unclear. In retrospect, my life turned out to be not much different than his.

In college, Professor Sadeski encouraged me to become an investigative journalist. She was spot-on, and the result has been a prodigious triumph.

The success of the book *FEARLESS: The Melinda Donne Story* had me wondering if another biography might be in my future. After all, I had an example of brilliance, courage, and love for mankind, right at home. I mused, wouldn't the story of a girl from the inner city who overcame tragedy and heartbreak to rise to prominence be a bestseller? With the right author telling the narrative, anything is possible.

The hardest part will be convincing Marjorie to let me chronicle her life. But then again, I convinced her to marry me, so in many ways, the hard part was already done.

Six months ago, Marjorie gave birth to a beautiful little girl, whom we named Franchesca. I now had the two most beautiful women in my life.

I sat back at my desk, turned, and looked out the window. The beauty of the day and the gratitude for all that I had accomplished overwhelmed me. I had become someone important.

Thank You for Reading
Saint Joseph

The author would like to acknowledge the assistance of many
others who helped complete this project.

Breanna McNair Proofreading & Editing
Beta Reading by Alexia Howell
Beta Reading by Isabella Warner
Beta Reading by Sherry Frances Domino
Cover Image from @gambar-ikam-gasa on Canva
Cover Image from Vladimir Yelizarov on Unsplash
Cover Image from Bruce Emmerling on Pexels

Please visit my website at:
www.Stairns.com

About The Author

J. Salvatore Domino is an award-winning author and blogger based in Scottsdale, Arizona, U.S.A.

After more than thirty years as a technical writer, he turned his attention to fiction. His journey from technical writing to the boundless realm of fiction is a testament to the power of transformation.

Demonstrating his storytelling prowess, he captivates the reader, inviting them into a world where the lines between the imagined and the real are artfully blurred. His characters are crafted to evoke strong reactions, often mirroring the complexities of real-life individuals.

His notable works include the cyber-crime series *The Algorithm Man*, a classic whodunit, *The DiMarco Incident*, and a raw crime fiction, *The Hard Place*.

Collectively, they reflect his versatility and ability to connect with a diverse audience.